S0-BOB-750

The Daily Astorian—On the Record

THEFT

Riverfront Books and Stationery in the
Roberts Building, 1117 Commercial,
Astoria. Wednesday, $6000 in office
equipment and software inventory was
stolen when intruders broke through
the basement door, Astoria police said.
Owner Georgia Madison was called to
the scene. Also on hand was Ben Stratton,
new owner of the Roberts Building.

Dear Reader,

Trust a Hero was born in the wee hours of a cold December morning when I was called by the police to the bookstore I managed in downtown Astoria. There'd been a robbery and the basement door had been ripped off its hinges.

Astoria is built over the rubble of a fire that destroyed much of the town in the 1930s. The result is a downtown that sits over a warren of tunnels that leads into many of our commercial area's basements. Burglaries are a major nuisance— particularly at 2:00 a.m.

That particular morning, as I rehung the basement door, I entertained myself by plotting a romantic mystery involving the tunnels and the heroic owner of a bookstore and her handsome new landlord. That's the best part about writing for a living— everything, even being dragged out of your warm bed at 2:00 a.m. is story material.

It was also a comfort to me that my imagination and my sense of humor could still function at that hour! I hope you enjoy the result.

Muriel Jensen

MURIEL JENSEN
Trust a Hero

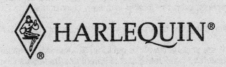

HARLEQUIN®

TORONTO • NEW YORK • LONDON
AMSTERDAM • PARIS • SYDNEY • HAMBURG
STOCKHOLM • ATHENS • TOKYO • MILAN • MADRID
PRAGUE • WARSAW • BUDAPEST • AUCKLAND

If you purchased this book without a cover you should be aware that this book is stolen property. It was reported as "unsold and destroyed" to the publisher, and neither the author nor the publisher has received any payment for this "stripped book."

ISBN-13: 978-0-373-36114-4
ISBN-10:   0-373-36114-9

TRUST A HERO

Copyright © 1990 by Muriel Jensen

All rights reserved. Except for use in any review, the reproduction or utilization of this work in whole or in part in any form by any electronic, mechanical or other means, now known or hereafter invented, including xerography, photocopying and recording, or in any information storage or retrieval system, is forbidden without the written permission of the publisher, Harlequin Enterprises Limited, 225 Duncan Mill Road, Don Mills, Ontario, Canada M3B 3K9.

This is a work of fiction. Names, characters, places and incidents are either the product of the author's imagination or are used fictitiously, and any resemblance to actual persons, living or dead, business establishments, events or locales is entirely coincidental.

This edition published by arrangement with Harlequin Books S.A.

® and TM are trademarks of the publisher. Trademarks indicated with ® are registered in the United States Patent and Trademark Office, the Canadian Trade Marks Office and in other countries.

www.eHarlequin.com

Printed in U.S.A.

MURIEL JENSEN

Muriel Jensen lives in Astoria, Oregon, with her artist husband, Ron. She has three grown children, many grandchildren, a black Labrador named Fred Astaire (because of his smooth moves) and three cats that just moved in over the years. She's written over seventy-five books and novellas since her first sale in 1983.

To Amy Wetherill Baker
and Julie Wetherill,
who inspired Linda and Lacey

CHAPTER ONE

BEN STRATTON FLIPPED ON the light switch and walked cautiously down the old wooden basement stairs. He was pleased to note that they felt solid under his feet. He glanced around as he descended and saw a bare bulb hanging on a chain, shelves neatly stocked with supplies and an orderly stack of unopened cartons against the concrete wall. Hundred-pound sacks of flour and sugar lay on pallets several inches off the floor. The owner of the Astoria Bakery was a tidy tenant—not very friendly, but tidy.

Ben walked across the scrupulously swept floor, seeing cracks in the concrete that had been laid more than sixty years before. He frowned. This close to the river there would be water seeping up when it rained.

He flicked on the flashlight he held and directed the light at a dark corner. There were cracks in the wall, too, but they were small, and he saw no evidence of dampness or the fine powder in the cracks that indicated current movement. Odds and ends of lumber were propped up against the wall. Moving to the opposite corner, he swept the light up a delivery shoot to inspect the underside of the double metal doors that opened onto the sidewalk in front of the building. He heard conversation and footsteps clanging on the doors as people walked by overhead.

Methodically, he swept the flashlight from beam to

beam. They appeared sound. There was no evidence of dry rot or any of the many insect infestations that could reduce wood to chips. It appeared David had made a good move when he purchased the Roberts Building.

"You doing all right down there?" A female voice called from the top of the bakery steps.

"Fine, thank you, Mrs. Hansen," he replied, grinning to himself at the owner's perfunctorily polite tone. He was sure she had concluded the moment he'd introduced himself as one of the new owners of the building that he planned to raise the rent or evict her or both. "I won't be much longer. I just want to have a look at Mrs. Madison's side of the basement."

"The light switch is at the top of her stairs." The door slammed, punctuating her brusque advice.

And they say people in small towns are friendly, he thought wryly. Moving out of the circle of light, Ben wandered slowly into the dark half of the basement that belonged to Riverfront Books and Stationery, picking his way carefully in the beam of his flashlight. His foot collided with something hard and solid, and he swept the light drown, finding a sea of cartons, invoices still attached. He smiled again. Obviously not as tidy a tenant as Mrs. Hansen. Winding his way through the boxes he found the stairs and climbed them, then flipped on the switch.

He looked at his watch: 8:35 a.m. He'd better get the lead out if he wanted to finish this tour before the other shop opened. He knew the Roberts Building's other tenant already considered her new landlords intruders in her life. He didn't want to contribute to her annoyance and natural suspicions by being around when it was time for her to open for business.

GEORGIA MADISON WALKED down Commercial Street toward the bookstore, humming to herself. It was a rare, sunny April morning and her long-awaited stock had arrived just the day before. It had been almost three months since the sale of the building in which she was a tenant, and the new landlord hadn't been heard from. Her fear of an exorbitant rent increase or eviction had begun to die down. Added to that was the extra bonus of finding on sale the very sweater that Lacey wanted for her birthday. Life was good.

Remembering the white cotton dress for herself she'd seen while shopping for the sweater, Georgia summoned her willpower and walked past the bakery without stopping for her customary blueberry muffin and coffee. Glancing in the window as she passed, she caught sight of Karen Hansen at her cash register and waved. Her short, plump neighbor smiled and waved back.

Georgia stopped in front of the double glass doors of Riverfront Books and Stationery and fit her key into the lock. Mentally, she listed everything she had to do today. Check in yesterday's freight, wrap Lacey's sweater, sign the birthday card, pick up the cake from Karen and water Bea's plants. Smiling wryly, she considered that modern woman's greatest freedom was the right to decide *which* eighteen hours to work in order to make time for everything she had to do.

Georgia pushed her way into the shop, then turned and locked the door behind her. Leaving the lights off, she dropped her purse on the counter and took a moment to look around her shop in satisfaction. After two years, the fact of her proprietorship still filled her with pride and a very elemental thrill she admitted was probably unsophisticated. The store satisfied a personal need that hadn't been necessary when Gary was alive, and a very practical need when his untimely death left her and the girls without support. .

She breathed in the smells of paper, wood and ink, the perfume of her financial independence. It was true that loans from her mother-in-law and the bank had helped make it possible, but she was paying the money back as promised and on time. In all the years she had worked beside her husband, keeping the books for the freight business that had been in his family for three generations, she'd been included in his plans and helped make decisions. But planning, deciding and implementing her own had provided a thrill she hadn't expected.

"Speaking of implementing..." she told herself aloud, heading for the basement stairs. If she didn't get busy with yesterday's freight, she wouldn't have it checked in and brought upstairs before it was time to open the store.

The sudden strip of light visible beneath the basement door alerted her. When she'd put her hand on the knob an instant ago, it had been dark. There was a sound on the stairs on the other side of the door, and her heart rose to her throat.

Then anger and resentment filled her as she remembered all the inventory she'd lost and the frustration she'd suffered at the hands of this thief. She also remembered what she'd heard at the police department's special seminar for merchants on dealing with the sudden wave of thefts downtown. "If you arrive at a robbery in progress," the officer had cautioned, "do not attempt to stop the thief yourself. Go to the nearest phone and call the police." She promptly pushed the advice to the back of her mind.

When she'd been robbed the month before last, the thief had taken her adding machine, her tape player and a whole case of her most expensive pens. Last month he'd taken her new adding machine, her new tape player and several cartons of computer software she'd been waiting for for four months. She was beyond being reasonable or cautious.

Certain the thief was some punk kid supporting bad habits by selling the inventories of the merchants on Commercial Street who worked hard for *their* money, Georgia decided to act. Quietly turning the knob, she pushed the door back suddenly with the full force of her 118 pounds. The door struck something solid, from which she heard a satisfyingly startled grunt, then there was the sound of something clattering down the stairs. She reached around the door, grabbed a fistful of what felt like flannel and yanked. "Come out of there you little parasitic menace to society!" she shouted, and with her free hand, grabbed the long-handled tool propped against the wall near the door. As she continued to yank, the perpetrator, encumbered by surprise and the steps, stumbled around the door and up into the store.

Georgia shoved him against the wall, then held the tool against his chest, her weight behind it, to hold him there. "I want to know what you were doing in my basement," she demanded in a hard voice, applying a little more pressure before he entertained any thoughts of trying to break away. He looked at her with startled hazel eyes, and she glowered back at him, realizing for the first time since she'd heard the noise that she'd done a truly stupid thing. This thief was not the youth she had imagined.

He was a man. A big man. In worn jeans and a blue-

and-gray flannel shirt with the sleeves rolled up, he appeared to have a good ten inches and probably seventy pounds on her. His light brown hair was tousled and dusty, and now that the initial surprise of her attack had passed, he did not look pleased. Georgia recalled that the police suspected the recent rash of burglaries was being coordinated by someone and was not the usual hit-and-run tactics of rowdy kids.

Fear began to dilute courage. It was a long way to the phone, the front door was locked, and she was holding a seasoned thief at bay with a window squeegee. With forced bravado, she asked again, "What were you doing in my basement?"

Ben tried hard to engage his sense of humor. When he thought about it, being pinned against the wall by a dark-haired woman half his size wielding a large windshield wiper was funny—as long as none of the guys he played tennis with found out about it. But he'd gotten up at five to drive up from Portland to look over the building Dave had purchased in the interest of making improvements. The owner of the bakery had been openly hostile, but this woman was making her look like a paragon of graciousness. There had to be humor here, but he couldn't quite bring it into focus.

"I'm here," he said with quiet care, "to make certain the building is structurally sound."

"Ha!" Georgia said. "You must think I'm structurally defective, if you expect me to believe that."

Ben looked at her short, dark hair, parted on the side and just skimming her chin in a loose wave, down the trim, subtly rounded lines of a lavender suit, along elegantly shaped calves to small feet in black, wedge-heeled shoes. His gaze went back to wide brown eyes that were now watching him with less anger than caution. "Hardly," he replied.

Apparently alarmed by his scrutiny, she applied more pressure to the squeegee. "Look, you..." she began to threaten.

"Mrs. Madison." He took a firm grip on the end of the handle closest to him and pulled it out of her hands without too much effort. "Now that you've rearranged my ribs, let's talk about this like civilized people." He propped the squeegee against the wall with a decisive thud and rested his hands on his hips. "I'm your landlord."

If he'd expected that news to change her attitude, he was mistaken. He was suddenly facing the business end of a pair of long-handled tongs, a device probably as old as the building. Its ends were sharp.

"I've met the man who bought the building," she said, beginning to look nervous despite her bravado. "You're not him."

Ben closed his eyes, summoning patience. "That was my uncle, David Wilson. He buys and I restore. We're partners."

She studied him a long moment, but she didn't drop the tongs. Taking them away from her, he decided, would require more skill than the squeegee.

"Oh, yeah?" she said finally. "Let's see your driver's license."

Instinctively, he put a hand to his back pocket. It was flat. "It's in my jacket," he said, watching the suspicion that had begun to recede in her eyes blossom again.

"And where's your jacket?"

"At the bakery."

"Sure."

Enough was enough. Ben grabbed at the handle, careful to reach beyond the nasty-looking points. But she was expecting the move this time and danced backward, jabbing him. He stopped, a long red gash on his forearm.

Ben bit back an expletive and studied the wound. It was nothing more than a good scratch, but it made him think twice about trying that again. "Mrs. Madison," he said wearily, "you're beginning to annoy me. You pay five hundred dollars a month rent, you haven't had a lease for the last two years, the building's furnace was on the fritz for the entire month of January, and you and Mrs. Hansen have had a running battle with the old landlord for a year and a half to repaint. Would a thief know all that?"

Oh, God. How else would he know that? Georgia's determination wavered, but she continued to keep him at a distance. "That sounds convincing, but I'm not entirely sure I believe you."

"Believe him." Karen Hansen suddenly appeared from the basement steps, wiping her hands on the apron that covered her baker's whites. She looked from her friend to her new landlord, obviously trying to decide why Georgia was holding the tongs on him and why he was bleeding. "I went downstairs to get a carton of napkins and heard the commotion. You threatened to raise the rent?" she asked Ben.

He folded his arms. "I had hoped to be finished before Mrs. Madison arrived, but she came in earlier than I expected, heard me in the basement and mistook me for a thief."

Karen burst into laughter, then stopped immediately, making a brave effort to look sober when no one joined her. "He is our new landlord, Georgia," she said, taking the tongs away from her friend. "Mr. Stratton, this is Georgia Madison, owner of Riverfront Books and Stationery—privately, a serial killer whose weapon is a pair of antique tongs."

Georgia glanced darkly at Karen, then looked into the hazel eyes she'd been confronting for the past five minutes, hoping to see a glimpse of humor there. It was minuscule, but she found it. He crossed the distance that separated them and extended his hand. The fact that the arm that connected it to his body was now bleeding made her groan as she took it.

"Hi," she said feebly, pulling him by the hand across the room to the bathroom beside her office. "Let me wash that off for you. I...suppose I can expect an eviction notice in the morning." She glanced at him with a cautious smile as the two of them crowded into the tiny room. Karen stopped in the doorway, folded her arms and leaned against the molding.

Georgia turned on the cold water and eased Ben's arm under it. He had to lean down to cooperate, putting them eye-to-eye across the sink. His hazel eyes studied her with new interest, and she looked away, concentrating on washing his arm.

"It's just a scratch," he said. "Worth a little more rent, maybe, but hardly eviction."

"You'll have to forgive her," Karen said from the doorway. "Her store's been robbed during the night four times in the last year, three times within the last four months."

Georgia turned the water off and reached to the rack for one of the fluffy towels she'd brought from home. She dabbed at his arm with it, then rested his elbow on it as she rummaged in the medicine cabinet over the sink for antiseptic.

Ben straightened, offering his arm when Georgia uncapped a bottle of iodine. "Mrs. Hansen let me into her basement to check for structural problems. Obviously we want to take care of those before doing the cosmetic work the building needs so badly. Since you share the same basement, I didn't think you'd mind me checking your side while I was down there. I went up the steps just to put the light on. I wouldn't have let myself into the store without your permission."

Now convinced he was innocent of thievery, Georgia looked him in the eye. His gaze was direct. She liked that; she was very straightforward herself. "So, what are you going to do with the building, Mr. Stratton? Rumor has it you and your uncle have office buildings up and down the Oregon coast."

"Rumor is right," he said.

"Is that what you plan for our building?"

Her contrition seemed to be giving way to a suspicion she'd probably held since Dave had bought the building. Ben was relieved that the tongs were out of reach. "We have no specific plans at this point, except to be sure the building is safe."

Georgia spread antiseptic liberally up and down the gash. The scratch wasn't deep, except for a small spot near the inside of his elbow, but she suspected that it stung furiously. Still, he didn't react. "You have two fiscally sound, responsible tenants right now, Mr. Stratton."

"He could divide the building into four smaller offices," Karen pointed out coolly, "give the building a face-lift and get a lot more rent."

Georgia tore the wrapper off a bandage and placed it over the deeper edge of the wound. The forearm she worked on was long, well muscled and tan. Obviously a wheeler-dealer type, she thought, with time to go to a gym and vacation in the sun—like the men who ruined Gary. Her task completed, she folded her arms and looked up at him. "Is that the plan?"

The atmosphere in the tiny bathroom was now thick with hostility; Ben felt it surround him. His tenants had obviously decided he was not to be trusted. That made him hostile, too.

He looked into Georgia's eyes, unsmiling, as he rolled down his shirtsleeves. "I just said we didn't have a specific plan."

Georgia and Karen looked past his shoulder at each other. He had little trouble reading the isn't-this-just-what-we-expected look on their faces.

"We're to believe," Georgia asked, "that a high-rolling buy-up team from Portland bought a decrepit old building in the boonies with the intention of leaving it as it is?"

Buttoning a cuff, Ben looked down at her with all the disdain she showed him. "Of course not," he said. "You could believe that we simply wanted an investment here, a good reason to weekend at the coast. You could believe that we want to be sure this old building is safe for you, and that we'd like to make it as attractive as possible so that it will be appealing to the tourists you depend on so that you and then we can make a profit. But small-town folks are always convinced that big-city people are out to take advantage of them. I wouldn't want you to buck a trend."

Never one to be unfair, at least not knowingly, Georgia had the grace to look ashamed. "Was that your plan?"

When he reacted with an impatient roll of his eyes, she added quickly, "I know. So far you don't have a plan. But if you did, might it include letting us stay here?"

He gave her a smile she didn't trust. "Half an hour ago, it did. Since then I've had a doorknob driven into my stomach, a squeegee into my ribs and sharp tongs into a main artery. Right now I'd cheerfully rent your spot out to rotating rummage sales.... If I can have fifteen more minutes in your basement, I'll be on my way."

Wordlessly, Georgia swept a hand toward the basement. Karen stepped aside to let him through the doorway. She and Georgia looked at each other as his footsteps sounded across the back room, then grew faint as he went down the basement stairs.

Karen walked into the bathroom to slap Georgia's arm. "Good work, Georgie. I've always wanted to peddle my wares out of a cardboard box in my golden years with you for company."

Georgia frowned at her. "You're the one who suggested he was going to change the building into an office complex."

"But I didn't leave the mark of Zorro on him, then suggest he was a liar."

Georgia's shoulders sagged. "If we had any chance of staying here in the beginning, I've probably blown it."

Karen put an arm around her. "Phil says not to worry about it until we know we have to leave."

"Your husband carries a gun. He doesn't have to worry about things. If people don't do what he wants, he can throw them in jail or shoot them."

Karen looked at Georgia. "He insists that being a police officer is more complicated than that. Now come on, cheer up." Karen drew Georgia out of the bathroom toward the shop. "Let me out the front door and I'll bring you back a blueberry muffin and a cup of coffee and you'll feel better."

"I'm trying to diet. There's this white cotton dress at Leon's—"

Karen interrupted. "I don't want to hear about it. I never wear anything white after hours or anything I have to diet to get into. And, anyway, how can you be dieting? Aren't you taking the girls for pizza tonight for Lacey's birthday?"

Georgia nodded, turning the lock on the front door. "I'm sure I'll burn off the calories maintaining order among four teenage girls."

"Your mother-in-law going?"

Georgia shook her head. "Bea's still in Cozumel with the senior citizens' tour. She'll be back in a couple of days."

Karen smirked. "Then there's a chance you'll have fun tonight."

Georgia swatted her friend's arm scoldingly. "Bea's a good-hearted lady. She's just…"

"Bossy."

"Yes. But if it hadn't been for her, I wouldn't have the store." Georgia sighed, then hugged her friend. "Thanks for coming to check on me. If you see Mr. Stratton again, tell him…"

"I'll tell him you have lapses of sanity." Karen opened the door, letting in a gust of cool morning air. It smelled of cedar and sun and the river a block away. Entwined in it were the wonderful aromas from Karen's bakery. "Actually, he's gorgeous for a landlord, isn't he?"

Georgia lifted a shoulder. "He's big. I didn't really notice that he was gorgeous."

Karen shook her head over Georgia's indifference. "Will you wake up? Gary's been gone over two years now, Georgia. It's time you started noticing men."

"Karen..." Georgia began.

"I know, I know. You and the girls are doing fine on your own, and the circumstances of Gary's death make it hard for you to... I mean..." Cornered by her own concern, Karen looked up at Georgia, wondering if she'd said too much.

Georgia made a conscious effort not to stiffen. Karen meant no harm. "When I'm ready for a relationship," she said quietly, "I'm capable of looking for one. I really am. So don't worry."

Karen took her hand and patted it. "I know you are, but Phil and I are worried about you. The longer you remain withdrawn—"

"I'm not withdrawn, I'm busy," Georgia said. Taking another whiff of the air from the bakery, she smiled at Karen. "Oh, what the heck. If you have time, bring me a muffin and coffee."

Karen gave her a look that told her she knew she'd been deliberately diverted and went off with a wave. Georgia left the door open, flipped the Closed sign to Open and turned on the lights, appreciating what a close call that had been. She'd almost had to talk about Gary's death.

After taking the cash drawer out of the safe and putting it in the register, she went to the long display window, pulling a few books out to make room for new stock. Glancing up, she saw Ben Stratton walk out of the bakery, shrugging into a light cotton jacket. He got into a red Chevrolet four-wheel-drive pickup and drove away.

Talk about close calls, she thought, watching the

truck turn down Twelfth Street. She had almost am-
putated her new landlord's arm. She could always
move to the shopping center. So the rent was twice
what she paid; the foot traffic was supposed to be twice
what they got downtown. But she didn't want to be in
the shopping center. She wanted to be here, where
she'd started, where she could see and smell the river,
feed the pigeons, kibitz with all the friends she'd made
on Commercial Street.

There was no alternative, she realized as she dropped
a stack of books on the counter. Somehow, she'd have
to straighten things out with Ben Stratton.

CHAPTER TWO

"NO MUSHROOMS!"

"Mushrooms are good! There aren't any calories in mushrooms."

"Could we *please* have one half with anchovies this time? I mean, it is my birthday."

"Anchovies? Yuk!"

"Wait, wait!" Seated at one end of the table occupied by her two daughters, Linda and Lacey, and Lacey's two best friends, Georgia raised both hands to try to reestablish order. The noise level in Mr. Fultano's was such that she had to shout to be heard. "Let's try to get together on this. Are there any two of you who want the same thing?"

The four girls in jeans and purple-and-gold Astoria High School sweatshirts stared back at her without response. Georgia was forced to admit that *had* been a silly question. She tried again. "Who wants the vegetarian *with* mushrooms?"

Linda, small and curvaceous at sixteen, raised her hand. She counted every calorie religiously, including the ones she was sure were in toothpaste.

"Without mushrooms?"

Lacey's friend Kristin raised her hand, round spectacles and retainer winking under the overhead light.

"And anchovies for Lacey. What about you, Dina?"

The tallest of the group, Dina was shy and stoop

shouldered from trying to hide her awkward height among her shorter friends. "Taco pizza, please, " she said.

"Okay." The choices memorized, Georgia stood. "Save the table, and I'll place our order. Diet Pepsi all around?" That, at least, was unanimous.

Georgia went to the counter and gave her order to a tall, redheaded young man. She dug a pen out of the bottom of her purse and opened her checkbook, then drew a mortified breath as she stared at the deposit slips that were all that was left in it.

The young man, who had just rung up her twenty-seven-dollar order, looked at her warily. "Changed your mind?"

"No, I'm out of checks," she groaned, routing through her billfold and coming up with $5.41. Then inspiration struck. "Is Mr. Fulton working tonight?" She served on a merchants' association committee with Robert Fulton. She was sure he'd extend her credit until the following day.

"It's his night off." The boy calmly dashed all her hopes, reminding mercilessly, "It's $27.50, ma'am. Shall I cancel the order?"

Behind her a group of obviously hungry young women in bowling uniforms fidgeted. Georgia turned to the table of giggling girls and groaned to herself. She would just have to drive home and back....

"Place the order." A long arm shot past her shoulder, a lean hand passing two bills to the relieved cashier.

Georgia spun around in surprise, finding herself nose to nose, or rather, nose to clavicle with her landlord. "Mr. Stratton." She felt caught between pleasure and embarrassment. His willingness to help her suggested he wasn't holding a grudge about that morning, and she had hoped for an opportunity to apologize for it. But it would probably have helped her case if she'd projected an image of competence and control; forgetting her checks hadn't done that. "Thanks, but I can't let you—"

"Please," he said. "I'd like to."

"Really, I..."

"I insist."

"Two large pizzas," the cashier repeated to Georgia, apparently considering it wise to make sure she hadn't changed her mind now that the man had appeared. "One half veggie with mushroom, one half without. One half veggie with anchovies, half taco. And a pitcher of Diet Pepsi."

She nodded, then turned back to Ben, planning to thank him. She opened her mouth, then closed it again when he held her to him as he reached over her shoulder to accept his change. He smelled of the leather of his jacket, she noticed, and a crisp, woodsy after-shave. It was the lightest touch of his hand at her back, a slight, brief flattening of her breasts against his chest, but her heart gave a formidable lurch. A reaction to surprise, she thought, ruffled but trying to appear calm as they moved along the counter to the clerk who would provide their drinks.

"Either you're very hungry," Ben said, "or you're not here alone."

She pointed across the room to where the four girls were huddled together, giggling. "It's my youngest daughter's birthday. Four growing girls can get very hungry."

Daughters, Ben thought, looking down at her ringless hands on the counter. He turned to the table and saw that the girls made a beautiful picture, like something an Impressionist might have painted: two pale, curly heads together with a brunette and a redhead, eyes flashing, bubbling genuine laughter—emerging femininity at its most touching. He felt a sudden ache for all he'd missed as a child, for all he was missing now. "The dark-haired one's yours," he guessed.

"And the redhead. She's the birthday girl, Lacey. the other is Linda."

Ben turned back to Georgia, letting his eyes wander quickly over her jeans and red sweater. He found it easy to forgive her for that morning. "I would never have taken you for the mother of two teenagers."

The boy behind the counter poured Diet Pepsi into a frosty pitcher. "I wouldn't have figured you for a landlord," she said, then laughed when his mouth took on a wry twist. "I guess I made that obvious."

The boy put the filled pitcher on a tray and pushed it toward Ben. "Your number is thirty-nine. Thank you."

Before Georgia could reach for the tray, Ben pulled it off the counter. "I'll carry this to the table for you, then leave you to your party."

As they approached the table, Georgia saw her daughters staring openmouthed at Ben Stratton.

"Girls," she said brightly, suddenly unaccountably nervous. "I'd like you to meet one of the new owners of the Roberts Building." The girls stared. "Mr. Stratton, these are my daughters, Linda and Lacey, and Lacey's friends, Kristin and Dina."

Ben put the tray in the middle of the table, smiling at the girls as he did so. "Good evening, ladies. Happy birthday, Lacey."

Lacey stood and offered her hand. "Thank you. Happy to meet you, Mr. Stratton."

"Ben," he corrected.

Georgia often prayed that her younger daughter would acquire a little subtlety to temper the honesty and enthusiasm with which she greeted life and everyone in it. But at the moment, her unqualified warmth and eagerness to talk covered her mother's nervousness. It also prevented Ben from leaving as he'd promised. She pulled up an extra chair. "Mom says you're going to make smaller offices out of the building and throw everybody out on their duffs."

Georgia folded her arms on the table and dropped her head on them. She heard Ben's light chuckle as Lacey went on. "You wouldn't really do that, would you? Mom's a widow and she works without anyone to help her so she can save money. It'd cost her a bundle to move. Are you married?"

Trying desperately to maintain a grip on the conversation but losing, Ben replied, "No, are you?"

The girls laughed. "No." Lacey rested her chin on her hand. "I'm not going to get married. I'm going to be a veterinarian and live alone on a big farm. But there is *someone* at this table who isn't married, either."

Linda rolled her eyes. "None of us is married," she said impatiently, "and you're embarrassing Mom. Right, Mom?"

Mortified, Georgia glanced at their guest and couldn't help laughing. "Yes. And probably Mr. Stratton, too."

He looked more amused than embarrassed. "I'm a bachelor and I like it that way," he said, filling the girls' glasses from the frosty pitcher. "And pretty as your mom is, I'm sure she's single because she wants to be."

Kristin, who was the youngest of seven children, looked surprised. "But, don't you want to have kids?"

"Oh, sure," he said, pushing a filled glass her way. "But my work keeps me going from place to place a lot. When you do that, it's hard to find a wife. And if you don't have a wife, you can't have children."

Tensely expecting one or all of the girls to take him literally and correct him on that, Georgia was pleasantly surprised when he added smoothly, "Of course, you *can*, but that's not good for anybody. Georgia?"

"What?" Her name on his lips, so easily spoken, startled her.

He gestured with the pitcher. "Pepsi?"

"Oh, yes." Realizing she was clutching her glass, she held it out for him to fill.

Lacey frowned. "I thought a landlord stayed around to watch his property. Why do you go from place to place?"

"Because my uncle and I own quite a few buildings on the West Coast. I travel around to all of them to check on problems and see that the buildings stay in good repair."

Linda, a dedicated homebody, asked, "Don't you get tired of that? Don't you ever want to just stay in one place?"

Georgia saw the slightest flicker in his eyes when he considered the question a moment. Then he shook his head, smiling. "When I do, I have a condominium in Portland."

"Number thirty-nine," a disembodied voice called over the loudspeaker.

"That's us!" Lacey was on her feet in an instant to

accompany Ben to the counter. They were back in a moment, deep in conversation about the merits of anchovies. With both pizzas in the middle of the table, Georgia began distributing napkins while Ben refilled soft drink glasses. Then he leaned over the back of Georgia's chair and smiled at the girls. "Thanks for letting me crash your birthday party, Lacey. I've got to be on my way."

All the girls looked disappointed, but Lacey, who loved or hated people instantly, grimaced. "Can't you stay? You can share my anchovies."

Georgia noticed that the look of regret on Ben's face also seemed genuine. "Thanks, Lacey, but I have to go. Happy birthday."

"Maybe we'll see you at the store sometime," Linda suggested.

He smiled. "Maybe. Meanwhile, take good care of your mom."

Linda shrugged as though she had assumed that demanding burden long ago. "I always do."

Georgia pushed her chair back. "I'll walk you out. Be back in a minute, girls."

Ben pulled her chair the rest of the way out and guided her to the door with a hand on her elbow. The weather had changed, and a light rain was falling. They stopped just outside the door in the shelter of the portico. The dark parking lot seemed suddenly still and strangely intimate.

"I want to repay you for the pizza," Georgia said. Her voice was a little breathy, and she cleared her throat. "Shall I just put it in with the rent, or will you be around tomorrow?"

He shook his head. "Please don't worry—"

"Now I'm insisting," Georgia said. "If you hadn't

been here tonight, I'd have had to go all the way home for my checks. The girls might have expired of starvation. And—'' she drew in a breath, squaring her shoulders ''—I wanted an opportunity to apologize for this morning.''

She had to have the softest brown eyes he'd ever seen, Ben thought. And the prettiest mouth—pink and supple and... He put aside his thoughts, realizing she was expecting a response to her apology. ''It's not necessary,'' he said, zipping up his jacket. ''I'm sure a woman alone, particularly one who's been robbed so often, has to be careful.''

''I didn't mean that,'' Georgia admitted with a wince. ''I meant...suggesting you lied about what you planned to do with the building. Not that you have any plans, but if you did...'' Having effectively stammered herself out on a limb, she stopped. ''Do you have any idea what I'm trying to say?''

He laughed softly. ''I think so. Where did Lacey get the red hair?''

Surprised by the question, she hesitated a moment. ''Her father,'' she replied.

Ben saw a glimpse of emotion in her eyes—loss, he guessed, but something else...a pain that didn't seem to be a part of grief.

''He could also talk himself into or out of anything,'' she said dryly. ''She's very frank and brave. Heroic qualities, but sometimes they make polite conversation difficult.''

He laughed. ''She's charming—they both are. Will you be at the Downtown something-or-other meeting in the morning?''

Her eyes widened in surprise. ''The Downtown Enrichment Association. Yes. How did you know about it?''

''I checked in at the Chamber of Commerce to pick up a map and a few brochures, and the manager invited me to sit in and learn what's happening in Astoria. That's a fanciful name for a group of merchants.''

Georgia nodded with a wry smile. ''We were a little tongue-in-cheek when we voted on it. The group is composed of some downtown businesses who think historical enrichment and preservation will 'enrich' our cash registers as well as our city. It's a fun group of people.''

''I'll look forward to meeting them. We can haggle about the pizza then.''

''All right.'' Georgia nodded, pleased with the way this encounter had turned out. He could still decide to evict them and make an office complex out of the building, but at least it wouldn't be her fault. ''Meeting's at seven at the Red Lion.''

He smiled. ''That's where I'm staying. See you then.'' With a brief wave he loped across the parking lot to the red truck.

''HE'S CUTE, MOM.'' Linda sat at the kitchen table with a cup of cocoa. She wore a white flannel nightshirt with Garfield in nap-attack mode on the chest. Her long dark hair had been brushed until it shone—a nightly ritual.

Beside her, Lacey, in an identical nightshirt, rested her chin in her cupped hands, her cocoa ignored. Her brown eyes were dreamy. ''He's a little old, but cute.''

''He's not old,'' Linda admonished. ''At least, not too old for Mom.''

Across the table from the girls, Georgia sipped her coffee, afraid to examine that remark too closely. It was late and she should send the girls to bed, but she relished these few moments of quiet they shared before retiring. Their lives were already getting busy with school activities and phone calls and overnights with friends. In a few years, they'd have lives of their own that would involve her only peripherally.

"Don't you think he's cute, Mom?" Lacey persisted.

Georgia put her cup down. "No," she said, then could not stop the smile that came as her daughters watched her expectantly. "I think he's gorgeous."

"All right!" Linda slapped the table in excitement, and Lacey leaned forward enthusiastically. "Do you like him? He seems so great!"

"Actually, I don't know him that well." Georgia suddenly felt the need to dampen their fervor. Their intense interest in her remarrying was something they all teased each other about. She didn't mind it because it meant they were getting over the loss of their father, but as a serious consideration, it was out of the question. "He'll be coming and going like he said at dinner. He enjoys being a bachelor, remember?"

Lacey, who always heard and remembered everything, corrected her. "That's not exactly what he said, Mom. He said he'd like to have kids, but it was hard to find a wife when you moved around a lot. He seemed to like being with us tonight."

"And with you, Mom," Linda said seriously. "He kept looking at your hair."

Georgia felt a blush start at her neck and fought it off by collecting their cups. Was that true? she wondered. "You're making something out of nothing. He's just a good-looking man who bought the Roberts Building."

A silence fell over them as Georgia rinsed out the cups. Then Linda, wiping off the table, looked at Georgia over her shoulder. "Do you want to get married again, Mom?"

Georgia gave the faucet a sharp turn and reached for a towel. "I don't know." She turned to face her daughter. "Don't you think it's kind of fun, just us girls?"

"Yeah," Linda admitted, her tone conditional. "Except when the dishwasher breaks down or it thunders or—" she sighed, rinsing the sponge under the faucet "—it comes times for the Senior Class Father/Daughter Tea. I know I don't have to worry about it until next year, but I won't have a father then, either."

Lacey came to put her arms around Georgia. She felt fragile in the nightshirt, and Georgia held her close. "Why did Daddy have to die?"

The girls had grieved over the loss of their father, but they have never whined. Despite the complete shock of the accident and the ugly days before and after the funeral, they had gone back to their obligations at school and around the house with a courage that had inspired Georgia to go on. Otherwise, after what she had learned, she might have given up.

"Because," she said gently, philosophically, "things happen to us in life that we can't explain and can't do anything about, except deal with them as gracefully as we can."

"That's crummy," Lacey said feelingly.

Georgia rubbed her back. "That's life."

Lacey pulled back to ask, "Do you miss him?"

Georgia nodded, tears blocking her throat when she had thought she'd cried them all long ago. Her grief had been entangled in the mysterious circumstances of his death and the ugly things they implied. Still, she could recall so clearly how completely they'd loved each other, how happy they'd been, how much he'd loved the girls and Bea. Her memories could negate every grim implication of the way he'd been found—yet, it had happened.

"Always," she admitted. "But I just collect my good memories and think about them—even let them hurt a little—and I feel better." That wasn't precisely true, but it sounded reasonable and she wanted her daughter to feel at peace.

"It doesn't really hurt anymore," Lacey explained. "It's just that…when I get to thinking about it…it's like…" Uncharacteristically at a loss for words, she looked to her sister for help.

"Like something's missing," Linda provided. "Something important."

Georgia pulled Linda into her free arm and hugged her. "I know. When it comes time for the tea, I'm sure Mr. Hansen or Ragnar will be happy to escort you."

Linda nodded. "That's nice, Mom. It'd just be better if it was my own dad, you know?"

"I know, sweetie, but we have reality to deal with here." Georgia hugged her again.

Linda nodded grimly, then looked Georgia in the eye with a burgeoning smile. "Reality is that half the kids' real fathers won't be there. Heather Berger will probably have to go with her grandpa, Jill Warner goes everywhere with Misty Henderson and her dad, and poor Shelly will have to go with that old guy her mom's going out with. If she hasn't traded him in for somebody else by then."

"He isn't old," Georgia corrected, struggling with a laugh. "He's just bald."

"He's weird," Linda insisted. "He talks about money markets and CBs and stuff."

Wondering what citizens band radios had to do with careful investing, Georgia suggested, "CDs?"

"Whatever. He has Shelly putting thirty percent of her allowance into the stock of some computer company in Connecticut."

"When she could be buying *clothes*?" Lacey was horrified.

"Anyway," Linda said with a sigh, "I guess I'd be lucky to have Mr. Hansen or Rags to go with."

"Can we have leftover pizza for breakfast?" Lacey asked as Georgia led them up the stairs to the bedrooms.

"No, but you can take it with you for lunch."

"Don't forget to sign my permission slip for the field trip," Linda reminded. "I left it on the refrigerator."

"Right."

"And pick up my drill team skirt from the cleaners," Lacey said.

"Right."

"Thanks for the party, Mom." In front of her bedroom door, Lacey turned to give Georgia a hug. "And for the great sweater. I'm going to wear it to school tomorrow."

"Good," Georgia said, hugging Linda. "Then at the end of the week I can pick *it* up from the cleaners, too."

Giggling, Lacey disappeared into her room. Linda hesitated a moment, looking in concern at Georgia from the shadows of the hallway. "Are you going to be okay, Mom?"

Surprised by the question, Georgia smiled, wondering if her mother-in-control facade had somehow slipped. "Of course, Lindy. Why do you ask?"

Linda shrugged, leaning back against the door frame to her bedroom. "I don't know. I never thought about it much before, but tonight, when we saw Ben with you, I realized that you must get very lonely without Dad. It's been two years now, and you never go out with anybody."

Touched that Linda had thought along those lines, Georgia felt the strange tension that had plagued her all day soften. "Well, at my age you have other things to worry about."

"But men are important to a woman's life."

The bold statement was made with such conviction that Georgia felt an instant's panic over just what had brought her daughter to that conclusion.

"I mean..." Not usually at ease with baring her soul, Linda folded her arms and looked down at her shoes, then up at Georgia. "I haven't ever been in love or anything..." Georgia let her breath out slowly. "But I've worked with a lot of boys at school on the student council and with that fund-raising thing last year for the band. Most of them don't even see me. But there's this one boy..." Linda shrugged and blushed. "Well... he makes me feel special...pretty."

Georgia's maternal antennae rose. "Why don't you invite him over?"

Linda shook her head. "It's nothing like that. I don't think he really likes me—he's just nice to me."

"I promise I wouldn't mention marriage," Georgia teased.

Linda giggled and rolled her eyes. "I just meant that when he smiles at me, I feel like there's a glow here." She put a hand to her stomach, alternately smiling and frowning as though her thoughts confused her. "But there're lots of pretty girls after him."

"Honey, you're pretty enough to compete," Georgia said firmly. "You have so many fine—"

"Mom." Linda stopped her with mild impatience. "You think I'm special 'cause you're my mother. But the truth is, I'm just not very pretty and kind of... weird."

"Linda!" Georgia put her hands on her daughter's shoulders and shook her gently, alarmed by how near she stood to the brink of womanhood and by how sincerely she believed herself to be ordinary when, in truth, she was such a special person. "You're not *weird*. You're genuine. You never pretend to be someone you're not. And as far as not being pretty, haven't you looked in the mirror?"

Linda sighed and rolled her eyes again. Vaguely, Georgia remembered looking in the mirror at that age and being convinced that an ugly, large-nosed freak looked back at her.

"That settles it, then," Georgia said, giving Linda a hug. "I can't get married again. I have to look after my little troll. Or, who knows? Maybe one day love will sneak up on both of us."

Linda pulled away, giving her a scolding glance. "This is the nineties, Mom. A woman goes after what she wants."

Georgia pinched Linda's chin. "Then maybe you'd better take your own advice. Good night."

She went back to the kitchen to sign Linda's permission slip and replace it under the magnet so that she would remember it in the morning. During the nightly ritual of checking the burners on the stove, the coffeepot, and window and door locks, Georgia let herself think about Ben Stratton and the thoughts he'd inspired in Linda.

Linda was wrong, of course. A man wasn't important to Georgia's life at the moment. Financially, she was doing fine; as a parent, she had a blessedly good relationship with the girls; and as a woman...well, as a woman she'd been alternately stunned, hurt, defensive, stubbornly loyal and completely confused since Gary's death. Until she had some answers—and the likelihood of that happening was negligible—she couldn't embark on another relationship. She had to know what had happened to the one she'd had.

Not that Ben Stratton would ever see her as Linda thought he saw her, anyway. She groaned softly to herself as she flipped off the lights and climbed the stairs. She had accused him of being a "parasitic menace to society," threatened him with bodily harm, then slashed him with a pair of tongs. She couldn't help the smile that formed when she thought about that. Hardly inspiration for romance.

Georgia went into her bedroom, stopping on the threshold as she'd done every night since the day Gary died. She wondered if this feeling of being a stranger in her own room would ever change. Without her husband it seemed to lose all familiarity to her. The shades of blue and cream with which she had so lovingly decorated it several years ago now reminded her of something someone had tried to recreate from a picture in a magazine, somehow losing the warmth and personality that had been intended.

Loneliness swept over her, harsh and very real. She knew how to deal with it, but for a moment she didn't have the energy. It was such a solitary struggle, and it seemed to go on so long.

Then she remembered Linda reminding her that "This is the nineties, Mom. A woman goes after what she wants." Pulling off her clothes and changing into a long, pink flannel nightgown, she had little problem mentally listing what took precedence in her life. She wanted her girls to be happy, well educated and on their way to promising futures. She wanted Bea to marry Rags and be happy, and she wanted to keep her shop—in its present location—and see it prosper.

She set the alarm on her clock radio and climbed into the middle of the cold bed, feeling better. It always helped, she thought practically, to know your priorities. It never occurred to her that she'd left herself out of them.

CHAPTER THREE

"GEORGIA! HERE!"

Breathless, Georgia stopped her headlong rush into the Red Lion's banquet room and turned her head toward the sound of the voice. Karen waved at her from across a room that was filled with most of the membership of the Downtown Enrichment Association. Georgia waved back, forcing her way through the group just as the association's president banged his gavel.

"You missed breakfast again," Karen said with a shake of her head, pouring coffee for Georgia as she settled into a chair beside her and dropped her purse on the floor. "What crisis befell the Madisons this morning?"

"Don't be smug," Georgia scolded with a smile, eagerly bringing the cup of coffee to her lips. "Someday, if you and Phil decide to have children, you'll know what it's like, particularly if they're girls. They can't find their shoes, the right blouse isn't pressed, their hair isn't right. It's hard to be anywhere on time. Did you save me anything to eat?"

Karen reached behind the coffeepot to something wrapped in a napkin and handed it to Georgia with a grin. "What are friends for?"

"All right!" Georgia unwrapped a fat bran muffin and dropped it onto the empty plate before her, putting the napkin in her lap. "If I had an orange juice, life would be good."

A tall, slender glass of juice suddenly appeared in front of her, deposited near her coffee cup by a large male hand. She followed the white cuff and the gray wool sleeve over her shoulder to the now familiar face of Ben Stratton.

"Thank you," she said in surprise as he took the chair opposite Karen. "That was thoughtful."

In a crisp white shirt, subtle tie and three-piece suit, he looked very different from the the dusty, carelessly dressed man she'd mistaken for a thief yesterday morning. His brandy-blond hair was combed back into order, an apparently stubborn side part taking over anyway, the strands it disturbed beginning to curl. His hazel eyes were bright, more gold than brown in the sunlight coming in through the wall of windows that looked out on the river. He smiled easily at her. "I'd like to take credit, but Karen knew you'd be wanting it. I just went to the buffet table to get it."

"Well, thank you both," she said, giving each a wry lift of her eyebrow as she privately wondered why she should suddenly feel breathless. "I've come to a sorry state when my best friend and my landlord can second-guess my needs."

Ben frowned. "Why a sorry state? Why not consider yourself lucky?"

Karen refilled Ben's coffee cup, then her own. "Because Georgia prides herself on always being on top of things. And if it wasn't for a propensity for tardiness, she would be. Knowing someone's read her mind probably makes her feel vulnerable."

Georgia was saved from having to defend herself when the meeting was called to order. The association's president, Jasper Johnson, an attorney who'd been a friend of Georgia's family since she was a child, conducted the usual preliminaries. The minutes of the previous meeting were read, the treasurer's report given—bringing its usual groan—and various standing committees' reports presented, drawing everyone's halfhearted attention while breakfasts were finished and gossip was exchanged in whispers. Then Jasper called Georgia to the podium.

In surprise, Georgia looked at Karen. "Did he call me?" she whispered.

Karen nodded, also looking surprised.

"Why?"

"I don't know." Karen made a shooing motion with her hands. "Your request for a grant to buy the Jeremiah houses has probably offended the Paul Rotherman Foundation, and they're going to tar and feather you and ride you out on the old Burlington-Northern tracks. Go."

"Georgia. Please." Jasper's voice boomed through the microphone as he looked over the crowd, finally spotting Georgia as she stood and began to weave her way through the tables to the dais.

Ben watched the back of Georgia's white woolen dress as she made her way to the microphone. Glossy dark hair swung as she moved, slim hips swayed with unconscious grace, and long neat calves and trim ankles drew his eyes. She smiled at good-natured jibes from friends as she passed and swatted one older man on the shoulder when he caught her wrist and said something that made the rest of the table laugh.

It was easy to see that she was loved, Ben thought, though he'd had sufficient evidence of that while Karen clucked for half an hour before Georgia finally arrived.

He allowed himself a moment of wondering what that was like. He usually didn't indulge those kinds of thoughts because they led to other painful memories of a part of his life he liked to think was behind him. Still, he couldn't prevent a moment's jealousy, a stab of envy for the woman surrounded by the love and respect of people she'd known most of her life.

"She's a favorite around here," Karen whispered.

Ben looked at the faces turned fondly, expectantly, toward her and smiled dryly. "Hard to tell."

On the dais, Jasper put an arm around Georgia. Ben watched her fold her hands self-consciously, smile at the watchful group, then lower her eyes as the president began to speak. She looked touchingly vulnerable, something he'd have never suspected the previous morning when she was rearranging his ribs with a squeegee.

"I'm sure you all remember," Jasper said conversationally, "last fall when we thought it would be a good idea to help the Columbia River Pioneers Museum acquire the two houses owned by Hiram Jeremiah on Duane Street behind the Roberts Building." He looked over the group with the comfortable confidence of long acquaintance. "We knew that two preserved historic homes right downtown would be good for our businesses. Of course, none of us could afford to buy the houses, and the current owner, living in San Francisco, was unwilling to donate them. We all decided that applying for a grant from the Paul Rotherman Foundation was a great idea." He stopped to acknowledge more nods and more approving murmurs. "But none of us was willing to write up the application. We were too busy, or we didn't know what to say. We talked about hiring someone to do it but decided it should really be done by one of us, someone who'd grown up here and who could express what it means to us in a way that would get us the money. So Georgia volunteered to do it.'' Jasper gave her a paternal squeeze and smiled out at his audience. ''Well, guess what came to my home this morning by messenger?''

Ben heard Karen's intake of breath and saw Georgia's head snap up and turn to Jasper. She put both hands to her mouth and waited with the rest of the now silent group. But Japser's pause for dramatic effect was a moment too long. Georgia grabbed him by both lapels and demanded in a whisper heard by everyone, ''Did we get it?''

''We got it!'' he shouted.

Georgia screamed and wrapped her arms around his neck. The audience rose in a body to shout and applaud. Laughing, Karen kissed Ben's cheek, then ran to the next table to share the excitement with friends. Ben watched the pandemonium and wondered how many places were left in the country where this kind of camaraderie, this kind of common caring took place. Probably not many. People loved and cared about each other everywhere, but it had been his experience that people valued their independence and found it difficult to work together toward the same goal.

A burly young man in jeans and a dark sweater reached up to the dais to bracket Georgia's waist and swing her down. She was swept from table to table with hugs and handshakes. After five minutes, the president reconvened the meeting.

Karen came back to the table, quickly followed by Georgia, who was arm in arm with a precisely groomed dark-haired man no taller than she was. Ben noticed that the man took hold of her hand as he sat at a right angle to her, across from him. He glanced up at Ben, giving him a friendly smile, but his attention was all for Georgia even after the meeting resumed.

A hand went up at the table nearest the podium. "Are we going to delay work on the houses until after Columbia River Days at the end of May?"

Jasper turned his head toward Georgia's table. "Mesdames cochairmen?" He smiled and corrected himself, "Cochairpersons?"

Ben was surprised when all the women in the group laughed, unoffended by the little chauvinist joke.

Georgia looked at Karen. "You explain it," she said with a smile. "I'm resting on my laurels." At which remark the little man covered their joined hands with his other one. Ben could not quite isolate or identify the strange feeling of annoyance rising in him without apparent reason.

Karen stood, a fashionable blue jacket over her bakery whites. "I haven't seen Jasper's letter, but it was our understanding when Georgia applied for the grant that it would be at least six weeks after approval before we have a check in our hands, so I'm sure we won't be able to start on the houses for some time."

The subject of building contractors was discussed then shelved until bids could be obtained and discussed at a future meeting.

"Okay." Jasper consulted his notes. "Last order of business. We need a volunteer to coordinate the Columbia River Days Princess pageant with Knappa, Seaside and Astoria high schools."

A hand went up at the back of the room, and Jasper smiled. "Ah, Mrs. Butler. A winner of the pageant herself in 19…?"

The pretty matron at the back of the room called back, "Am I under oath?"

Everyone laughed and someone shouted, "The question should be, are you under warranty? All those teenage girls!"

"I can handle it," she boasted. Her approval was made unanimous by a round of applause, and the meeting was adjourned.

The small man across the table from Ben immediately took the opportunity to pull Georgia closer and kiss her cheek. "I can't believe you pulled it off! Remember how hard I tried to get us a grant two years ago and got nowhere? And I'm supposed to know how to do that stuff."

"Well, you should have asked me for advice," Georgia teased, turning to Ben, her cheeks flushed with modest pleasure in her success. "Mr. Stratton, I'd like you to meet Walter Bishop, curator of the Columbia River Pioneers Museum. Wally, this is Ben Stratton, the new owner of the Roberts Building."

Bishop stood, offering his hand, and Ben reciprocated.

"Do you believe this woman?" Bishop asked, his thin-featured face flushed with pride. "The grant will mean so much to us." He grinned at Georgia. "And who'd have thought it from the girl who ducked class to go to Young's River Falls with a quarterback."

"Come on, Wally." Karen took his arm and began to propel him toward the door through which everyone was crowding, hurrying to get to their cars to reach their shops and businesses in time to open. Georgia and Ben pressed in behind them.

Georgia looked up at Ben. "If you noticed the three old houses right behind our building, Wally owns the only one of the three that's painted. It once belonged to Godfrey Mitchell, an early river pilot here. The other two are the Jeremiah houses we were talking about.''

As the crush moved forward, Wally told Ben over his shoulder, ''I still have years of work inside, but it's a wonderful house. Georgia and I fought over it, but I won.''

''Only because you had the cash deposit.'' Georgia grinned at him. ''All I have are two kids who insist on eating and a voracious oil furnace.''

Nearing the door, Karen and Wally squeezed through an opening to their left just as a large man in front of Ben and Georgia swung a raincoat over his shoulders. Ben pulled her close, raising his hand in front of her face and ducking his head to cover hers as the thick, button-studded fabric flew at them. It slapped harmlessly against the side of Ben's head, and the man immediately turned to apologize. He was tall and thickly built. His contrition seemed to lessen when he saw whom he'd struck. He stopped beyond the door on the landing while everyone else rushed around them down the steps to the parking lot. Pale blue eyes looked at Georgia with animosity, and Ben put a hand on her shoulder, coming alert. Suddenly the warm, small-town atmosphere was shattered by the jarring note of the man's anger. He looked up at Ben in a moment of interest that contained no courtesy or even civility, then lowered his eyes to Georgia.

''So, the house hugger gets two more.''

Ben felt Georgia's shoulder stiffen under his hand. ''It's a place of history, Rob. You can put your restaurant someplace else.''

''I wanted to put it on Duane Street. It was a good

commercial location and would have relieved us of two eyesores. You messed it up for me.''

Ben watched in admiration as Georgia smiled, making no effort to hide the fact she was pleased. ''I know.''

The man bristled, glancing at Ben, then back at Georgia. ''Good thing the cool widow's got herself a bodyguard. She might need him.'' He turned and hurried down the steps to a red Mercedes.

Georgia turned to Ben with a grin. ''Thank you,'' she said. ''If you hadn't been here, I think I'd have been fish food.''

He could see no real fear behind her brown eyes, but she looked just a little shaken. Ben retained his hold on her shoulder and started down the steps. The early sun had gone into hiding, and a sky now heavy with pewter clouds was spitting rain. ''There seems to be one person in Astoria who doesn't love you. Where's your car?''

She pointed across the lot to the blue station wagon, and they started toward it. ''Rob MacKay is always at odds with everybody. He wants to bring in a Super Steaks franchise, which is a great idea. But he wants to tear those old houses down to make room for it. Wally and I have been fighting him for a year.''

''Why didn't he snarl at Wally?''

They stopped at the station wagon, and Georgia leaned against the door to face him. She rubbed her wool-clad arms against a cool breeze coming off the river, then pointed to Wally and Karen, already at their cars. ''Fortunately for Wally, he was out of the way. Actually, I offend Rob more because I'm a woman, I suppose. He hates to be outmaneuvered by anybody, but he dislikes me particularly.'' She shifted suddenly, putting her large leather purse on the front fender and routing through it. "About the pizza..."

"Forget it," he said. "You can take me for pizza when I come back to town."

She turned, a frown between her eyes. She replaced it immediately with a tentative smile. "You're leaving now?"

"I've got to get back. I'm supposed to be in Salem tomorrow." He looked at her seriously. "You watch out for that MacKay character. I don't like his looks or his attitude."

She dismissed him as a threat with a wave of her hand. "I've been arguing with him for years. Well—" she held a hand out to him "—it's been nice meeting you...." She laughed. "And I apologize again for yesterday morning."

He engulfed her small hand in his, not surprised to note that, despite its size, its shake was sturdy. "It's all right. It's nice to know someone's guarding the building."

"When will you be coming back?" she asked, then added casually, "I mean, you still have to decide what to do about it."

He smiled. "I know what I'd like to do," he said noncommittally, "but I have to discuss it with my uncle. I'll be back in a couple of weeks to have a tenants' meeting with you and Karen."

Georgia nodded, wishing he could offer a little more reassurance but understanding his position. She pulled her keys out of her purse and opened her car door. "We'll see you in a couple of weeks, then. Goodbye." In a matter of seconds, Georgia was in the car and heading east on West Marine Drive back to town.

Her hands were steady on the wheel, but something

deep inside her was trembling. Residual fear from that encounter with Rob MacKay? she wondered. Partly. But part of it was a disjointed memory of having her head pulled into Ben Stratton's shoulder. The left side of her face had rubbed against the roughness of nubby wool, while the right had been pressed into a warm hand. The smell of his woodsy after-shave was a fresh memory in her nostrils even now.

As her mind replayed the scene that had followed with Rob MacKay, she could feel the weight of Ben Stratton's hand on her shoulder.

God, she thought worriedly as she braked for a red light. *Have I been alone too long?*

"YOU WANT TO WHAT?" The voice at the other end of a perfect telephone connection shouted, as though something had interfered with his hearing.

"I'd like us to just give the building a new front and leave it as it is." Ben spoke from the sofa of his motel room, looking out the double glass doors to the fishing boats bobbing at anchor in Astoria's west mooring basin. In the darkness, light bloomed from several of the boats, and the rest were highlighted by the floodlights from the motel. It was a pretty sight that eased the tension he usually felt when he was on business. "It has two thriving tenants at the moment, and they've just gotten some kind of grant to restore a couple of old houses. They're really into preservation. I'd like to give the building a new front appropriate to the historic atmosphere here and wait on any major changes."

"Ben," his uncle said reasonably, "I always trust your judgment on these things, but we are in the business of acquiring and restoring to make a profit."

"We have a building you bought for a song. It's in

good repair, and for the price of a face-lift, we'll get steady rents. We can always subdivide later if I'm proven wrong.''

There was a moment's pause. ''You're sure?''

''Yes.''

''All right. Will you be back in the morning?''

''No, I thought I'd hang around a few days and talk to an architect, then bat his ideas around with a builder.'' Ben hesitated, waiting for David to protest. When he didn't, he added, ''You'd better send Kimball to Salem. I could be tied up for a few days.''

That did make David react. ''Ben, is there something you want to tell me?'' he asked.

Ben smiled to himself. He could imagine David, who liked detail in everything, pulling at his thin gray hair. ''You sent me to do a job,'' he replied easily. ''I'm just trying to do it right. If my staying is a problem, I can leave early in the morning and be in Salem before lunch.''

''No....'' David said uncertainly. ''You do what you have to do. I can send Kimball. Just keep in touch.''

''Don't I always?''

''When it suits you.'' David's reply was not so much a criticism as a statement of fact.

Ben smiled again. ''All right, Unc. I'll give you a call as soon as I know anything I can pass on.''

After bidding his uncle good-night, Ben hung up. Pushing the double glass doors open, he stepped out onto the small fenced-in area that separated the motel from the riverbank. He drew in a deep breath of air and was surprised to find nothing offensive in the smell of diesel and fish. Woven into it was the tang of evergreen, the sweetness of an early spring night and the mysterious fragrance of the river.

Leaning his hands on the wrought iron railing, Ben looked out at the boats and wondered why he was still here. All the things he told David he wanted to do, he could have done by phone. Something he couldn't quite define had made him stay.

Astoria was a pretty town filled with nice people. That was true, but Oregon was full of pretty towns and nice people. Ben straightened, folded his arms and acknowledged to himself that Astoria had Georgia Madison in it. He had a vague memory of silky hair that smelled of something sweet and herbal against his face when he'd shielded her from MacKay and his errant raincoat. The soft skin of her forehead had grazed his chin; her hand had made a startled movement to his chest and he'd felt the warmth of it through his shirt and undershirt. His hand went to the spot now, rubbing as though the feeling lingered. He remembered also a subtle look of disappointment in her eyes when she realized he was leaving.

You're a loner, he told himself severely. *You've never been loved, you don't know how to give love, you have no business looking for it.* Ben instantly denied to himself that he was looking for anything, except signs of structural problems in the Roberts Building. Following that thought was the mental image of a frightened but courageous Georgia holding him against the wall of her back room with a squeegee. He laughed into the darkness despite himself.

Turning back into the room, he closed and locked the doors, then drew the drapes. The trouble with the world, he'd often thought, was that people analyzed too much. They overlooked simple pleasures or successes or ruined them by picking them apart to determine why they were. He wasn't going to do that, he decided, heading determinedly toward the shower. He wanted to have another look at the building, maybe look up photos of old Astoria to get some ideas for the renovation. If he saw Georgia Madison again in the process, that would be a bonus. But he wasn't looking for anything.

"LAST CALL, LACEY!" Georgia shouted from the bottom of the stairs, pulling on a silky fuchsia raincoat. "One more minute and we leave without you!"

Linda, calm and organized, books in her arms, purse and gym bag hanging over her shoulder, said dryly, "She probably has an eyelash out of place."

"Or she rewashed her hair." Georgia checked her purse for apple and granola bar. "She thinks it'll dull the color."

Linda laughed without humor. "She wishes she had my color. Can you imagine? This—" Linda held a glossy, wavy strand of rich brown away from her head with disdain "—in place of that red?"

"Careful," Georgia cautioned. "Your hair is just like mine."

"It looks good on you because you're…mature," Linda explained diplomatically. "But the guys at school notice great bodies and great hair. Guys in my class are already looking at Lacey."

In the process of bustling Linda toward the door, Georgia stopped, sensing they'd bumped up against a sensitive subject. Though almost two years younger, Lacey was already three inches taller than Linda. Her graceful neck, ghostly slender torso and long limbs were giving every indication of developing into a spectacular body. Georgia suddenly wondered if that contributed to Linda's blurred self-image.

"Does that bother you?" she asked gently.

Linda looked up at her and gave her one of those smiles that told her she saw through the question to what her mother really wanted to know. "It doesn't make me hate her, if that's what you mean. Who could hate Lacey? But I am jealous." She sighed, watching as Lacey, looking like something out of *Seventeen* magazine in black jeans and a lavender-and-black sweater, appeared at the top of the stairs. "I take care of my clothes, put my makeup on carefully, do my hair, and I always feel pretty when I leave the bathroom. Then I run into Lacey and suddenly feel ugly."

Georgia took Linda's chin in her hand and looked down into her eyes. "Am I ugly?" she asked.

Knowing what she was getting at, Linda rolled her eyes, trying to pull away, but Georgia held fast. "Answer me," she said mildly. "Am I ugly?"

"No, Mom," Linda replied reluctantly, "you're not ugly."

"You'd even be pretty," Lacey, who had just come downstairs to join them, contributed enthusiastically, "if you'd take your hems up a little, tighten your—" She stopped midsentence when Georgia shot a quelling look at her.

Georgia turned her attention back to Linda. "Remember how your father always used to say you were cloned from me?"

Expecting that memory to cheer Linda, Georgia was surprised and dismayed when Linda's eyes filled with misery and her bottom lip gave an alarming quiver. Then Linda shook her head. "He probably didn't mean it," she said, and turned to walk out the door.

Georgia caught her arm and stopped her, surprised by Linda's reaction. "Why do you say that?" she asked.

Linda looked into her eyes for a moment, swallowing with obvious difficulty. She glanced at Lacey, then said with a sigh, "We're going to be late for first period, Mom."

Georgia worried about that exchange as she drove back to town from the high school. Linda's grief over her father had always seemed complicated by something else, something Georgia couldn't understand. She'd always attributed it to Linda's age. Adolescence was a time of such emotional upheaval that a serious loss was bound to hurt longer and require a slower return to normalcy.

Usually, Linda gave every indication of having recovered, but once in a while, like the other night and this morning, Georgia would glimpse something in her—some buried pain that had been ignored and was now ingrown. She was a good and dutiful child but much more private than Lacey, and Georgia tried to give her latitude there, tried not to force confidences she wasn't willing to share. But she might have to take a different tack here, she decided.

Parking her car in her usual spot, two blocks from her shop on a side street to leave the convenient parking for shoppers, Georgia walked briskly to Commercial. Maybe one day, she thought wryly, the Downtown Enrichment Association could do something about downtown parking.

Waiting for the light to change on Duane Street, she glanced to her right, where the two rickety old houses sat, and smiled with satisfaction. "You're going to live," she told them quietly. A well-dressed woman with a hat stopped beside her, glanced in the direction Georgia had been looking and saw no one to whom she might have been speaking. When Georgia smiled and said "Good morning," the woman gave her a quick, humoring smile and decided to cross in the other direction. Georgia laughed and walked on.

Running into the bakery, Georgia waved at Karen, who was busy transferring a sheet cake to a box, and ordered her usual muffin and coffee to go. In front of the bookstore, she balanced purse, bag and coffee to find her key and turn it in the lock. She had almost an hour to check in the stock she'd been meaning to get to for two days.

The door unlocked, she shouldered it open, then stopped two feet inside to gasp in shock and dismay. Her cash register was on the floor, every standing rack was on its side, and cards and notes were spewed all over. Half the books had been pulled off the shelves and strewn around, computer disks had been bent and tossed everywhere, and reams of paper had been torn and thrown like confetti. She put a hand to her pounding heart. Fear rose in her throat and she took several steps forward.

"Stop!"

CHAPTER FOUR

GEORGIA SPUN AROUND, backing away at the sound of a masculine voice. Relief washed over her when she recognized Ben. Forgetting that he was supposed to have left for Portland yesterday, she knew only that she was glad to see him. She went toward him, hands outstretched. "Somebody trashed my store," she said in a voice that was half hurt and half indignant.

Taking her hands, Ben pulled her out onto the sidewalk. "Go to the bakery and call the police," he said.

"No, I want to..." She tried to go past him, back into the shop. The store had become so much a part of her, she felt a need to walk through it, assess the damage, check the basement.

Ben stopped her with firm hands on her shoulders. "No," he said implacably. "Go call the police. I want to make sure there's no one inside."

She looked up at him stubbornly. "It's my shop," she said.

"It's my building," he returned quietly. "Go to the bakery, call the police, then wait out on the sidewalk." When she hesitated, he added, "Please, Georgia."

It had been two years since Georgia had had to bow to someone else's will, but she did it, however grudgingly.

Ben picked his way through the mess, heading for the back room and the basement stairs. Everything that could be overturned had been, and all stationery racks and shelves had had their contents thrown onto the floor. There was cruel and wanton destruction in the torn paper, ink splashed against the back wall and small pieces of office equipment that had obviously been thrown and stomped on.

Going cautiously down the basement steps, Ben found that the cartons he'd stepped over two days ago were intact, but the shelves had been overturned, contents strewn across the concrete floor. What could be broken had been.

Uneasiness began to grow inside him when he saw that the bakery's half of the basement was completely untouched. Any thought that this was a random act of vandalism was dashed by the orderliness across the room.

After a complete tour of the basement, Ben was satisfied that the perpetrators were no longer in the shop. He ran back up the stairs, stopping at the top at the sight of a green smock hanging on a hook in the back room. A knife had cut it into fringe. His feeling of uneasiness became full-blown fear for Georgia and an anger so fierce he had to concentrate on quelling it to think straight.

He went back across the littered floor to the sidewalk, where Georgia waited with Karen. Standing on the other side of Georgia was a stout, gray-haired woman with a ferocious frown and the air of a top sergeant with an intestinal disorder. The fact that she had a brightly colored piñata under one arm and a serape over her other shoulder contributed to Ben's confusion. Before he could say anything, the woman demanded, "Well, young man. Who do you think you are to keep us cooling our heels out here?"

Georgia smiled thinly at Ben. "Ben, I'd like you to meet my mother-in-law, Beatrice Madison. Bea, this is Karen's and my new landlord, Ben Stratton."

"Good morning, Mrs. Madison," Ben said. "Or should I say, *¿Buenos días?*"

"Good morning," Bea replied without expression, apparently unimpressed with his attempt at humor. "I'd like to go in now and look around."

"We'll wait for the police," Ben said, smiling but firm. "They should be along in a minute."

"Young man," Bea said, squaring her impressive proportions. "This shop is my daughter-in-law's livelihood, and I have a financial investment in it, as well as an emotional investment in her. As you are merely passing through Astoria, making a little money off the locals as you go, I fail to see how that empowers you to keep me out of here."

Ben looked down into the woman's affronted blue eyes and ignored the insult to his absentee landlord status, striving for patience. Though he found her corseted body and Victorian demeanor a refreshing change from the Nike-clad, tennis-playing grandmothers who populated much of the West Coast, he recognized spoiled willfulness when he saw it and didn't mind exerting his own. "Your financial investment happens to be in my building," he said evenly, "and you and your emotional investment are safer out here until the police arrive. The floor is littered with junk you could easily turn an ankle on, and it would be best to leave everything undisturbed for the police. They might see something we wouldn't notice."

She glared at him mutinously, then, apparently giving the matter thought, had the grace to agree that he was right. "Very well," she said. She handed the piñata and the serape to Karen. "May I use your telephone to call Mr. Jyhla?"

Karen nodded. "Of course, Bea."

When her mother-in-law disappeared into the bakery, Georgia pulled her raincoat more tightly around her. "I'm sorry," she said. "Bea's used to having things her way. She's really a very kind person."

Karen looked up at him and shook her head. "No, she's not." Prepared for Georgia's predictable defense of the woman, Karen turned, forestalling her. But the appearance of a police car at the curb prevented an argument.

A tall officer with boyish good looks and a shorter, dark-featured man with the look of a seasoned veteran, though Ben guessed he wasn't yet forty, emerged from the car. As the young man peered inside the shop, Georgia introduced the veteran as Phil Hansen, Karen's husband.

"How far in did you go?" he asked Georgia.

"Ben went inside and down to the basement. He didn't see anyone."

The man gave Georgia's shoulders a squeeze, winked at Karen, then went in with his partner, gesturing for the others to follow. At the sight of the damage, Phil whistled and pushed his hat back on his head. "Stay near the counter," he advised, "until we look around."

"I'll get you some fresh coffee." Karen dropped Bea's gifts behind the counter and headed off to the bakery. She and Bea passed in the doorway.

"My God!" Bea exclaimed as she took several steps into the shop. She put an arm around Georgia and patted her stoutly. "You poor dear. Don't worry about a thing. I'll help you clean up and we'll find a way to replace your stock until your insurance comes through.''

"Thank you, Bea.'' Georgia hugged her. "But don't *you* worry. I can take care of things.'' She pointed her mother-in-law toward the chair behind the counter. "Phil asked us to stay here until they're finished looking around. Why don't you sit down?''

Bea walked around the counter toward the chair, then gasped in alarm when she started to fall. Ben caught her plump forearm and steadied her with an arm around her waist. She looked up at him in annoyance, then, when he kicked aside the clump of papers she'd stepped on to reveal part of the broken ribbon cartridge that had caused her to turn her ankle, she sighed and admitted grudgingly, "Thank you, young man. It seems you were right.''

He inclined his head. "You're welcome. Are you hurt?''

She leaned on him and flexed her ankle. "No, I'm fine, just clumsy.''

"Then I'd better help you to the chair.''

She frowned at his impertinence, then, looking into his eyes, apparently saw the amusement he was trying to conceal. "Your name again?'' she asked imperiously.

"Stratton,'' he replied. "Ben.'' He sat her in the chair, and she tossed her head back. He imagined what a handful she must have been at nineteen.

"Thank you, Ben,'' she said. "You may call me Bea.''

Certain an honor had been conferred on him that was restricted to very few, he accepted it with appropriate gravity. "Thank you, Bea. Ah, here's Karen with coffee.''

While Karen handed Bea a paper cup of coffee and offered her a pastry from a small tray she'd brought, Ben walked around to Georgia. Before she knew what he intended, he lifted her onto the counter. "You look as though you need to be off your feet," he said, seeing her surprised expression. "Try to relax. I know it's been a shock and the cleanup looks horrendous, but I'll stay around to help you."

Georgia wanted to scream and cry and carry on. She didn't want to sit and wait, all controlled and mature, while Phil and his partner went over her store. She wanted to knock down the few books that remained standing. She wanted to kick and rave about the cruel and selfish vandals who had done this to her. Something about Ben's strong hands lifting her onto the counter as though she weighed no more than a child, and the gentle empathy in his eyes, contributed to that feeling. Instead of making her feel stronger, he made her want to throw her arms around him and cry.

Ben took the coffee Karen offered him and handed it to Georgia. He smiled into her uncertain expression. "Think of it as a good excuse to ask the landlord to repaint."

She took the lid off her cup and gave him a dry glance. "Repainting inside isn't the landlord's job."

He shrugged, taking his own cup from Karen. "You've never had me for a landlord before."

Karen offered them the platter of pastry. "Our previous landlord wouldn't even paint the outside. Georgia, have an apple fritter. It looks like it's going to be a long day."

Georgia put her hand to her now queasy stomach. "I don't think I can eat anything." Then her frown deepened and she looked around. "But I had a blueberry muffin in a bag and a cup of coffee when I came to work this morning.''

Ben pointed behind him. ''I stepped over it. You must have dropped it when you saw what had happened.''

Karen put the platter on the work surface behind the counter. Then she came back around the counter and looked at Georgia. ''Do you think MacKay did this?''

''No,'' she said. Her expression and her voice registered surprise that Karen had suggested he was responsible. ''I know he thinks I'm an obstacle in the path of his financial success, but... I mean, we all went to school together—you and Wally and Rob and I. I can imagine him asking the city council to rezone this particular part of the block residential just so I'd have to move, but I can't imagine him doing—'' she waved a hand at the wanton destruction ''—this.''

Karen looked at Ben. ''She gives him too much credit. She does that with everyone. I don't like the looks of this.''

''Frankly, neither do I.'' Phil Hansen came to lean a hip against the counter while his partner went out to the patrol car. In his hands were the shreds of the green smock. ''Do you have any idea what this is about, Georgia?''

''No,'' she said, taking the smock from him. ''Isn't it just...vandals?'' The last word came out weakly as she held up the smock and saw the work a knife had done. She felt herself go pale.

Ben took the smock from her. ''Drink your coffee,'' he ordered quietly, then turned to Phil. ''Did you find anything?''

Phil held out a hand with several minute pieces of straw in it. ''A few pieces of this in the back room.

Otherwise, it looks like the usual under-the-street entry that's become part of our weekly routine around here."

Ben frowned at him. "What do you mean?"

"Astoria's built over the remnants of the turn-of-the-century city. There's an underground network of catacombs that provides entrance to most of downtown's basements for every punk, thief and vandal in the county. When life gets dull for the less reputable element in town, we can always count on a rash of break-ins. They've been working hot and heavy for the past few months."

"Can't you seal off the underground?"

Phil shook his head. "It would be an expensive proposition. The merchants think the city should do it and the city thinks it's the merchants' responsibility. Impasse. Anyway..." He glanced at the mess behind him, bounced a look off Ben that Georgia couldn't quite decipher, then focused on her gravely. "I don't like the look of this, Georgia. It isn't just random vandalism. It's aimed directly at you."

"But, why?" she asked. "I know I've upset Rob MacKay, but I can't believe he'd do this."

Phil smiled. "Karen told me about the grant. Congratulations. Rob MacKay, huh? I'll talk to him."

"He has horses," Karen said, standing beside her husband, her arms folded.

When everyone turned to her, waiting for her to explain that apparent non sequitur, she reached into her husband's hand to pick up a piece of straw between her thumb and forefinger and said, "Straw is used in horse stalls."

Phil smiled down at Karen. "How'd you like to be a cop, lady? Great hours, great pay."

She patted his cheek. "Then who'd make your doughnuts, flatfoot?"

Phil reclaimed the piece of hay and put it in his shirt pocket. "Good point. Georgia, maybe you should stay with someone for a while," he suggested, "until I can check this out a little further." He shook hands with Ben, winked at Georgia, kissed Karen's cheek and told her he'd see her at dinner.

As Phil went out to the patrol car, Karen gave Georgia a hug. "I'd better get back to work. You know, Phil was right about you staying with someone. Why don't you and the girls move into our family room?"

Georgia shook her head firmly. "Thanks, but I can't do that. We'd need something the size of the armory just for the girls' clothes for a few days."

"You're coming home with me," Bea said from her chair behind the counter. "And I won't hear any arguments."

Karen gave Georgia a silent, speaking look, then hugged her again. "Well, if you need anything at all, I expect you to call me."

Georgia followed her to the door and prepared to lock it, knowing she'd have to remain closed for the day to clean up. But a hand pushed against the door, and she found herself looking through the glass at Ragnar Jyhla. She opened the door for him and was instantly wrapped in his hug. He was a tall, spare man in jeans, a denim jacket and a baseball cap. A ruddy complexion, graying blond hair and a surprising impression of muscle for a man in his sixties spoke of Rags's Scandinavian ancestry and years spent at the helm of a ship. He and Bea had been seeing each other more than a year.

"Hi, Rags," Georgia said, reaching behind him to

lock the door. She drew him toward Ben. "I know Bea called you, but you didn't have to rush right over."

He looked around, his wrinkly lidded gray eyes widening at the mess. "Good God!" he gasped. "What happened?"

"The police think someone's out to get her." Bea walked into the arm he immediately curled around her. "She's going to stay with me for a while."

"Thank you, Bea, but I can't do that," Georgia said with as much determination as she could muster. She owed a lot to Bea, and more than that, she admired and respected her. Despite her mother-in-law's propensity for taking over, Georgia seldom fought her, knowing she meant well and was motivated by love for her and the girls. But this time she would have to be firm. She was about to offer several reasons why it was impossible, but was prevented from doing so by Rags, who appeared to be staring at Ben with a combination of surprise and pleasure.

"Rags, this is…" she began.

"Ben Stratton," Rags said, covering the small space that separated them and offering his hand. "The best backhand on the Portland Tennis Club courts. How the hell are you, and what are you doing here?"

Apparently as pleased to see Rags as the man was to see him, Ben laughed and shook hands with him as Georgia watched in surprise. "I'm great. Dave and I just bought this building," he said. "I happened to be around this morning when Georgia discovered the mess. I forgot that you live here part-time."

"River pilots usually have a foot at each end of their route. When I'm not in Portland, this is where you'll find me."

Ben glanced at his arm around Bea and grinned. "And you have a lady in every port along the way?"

Rags tightened his arm around her. "No, just this one. This is what happens to you when your friends can't stand your single status. They invite you to dinner, put a beautiful woman in your path and watch you try to weigh anchor."

Ben looked at his broad grin and appearance of general good humor. "You don't look as though you're suffering."

"He's never been better fed," Bea assured Ben, her chin angled, "or better cared for."

Ragnar frowned down at her. "Then why don't we make it permanent?"

Bea blushed and gave Rags a sturdy slap on the chest. "Rags, really. I explained that I have... responsibilities. I just can't run off to Portland. And this is not the place to discuss it."

Ragnar looked from Georgia to Ben. "We're among friends. I want you two to know we fought about this all over Mexico, and I want to go on record as having offered to make an honest woman of her." He shook his head at Ben and sighed with exaggerated regret. "Women are hard to deal with today. They have so many responsibilities that don't include us. How have we managed to slip in status?"

Ben laughed. "Apparently something got by us while we were playing tennis."

Bea cast a murderous glance from one man to the other. "We have a full day's work here, gentlemen. The sooner we begin, the sooner Georgia can get home and pack."

"We're not moving in with you, Bea," Georgia said, feeling almost too weary to face off against her mother-in-law. "The girls have all kinds of things going at school, and I can't disrupt them like that. I'm sure this was just somebody's crude attempt to...to frighten me. I'm sure they know it's worked, and now they'll leave me alone."

Bea squared her shoulders. "Georgia, Officer Hansen suggested that you need protection."

"My house is secure. We'll be fine."

"Think of the girls."

The safety of her daughters was enough to make Georgia think twice, but then she had to consider the danger she would face at the hands of her girls were she to suggest that they all move in with their grandmother. Bea would be after them to keep their music down, wear longer skirts, give up volleyball for more academic pursuits. It would never work.

"You're moving in with me," Bea said, "and that's final."

Seeing the look of desperation in Georgia's eyes, Ben suggested, "Why don't I move in with Georgia for a while?" When both women's eyes rose to his in alarm, he added easily, "I've decided to stay in town for awhile anyway. I have to see an architect and contractors, and working out of a motel room is less than convenient. You must have a spare room or an extra sofa." When Georgia said nothing but continued to stare at him as though he'd suggested they share a hot tub filled with champagne, he said, "A corner in the garage?"

"What I have," Georgia said, "are two teenage daughters to whom I am constantly preaching the value of exercising caution around men they don't know."

"I know him," Rags said quietly. "We play doubles in the tennis club's celebrity tournament every year to raise money for Waverley Children's Home." He grinned. "My wily trickery and his young legs are a deadly combination. We've even shared the court with the governor a time or two."

"But..." Bea began to protest.

"Face it, Beabee," Rags went on. "Ben could certainly provide better protection for Georgia and the girls than you could—unless, of course, we're dealing with a criminal who's susceptible to intimidation."

Georgia was surprised when Bea took no offense at Rags's suggestion or his teasing jab. She simply seemed to be considering the truth of what he's said. "I suppose his being seen with her might even discourage someone from threatening her further."

"Exactly."

"All right. Ben, you'll move in with Georgia and the girls tonight. Gary had a small workshop in a shed behind the house that hasn't been touched since he died. It has all the comforts of home. There." Dusting off her hands as though satisfied that was settled, Bea gave further orders. "Georgia, we'll need large plastic garbage bags to get some of this junk off the floor so we can assess the damage. You two youngsters can do the bending, while Rags and I record what you've lost for the insurance company and to facilitate your reordering."

As Ben and Ragnar righted a card rack and Bea sorted through the rubble for the cards that belonged on it, Georgia picked her way to the back room, where she kept garbage bags. Her thoughts and her feelings were too chaotic for her to analyze how she felt. The only thing that registered clearly was a sense of panic. Her daughter was troubled, her store had been trashed, it looked as though someone would take great pleasure in making her suffer unspeakable emotional and probably physical agonies, she was in charge of a county-wide event that would bring thousands of people to Astoria, and a man she'd known for two days and had seen for probably a total of an hour in that time was moving in with her for an indefinite stay. The urge to cry and scream and kick had left her. Now she felt a desperate need to run away.

"HE'S GOING TO *LIVE* HERE?" Lacey blinked, looking at Linda to make sure she hadn't misunderstood.

Linda, who liked to get things straight, asked, "You mean, Mr. Stratton, your landlord, is moving in with us?"

Georgia abandoned the onion she was trying to chop and turned to the girls, who still wore their knee socks, athletic shorts and Astoria High volleyball shirts. "I mean that he's going to live in Daddy's shop until the police can find out who trashed the store."

"Why?" Lacey asked.

Trying to minimize the suggestion of danger to herself, Georgia turned back to the onion. "I don't know. Mr. Hansen suggested that someone stay with us. The other alternative was moving in with Grandma for a week."

Lacey thought a moment, then threw her arms around Georgia. "Thank you, Mom. I mean, I know how you are about men and everything, but we'd have died at Grandma's."

Ignoring the onion once again, Georgia frowned at her youngest. "How am I about men?"

"You don't like them," Lacey replied without hesitation. "I mean, I know you said you *liked* Mr. Stratton the other night, but you don't like him like we like boys. You think he's cute but you wouldn't want to marry him. Can you be considered an old maid even though you've been married once?"

"No," Georgia replied. "Just an old widow. Could you two get changed and set the table, please?"

When Lacey ran upstairs, Linda lingered a moment, putting her arm around Georgia's shoulders. "Are you in some kind of trouble, Mom?"

"Not exactly," she replied, slanting Linda a smile. "Mr. Hansen just thought it would be good for us to have a man around for a while."

Linda nodded thoughtfully. "It would."

Anxious to divert her from her concerns, hoping she'd want to discuss this morning's upset, Georgia asked, "Did you have a good day today?"

"Practice was a killer," Linda replied, reaching into the colander of vegetables draining in the sink and pulling out a slice of cucumber. "Shelly jammed her finger. That's because she always covers her face when the ball comes at her instead of trying to bump it back."

"See that boy you told me about?"

"Yes." She took a carrot spear. "He just didn't see me. Story of my life. We're going to vote for Astoria High's Columbia River Days Princess tomorrow. Shelly thinks she'll get it."

Georgia cupped the chopped onions in her hand, carried them to the frying pan on the stove and added them to a browning pound of hamburger. "That's modest of her," she said.

Linda followed her, shrugging. "She's just being realistic. She looks like Kim Alexis, she has a great body and wears a C cup. The guys'll all vote for her."

Georgia stirred the onions into the hamburger and

sniffed the resulting aroma. "I thought you said a lot of the girls don't like her."

Linda stared thoughtfully into the pan, nibbling on the carrot spear. "The popular girls like her 'cause she's one of them. The girls in my crowd think she's a snot, but we don't have any power. And they don't understand her, anyway."

"What's to understand?" Georgia asked, remembering all the times Shelly had slighted Linda in one way or another. "She uses you when she needs help studying or preparing a project for cooking class."

"I know," Linda admitted without any apparent resentment. "But we kind of understand each other. Her dad's gone, too. I mean, he just left her mom, but Shelly hasn't seen him in two years, and that's kind of like he's dead. A lot of the other kids have stepfathers, but at least they have them. Shelly misses her dad, too. And her mom's never around."

Georgia stopped stirring to look down at Linda, now certain that her grief ran deeper and was more complicated than she'd ever expected. To her surprise, Linda grinned up at her, shaking her head as though Georgia were cause for amusement.

"You're so *intense*, Mom. It's not like I expect you to get married tomorrow because I miss Dad. I was just trying to explain to you how I felt. When you look all upset like that, it makes me not want to tell you."

"I want you to tell me how you feel," Georgia insisted, putting an arm around her shoulders. "Don't spare my sensitivities. Mothers get upset, they worry about their kids—it's our job. I just hate to think you're unhappy."

"I'm not unhappy," Linda said, stirring the mixture Georgia was ignoring. "I just get lonesome sometimes.

You are going to drain the fat off this before you add the spaghetti sauce?"

Knowing that was Linda's way of concluding the discussion, Georgia nodded, reaching overhead for a colander. "Yes, Miss Fonda, I am. Go get changed for dinner."

Linda started to run off, then stopped in the doorway to the back hall and the stairs. "Did Lacey tell you about the cold water faucet?"

"No."

"It wobbles. She tried to fix it, but it still feels a little weird to me."

"All right. I'll have a look at it." Georgia drained the meat first, then, filling the coffee decanter, she had to give the faucet an extra turn in order to produce water. She frowned at it, considering the advantages of simply calling a plumber over trying to do something about it herself and saving the hundred dollars. A knock on the back door distracted her. "Come in!" she called.

Ben walked into the kitchen, looking freshly showered and very large. For an instant she remembered Gary walking in like that after a Saturday afternoon in his workshop, looking fresh and hungry. Startled by the memory, she couldn't speak for a moment.

"Your husband was a lucky man," he said, coming over to the sink, where she stood. "That shop has every tool imaginable, a comfortable sofa, a television and a shower. My first apartment wasn't that elegant."

"After college?" she asked, making an effort to behave naturally. She opened the cupboard to her right, pulled out a jar of spaghetti sauce and twisted the lid.

"No, I was about sixteen and had gotten my first paycheck after working a month on a charter boat."

When the lid refused to give, he took the jar from her, gave it a twist, then handed it back to her. It came off easily.

"You were on your own at sixteen?" she asked in some surprise. He had the look of a man who'd come from a privileged background.

"I was happy to be," he replied, his tone implying that was as far as he wished to discuss it. He leaned a hip against the counter while she went to the stove and added the sauce to the hamburger and onions. "Anything I can do to help?"

"The girls will be down in a minute to set the table. We will need another chair, though. There's a straight-backed one in the corner of the living room."

"Right." As he went off for the chair, Georgia took a moment to draw a deep breath, thinking that around him she always felt as though she had emphysema. She reached into a bottom cupboard for a large saucepan in which to cook the noodles, put it in the sink and turned the faucet on. Two things happened simultaneously. The faucet came off in her hand, and a spray of water the size of a whale's spout hit her in the face. Her scream was choked back by a mouthful of water as she groped blindly to cover the hole. Then a firm hand pushed her away and the rocket of water became a high-tension spurt under Ben's other hand.

Already as wet as she was, he turned his head to the girls, who now stood wide-eyed on the other side of the table. "Linda," he said calmly to Lacey, who was closest, "turn off the water supply in the basement."

"I'm Lacey," she replied, remaining where she stood.

Flinging her drenched hair back, Georgia heard his

frustrated half laugh. "Would you do it anyway, please?"

"I'll go." Linda ran down the basement steps, and the squeak of a seldom-used valve could be heard. The spurt of water under Ben's hand remained constant.

"Turn it the other way!" he shouted in the direction of the stairs.

After more squeaking, the flow of water stopped. He removed his hand carefully. A trickle of water escaped, then stopped completely. He turned to Georgia, the front of his shirt drenched, his face and hair dripping.

Looking as though she'd been completely submerged, Georgia smiled at him and asked, "Do you still think this'll be more convenient than your motel room?"

CHAPTER FIVE

BEN TRIED NOT to stare at the sight of Georgia eating spaghetti with a towel wrapped around her head. Without the distraction of her glossy hair, her eyes seemed wider, her cheekbones more pronounced, her smile more devastating. She continued to look at him warily, but the small crisis had eased the tension caused by his presence. And the five minutes it had taken him to replace a faucet washer and tighten the faucet handle had earned him a look of surprised respect from Georgia and her girls.

"Do you think you could fix our stereo?" Lacey asked clearing away dishes while Linda scooped ice cream into dessert glasses. "You have to turn it up really high to hear anything, and sometimes it makes this awful noise."

"Lacey…" Georgia began to scold.

"It's all right." Ben smiled across the table. "I'm a better plumber than an electrician, but I don't mind looking at it."

Linda distributed ice cream around the table, and both girls sat down again. "Why would you want to own a building in Astoria?"

"Because it's beautiful here," he replied. "Having business here will give me a good excuse to come up often."

"But it rains all the time," Lacey pointed out.

Ben shrugged. "I lived for a couple of years in Los Angeles, where it's sunny all the time. You can get tired of that, too."

Lacey looked doubtful. "Really? I'm going to have a farm in Bend, where it's sunny. And I'll have animals all over the place."

With the child's looks, Ben thought she might already be contemplating a modeling career in Paris. He thought it refreshing that she seemed unaware of her special beauty and longed for something as wholesome as a farm and animals.

"What about you?" he asked Linda.

"I'm going to have a restaurant and lots of kids," she replied. Then she slanted Georgia a teasing look. "And a dishwasher that works." Immediately after the words were spoken, she straightened in her chair, turned to Lacey, who seemed to read some message in her eyes, then both girls turned to Georgia and cried simultaneously, "He can fix the dishwasher!"

Georgia smiled apologetically at Ben. "I'm sorry. We've been handyman poor around here for a long time, and they're a little delirious over your skill." She darted a threatening look at Linda and Lacey. "Please don't touch the dishwasher, Ben. The girls aren't expected to do that much around here, and dishes for the three of us—well, four of us—isn't going to kill them."

"What's the matter with the dishwasher?" he asked.

Before Lacey could reply, Georgia cast her a quelling look. "It doesn't matter. It's as old as Lacey is. Probably just time to throw it away."

"And me, too, I suppose," Lacey teased.

Georgia smiled at her. "Not till after you've done the dishes."

When Ben insisted on looking at the girls' stereo after dinner, Georgia took a thermos of coffee and a space heater to the workshop to make it more comfortable. Spring in Astoria was cold and damp. The sofa didn't open into a bed, but she put sheets and an old comforter on it, then a doubled-over blanket on top of that. She left another folded at the end of it, then made a mental note to bring fresh towels.

When she returned to the kitchen, the strains of "Tony, Tony, Tony" came vibrating down the stairs clearly and with considerable volume.

"Just a loose wire," Ben reported.

Shaking her head at the end of the auditory peace the faulty stereo had provided, Georgia laughed softly. "Thank you so much for fixing it. I hope you'll think of me while you're safely removed from potential eardrum damage in the workshop."

He grinned at her and she fought an attack of breathlessness with sudden briskness. "I left a thermos in the workshop for you and a space heater. I'd appreciate it if you'd turn it off before you go to sleep. Wait here, and I'll get you some towels." Before he could say anything, she ran downstairs to the dryer and back up again. She handed him two dark blue bath towels and a washcloth, thinking that now, at least, she had a reason to be breathless. "Breakfast is at seven," she went on, "and there isn't usually a moment's leeway. We have getting ready for school and work timed down to the second."

He was being dismissed, Ben realized, and turned to the back door.

"Thanks for fixing the faucet and the stereo," Georgia said quickly. "Had I been alone with the girls, I'm sure we'd have drowned."

He smiled, opening the door. "I'm sure Bea would have held me personally responsible, and I shudder to think what I'd have suffered." He turned to leave, then hesitated a moment. "How long have Bea and Rags been seeing each other?"

Georgia smiled fondly. "Over a year. She loves to cook for him, and he loves to tease her, as you saw. She doesn't let anyone else get away with that."

"You think he'll talk her into getting married?"

Georgia shrugged. "Bea's pretty independent, and Rags is indulgent, but he doesn't let her push him too far. I suppose she wants to be sure. Meanwhile, I'm glad they have each other. Everyone needs someone to care about them."

Ben nodded agreement, able to attest to that truth firsthand. Reluctant to leave the cozy kitchen and Georgia's smile, he made himself smile and do just that. "See you in the morning," he said over his shoulder.

Moving to the back door window, Georgia watched him walk toward the shop, his long strides eating up the shaggy lawn, his tight, narrow hips in old jeans moving to the distracting rhythm of his easy pace. Suddenly aware of what she was doing, she slapped the small curtain down and ran upstairs to ask the girls to lower the music.

In the workshop, Ben did a slow circuit of the small room, hands in his pockets, getting a feel for the man who had once spent long hours working there. The pegboard wall of carefully placed tools showed that he'd taken care of his possessions, but there was a comfortably messy air about the rest of the place with which he could identify. A pile of chairs in the corner in various stages of dismemberment, an overturned, legless table and a strange-looking hoop on a broken stand, the use of which he couldn't imagine, stood around the shop, probably attesting to a very human tendency to procrastinate.

On the wall over his workbench, next to a two-year-old poster-sized calendar from Astoria Builders Supply, was a framed photo of Linda and Lacey taken on the front steps of the house. He leaned on the workbench for a closer look. On the steps behind them was a smiling Georgia, her head leaning on the shoulder of a man who sat beside her. Linda leaned back against his knees, squinting against the sun, and Lacey rested against Georgia, looking just as she did now, delighted with the world, though a little baffled by it. It was a beautiful family portrait capturing the love and confidence in each other he was sure must be the backbone of every solid home.

Ben felt an acute sense of jealousy mingled with awe and admiration. It was nice to know those things did exist, though they weren't part of his experience. He found it oddly comforting to know that Georgia and the girls had had a husband and father they had loved and on whom they'd been able to depend. It also made him more able to appreciate what they had lost and how bereft they must feel.

A nice guy had occupied this space, Ben thought as he moved restlessly across the room. A guy who'd loved his wife and kids and been loved in return. Jealousy nudged him again, but he smiled to himself as he walked back to the stack of chairs. He had long ago decided that bitterness was destructive and counterproductive, but a little jealousy never hurt. The world was full of things he couldn't have; he'd have to be dead not to resent it occasionally.

He picked up a chair that matched those around the

dining table and saw that it was missing a turned rung on the bottom. He found the piece in a pile of things beside the chair and carried both to the workbench. It was going to be a long evening, he decided. He might as well make himself useful.

BREAKFAST REMINDED BEN of a raid. In the old movies about the twenties, people were always running back and forth and screaming as the police burst through the door. When Ben rapped lightly on the kitchen door and got no answer, he turned the knob and found it unlocked. Lacey was running past, red hair flying, shouting, "You said I could borrow it!"

Linda followed her, a curling iron in her hands, half her dark hair bouncing with curls, the other half hanging straight. "You can't borrow my Generra! You've got your own new sweater. Oh, hi, Ben."

"Hi," he replied tentatively. "You guys all right?"

She smiled at him. "Lacey's going to be dead. Mom'll be down in a minute. Have some cereal."

As both girls disappeared upstairs, Ben went to the table, where a box of cereal and a carton of milk stood. Georgia ran into the kitchen in her stocking feet, wearing a silky blue blouse over a slip, adjusting an earring. At the sight of him, she stopped, gasped and closed her eyes.

"It's all right," he assured her quickly, putting a hand over his face. "I've closed my eyes." He had, but not before he'd had a deliciously tantalizing glimpse of thin, satiny fabric molded to slender hips and long thighs. "If you'll put a bowl and spoon on the table, I won't even look up until you've done what you came in to do. Incidentally, Linda is chasing Lacey with a curling iron. I just thought you should know."

He heard a small laugh. "She must have tried to borrow her Generra sweater."

He almost dropped his hand in surprise, then caught himself. "How did you know?"

He heard a bowl and spoon clatter onto the table. "I'm their mother." He heard the sound of liquid pouring, heard it a second time, then the sound of Georgia expelling a small sound of relief. "Ah, caffeine. Okay, Ben. Count to five, then you can open your eyes."

He dutifully counted to five and lowered his hand to find himself alone in the kitchen. There was a bowl, a spoon and a banana at his place, and a steaming cup of coffee. Music blared from upstairs, the telephone rang twice, and a black cat with large amber eyes leaped onto the table, rubbing against his elbow with bold familiarity as he poured milk into his cereal.

Linda reappeared, shooed the cat off the table, then dropped books and jacket at her place and poured herself a glass of juice. "Sorry about that," she said, smiling at Ben as she stood and drank her juice. "Midnight lives next door but likes to sleep in our basement. He comes up to see what we're eating."

Lacey appeared, dropped her things beside Linda's and scooped up the cat. "And meany always chases him away."

"Not away," Linda corrected. "Just off the table."

"Poor baby," Lacey cooed over him, holding him in one arm while she rummaged through a fruit bin near the stove and pulled out an apple. "Mom down yet?"

"Ah...just for a minute," Ben replied. "I don't think she was quite ready yet. Aren't you two going to eat anything?"

Linda looked at him in surprise and held up her glass. "Juice."

Lacey bit into the apple.

Georgia appeared a moment later, dotted each girl with a kiss, petted the cat and refilled her coffee cup. She glanced at her watch. "Good morning, Ben. You girls about ready?"

Both heads nodded and Midnight was deposited out the back door. Georgia ran from the room again, and when she reappeared wearing a gray jacket that matched her skirt, the girls were nowhere in sight.

Expecting her to be upset, he was surprised when she simply leaned against the back door and waited. "Brushing their teeth," she explained. Then she glanced at his sweater and slacks. "Are you coming with us?"

He took his leather jacket from the back of the chair. "I'm your bodyguard, remember?"

"Well, that doesn't mean you have to stay with me every minute." She opened the door as the girls thundered down the stairs, grabbed their things and ran out to the car. "Surely you must have things you want to do on your own."

He ushered her out and turned the lock before closing the door behind him. "What I have to do involves the building," he said, keeping pace with her hurried strides around the house to the driveway. "Fortunately, that's where you'll be."

Georgia halted in her tracks. "Your truck's in my way."

"I'll drive," he said, digging keys out of his pocket.

Georgia would have protested, but the girls ran delightedly to the truck, exclaiming over its size. "Wait till the kids see us arrive in a red four-by-four with custom wheels!'' Ben opened the passenger door and the girls scrambled in.

Finding Georgia still hesitating, Ben caught her hand and pulled her to the driver's side. "My skirt's too..." she began to explain, indicating the high step and the slim cut of her skirt.

Ben tossed her purse to Lacey, then lifted Georgia onto the seat. "Watch your head," he cautioned.

Completely ruffled, Georgia sat silently while Ben and the girls talked across her, Linda giving him directions to the high school. Georgia was so close to his body she felt painted onto him, and breathing became even more of a problem for her than usual when he was around.

Their arrival in the school's parking lot caused the stir among the kids the girls had predicted. Linda opened her door, and Georgia watched as a tall, dark-haired young man in a letterman's jacket came to help her down and concluded that he was the boy Linda had told her about. He seemed much more aware of Linda, Georgia thought, than the girl realized. There were four boys to help Lacey down, and Ben had to wait a moment while an appreciative group walked around the truck and asked a few questions.

It wasn't until they'd headed back to town and Ben stopped at a red light, then glanced down at her that Georgia realized she was still painted to his side.

"You made their day," she said casually, scooting over.

He studied her for a moment, his eyes moving distractedly over her mouth, then her hair. "You should seriously consider a twenty-four-hour guard for them," he said, turning back to the road and accelerating when the light changed. "They're a dangerous combination of beauty and warmth. Did you have anything this morning besides that coffee?''

"No. I never do. Except an occasional blueberry muffin.''

He sent her a frowning glance, then looked back at the road. "You look a little peaked this morning. Didn't you sleep well?''

"No,'' she replied again. "But I never do that, either. It's nothing unusual. I have one of those systems that runs on coffee and adrenaline.''

"You open at nine-thirty?'' he asked, glancing at his watch.

Second-guessing him, Georgia turned in her seat to face him. "Yes, but I usually use the extra hour to catch up on paperwork or check in stock. I have stuff downstairs I've been trying to check in and bring upstairs since the day you turned up in the basement. I've got to get to it.''

"Why can't you do it later today?''

"Because I work alone,'' she explained patiently. "I can't work downstairs when a customer could walk in and need my help or rip me off. And the boxes are too heavy for me to carry upstairs and work on them in the shop.''

"I'll carry them up for you and help you check them in,'' he volunteered, turning into the parking lot of the Dutch Cup, a neat little restaurant with a view of the river. "You know, it's not good for your girls to choke down juice and rush off to school.''

Georgia sighed. "Did Bea coach you to say this? I'd rather they had solid breakfasts, but they're at a point in their lives when they'd rather make sure their hair is perfect than eat breakfast from the required food groups. I always make sure they have enough money to eat well from the cafeteria at lunch.''

He pulled into a parking spot and turned to grin at her. ''What do you do for lunch with no one to relieve you or run out to get you something.''

''I always have a granola bar in my purse,'' she replied.

Ben rolled his eyes, pushed his door open and jumped down. He turned to reach for her to help her down. She drew back, her expression suddenly haughty. As that was something he hadn't seen in her, he leaned an arm on the truck frame and waited.

''You're my landlord,'' she said evenly, ''not my husband. I haven't had to answer to anyone or do anything I haven't wanted to do in a long time. I'm comfortable with that. If we're going to be spending time together for the next few days, you're going to have to come to terms with it.''

Because she had spoken so calmly and so rationally and Ben had proved himself so far to be a rational man, Georgia fully expected him to get back in the truck and drive her to the store. Instead, he took hold of her arm, pulled her toward him and lifted her down.

''I'm also your bodyguard,'' he said quietly into her startled expression. ''And I'm a conscientious man. I feel as responsible to protect your inner body as I do your lovely arms and legs. If I carry you in there slung over my shoulder, we'll probably upset everyone.'' He locked the truck door, slammed it, then put an arm around her shoulders and started for the restaurant. ''So let's be civilized, all right?''

Ben had finished his breakfast and Georgia was half-way through a cheese omelet and toast before she could bring herself to speak to him. She was definitely annoyed by his presumption, but her feeling of confusion was stronger. It had been a long time since anyone— a man, particularly—had forced her into anything because he cared. Gary had been kind and gentle, though fairly forceful, and she'd forgotten the luxury of being that precious to someone. It was unsettling and curiously exciting to be outwitted by a man who had your best interests at heart.

"It could be," Ben said, "that you don't sleep well because you don't eat right."

"I don't sleep well," Georgia said, "because I've no one to sleep with." She heard the words come out of her mouth and looked up at him, daring him to misunderstand what she meant. When she saw that he didn't, her confusion deepened.

"I can only imagine the depth of your loss," he said gently. "I'm sorry."

She felt tears scrape her throat and sting her eyes. She sniffed them back, took a last sip of coffee and prayed they wouldn't fall. "Are you ready?"

"Why do you do that?" he asked, making no move to leave.

"What?" she asked wearily.

"Get angry when someone understands how you're feeling." When she hesitated over an answer, he took a guess. "Because you don't understand yourself, maybe? Because you run around so frantically so you don't have time to analyze it?"

Georgia tried not to react in any way that would betray how on target he was. She replied coolly, "Because my deepest feelings are hard for me to share. Particularly with a man I've known all of three days. Why do *you* do that?"

"What?"

"Come to my defense like a storybook hero? This is real life, you know. I'm a widow who pines for her husband. There's no future in this for you, if that's your plan."

He studied her a moment, then gave her a smile that made her feel young and silly. "It's interesting that a woman wants to be accepted on her own terms, and when a man does that, she's sure he has sexual motives. You were in a mess and I wanted to help you. Now that I own your building, our financial futures are somewhat entwined. In helping you, I'm helping myself."

Georgia looked into his steady hazel gaze and found no reason there to disbelieve him. What was the matter with her? she wondered a little worriedly. Had all her social skills atrophied? "I'm sorry," she said with a sigh. "That didn't sound very grateful, did it?"

He grinned and stood, offering her a hand up. "No need to be grateful. Just don't accuse me of lechery. I'm very sensitive."

Ben paid for their breakfast, then walked Georgia out into the parking lot. He stopped at a newspaper box, digging in his pocket for change. "Let's see if there's anything in the paper about—" The sight of Georgia, halted and turned toward him in the middle of the driveway, and a speeding Camaro, bouncing over the sidewalk toward her, stopped him in mid-sentence.

Ben heard the roar of the car's powerful engine and saw Georgia's look of confusion then fear as she saw the car barreling down on her. He took two long strides, then threw himself at her as the car burst past them, twisting his body to take the brunt of the impact as they crashed to the ground.

Ben lay still for a moment, waiting for his heart to settle down, his primary relief the comforting weight of Georgia's body atop his. He could feel her heart pounding against his and see the lingering shock in her eyes when she braced herself with a forearm on his chest and looked down at him.

"It occurs to me," she said gravely, as people began to run toward them from the restaurant, "that as a bodyguard, you're underpaid."

CHAPTER SIX

"GEORGIA, I DON'T KNOW what the hell is going on." Phil made notes on his small pad while leaning against the open door of Ben's truck. Georgia sat sideways on the passenger seat, her legs hanging down so that her feet, one of them shoeless, rested on the chrome running board. "You didn't even get a glimpse of the driver?"

"It happened too fast," Ben said, leaning against the truck's frame. "It was a Camaro, but it never occurred to me to look up at the driver."

"If Ben didn't have good reflexes," Georgia told Phil quietly, "I'd be dead, or very messy."

"MacKay's out of town," Phil said. "Has been since the day of the Downtown Enrichment Association meeting. We have no idea where he went. He seems to have disappeared."

Ben straightened. "Convenient. He could have hired someone to trash her shop and run her down."

Phil raised an eyebrow and flipped the pad closed. "That's possible. He's a hothead with big ideas, and I know he and Georgia have gone head-to-head over a few things, but somehow this just doesn't seem like his style. Meanwhile—" he slapped Ben on the chest with the pad "—good work. Keep it up till I find out what's going on here." He leaned into the truck, kissed Georgia's cheek, then joined the officer who was taking a statement from the woman who'd seen the incident from the restaurant window.

Georgia looked up at Ben hopefully. "Did you find my shoe?"

He shook his head, a little concerned by her utter calm. "Apparently it flew off your foot when I grabbed you. The lady sitting by the window said she saw the car hit it midair. It could be in the river."

That information suggested the hairbreadth by which Georgia had missed being hit and the impact with which the car would have struck her. Since their stop at the restaurant was not part of her usual routine, the attack suggested she had been followed from home. She looked up at him, that reality reflected in her eyes. But her only reaction was a sigh. She swung her legs into the truck. "Well, I'm already half an hour late opening. Breakfast was a great idea, Ben."

Georgia stared straight ahead while Ben continued to study her a moment before closing her door and walking around the truck. As he drove silently to the shop, Georgia knew he was the only reason she was alive at this moment. Still, the suggestion to stop for breakfast had been his, and it was easy and comfortable to blame him. She didn't understand and couldn't quite believe what was happening to her. Shifting responsibility for it onto someone else relieved her of the burden.

Wearing the low-heeled shoes she always kept at the store, Georgia worked like a demon. Ben carried box after box up from the basement for her, then checked items off the invoice as she unwrapped her purchases and read their stock numbers. Otherwise, they didn't speak at all.

Ben left shortly after one, and Georgia tried to ignore

his absence, imagining him back at the workshop, packing his bags. That was fine, she told herself. She'd gotten along before he'd come to town.... Of course, no one had been trying to kill her then. The telephone rang before that fact could settle in her mind and destroy the fragile composure she'd constructed over frayed nerves. It was John Kirby, the owner of Estuary Architects. He wanted to make an appointment with her and Karen to discuss the design of the building's new face.

She frowned, wondering why he wanted to speak to her. Apparently sensing her confusion, the gentleman on the other end said, "Mr. Stratton called me. He said he'd like the two of you in on the discussion. This afternoon okay? About two-thirty?"

"Yes, I think so," Georgia replied. "I'll call Mrs. Hansen to be sure. But I'm not sure about Mr...."

At that very moment the bell over her door tinkled, announcing the arrival of a customer. She looked up to see Ben closing the door behind him, a large white bag balanced on one hand. Guilt and remorse filled her. She held the receiver against her chest. "It's Estuary Architects. They want to know if it's all right to come by at two-thirty this afternoon to talk to us."

He placed the bag on the counter beside her, and she got a subtle whiff of a beefy scent. He wore the same neutral expression he'd worn since they'd driven back to the shop. It made her feel deprived and uncertain. "Is it all right with Karen?" he asked.

"I'll check with her." Into the receiver, she said, "It's fine with Mr. Stratton. I'll check with Mrs. Hansen. If you don't hear from me, two-thirty will be fine."

A call to Karen brought the same reaction Georgia had experienced. "He wants to talk to *us*?"

"Yes," Georgia replied, unwilling to admit her own surprise with Ben standing two feet away, pulling paper cups out of the bag.

"Why?"

"Oh, our valuable input, I'm sure," she replied casually. "Can you be here?"

"You bet. I'll bring coffee and cookies."

"Great." Georgia replaced the receiver and smiled brightly at Ben. "She'll be here."

"Good." He handed her a tub-shaped cup, his index fingers holding several packages of crackers to the lid. "Beef barley soup."

"Thank you." She took it from him, removed the lid and sniffed the wonderful aroma of beef and vegetables. A shopper came to the counter with a thin volume of poetry. Georgia rang up the sale, bagged the purchase and sent the customer on her way with a smile. Then she turned to Ben. He leaned a hip on the counter and sipped from the cup. "I thought you'd left to go back to the workshop and pack your things."

He raised an eyebrow. "Why?"

"Because I was so rude and ungrateful."

His hazel gaze held hers for a moment, his expression remaining quiet. He shrugged. "We storybook heroes deal with dragons all the time."

"I'm sorry."

"Forget it."

Not entirely satisfied that the comfortable communication she'd come to enjoy with him had been reestablished, Georgia pushed a little harder. "You're still angry."

"I'm not angry," he denied. Then he looked at her,

the first frank look he'd given her in hours. "Hurt, maybe."

She nodded, accepting that he had a right to be. "I don't blame you. In my own defense I can only say I was frightened and upset, and I'm not used to someone caring. Oh, I have great friends, but I mean…" She drew a breath and admitted honestly, "I'm not used to a man caring."

"Then we're both confused." He reached into the bag and brought out two wide-bowled plastic spoons, handing her one. "I'm not used to caring. I can't explain my motives because I don't understand them. But I can promise you they hold no danger for you."

Georgia sighed, satisfied they were on an even footing again. Honesty seemed to be what they shared best.

It didn't occur to either of them that he could be wrong.

JOHN KIRBY'S PLANS for the Roberts Buildings' facelift brought smiles to Georgia's and Karen's faces as they studied the blueprint spread out on Georgia's counter. Kirby indicated the roofline with his pen. "The face will be weathered-look board and batten. If you don't mind giving up your big display windows, I'd suggest that we put in bay windows of small-paned glass—the bookstore's on the west side and the bakery's on the east. I suggest you removed your old awnings and build out a boardwalklike roof or put a shingled roof over the bays. Replace your commercial doors with ones typical of the atmosphere." He turned to Ben. "I'd use stone up to the windows, but that would be expensive."

Georgia and Karen looked at each other again in

wonder, then turned simultaneously to Ben. "Well?" he asked.

Georgia was speechless. Karen never suffered from that condition. "The plan is more than either of us ever hoped for. We were ready to settle for fresh paint." She put a hand on the blueprint. "This would be exquisite, but don't bankrupt yourself."

Ben nodded. "I have to talk it over with my uncle, but I wanted to make certain you two approved before I took it to him." He turned to Kirby. "I'll let you know tomorrow afternoon."

Karen left in a daze, and Georgia finished the day that way. As she rearranged the window with new stock, Georgia tried to imagine a neat bay window of small-paned glass, herself looking out on a barrel of flowers near her door. It was what she and Karen dreamed of—class and elegance. And they weren't going to have to mortgage their homes to get it.

It was almost four when Linda burst through the shop door, her books clutched to her chest, her purse and gym bag hanging crazily from her arm. "Guess what?" she demanded.

Georgia looked from Linda to Lacey, who'd gone behind the counter to put her books and bags down, to Linda's friend Shelly. Georgia's gaze lingered a moment on Shelly's platinum elegance. The girl always made her feel that her daughter was keeping company with Lolita. Georgia looked at Linda again, wondering what could possibly have put that flare of excitement in her eyes. Then she remembered the pageant.

"You were chosen as Astoria High's Columbia River Days Princess!" Georgia guessed.

Linda rolled her eyes, and Shelly looked at Georgia as though she were crazy. "*I* got that, Mrs. Madison."

Of course.

"Ms. Moss put me in charge of the high school's cookie concession for Columbia River Days!"

"Oh!" Georgia tried to look delighted, though that sounded like a lot of work to her. But Linda loved work. "Darling, that's wonderful."

"I've got to plan what we're going to make and figure out a budget. Can I use the adding machine in your office?"

"Of course."

The two girls headed for the stairs, then Linda stopped in her tracks and Shelly collided with her. "Mom, we have to go grocery shopping before we go home," Linda said urgently. "I want to try some recipes tonight."

Georgia turned to Ben, who was just coming up the basement stairs with the last box of freight. "Ben drove this morning, honey. You'll have to ask him."

Ben looked in puzzlement from Georgia to Linda, his glance hesitating for a moment as it passed over Shelly. "Ask me what?"

Georgia watched in delight as Linda went through her "Guess what?" routine all over again. The girl had been so serious about things since her father's death. It somehow restored Georgia's faith in herself as a mother to see Linda reacting with youthful excitement and anticipation—the fact that it was all generated by a responsibility she was anxious to execute well was a mother-bonus.

"All *right*!" Ben grinned at Linda. "Good for you."

"I need to get some stuff at the store before we go home so I can try some recipes tonight. Mom says since you drove…"

He nodded before she could finish. "Sure. No problem."

"Thanks." Beaming, Linda headed for the office, Shelly following.

As Ben carried the box to the floor behind the counter where Georgia had cleared a spot, Lacey hiked herself onto the safe and folded her arms, her long legs dangling. "Are you sure she's ours?" she asked.

Georgia knelt beside the box as Ben slit it open with a knife blade. She smiled up at Lacey. "I've often suspected you were both left by alien storks. Why?"

Lacey pointed a hand in disgust in the direction in which her sister had disappeared. "She came in second to Hot Hips for pageant princess, and she's not even upset about it. But they put her in charge of all that *work* and she's happy!"

Georgia was so surprised by the news that Lacey's forbidden name for Shelly went unnoticed. "She was runner-up?"

"Yeah." Lacey shook her head. "She doesn't get anything for that, but it means she was *almost* a princess. Instead, she's got all that work to do. Her whole cooking class is excited about it now, but when it comes time to do it all, nobody'll want to help her and she'll have to do it herself." Lacey frowned at Georgia. "Linda's weird sometimes, you know? I'm going to Columbia Chocolates for some macadamia clusters. Anybody want anything?"

As Lacey loped off, Georgia stared worriedly in the direction of her office.

"What's the matter?" Ben asked, pulling the packing slip off and pressing the sides of the box flaps open.

"She was almost a princess," Georgia said wistfully, not even realizing until that moment that she harbored every mother's secret wish that her daughter be recognized for the grace and beauty she knew she possessed.

"You're wrong about that," Ben said.

She turned to him in surprise.

"That's the sweetest, most responsible kid I've ever seen," he explained. "She is royalty. And that football jock who helped her out of the truck this morning knows it, too."

IF THERE WAS SUCH A THING as orderly chaos, Georgia decided at nine o'clock that night, her kitchen was it. Every flat surface had a bowl or a cookie tin on it, and anyone foolish enough to wander in when delicious aromas began to radiate from the room had been pressed into service. The flour sprinkled on the counter to facilitate the rolling out of butter-cookie dough had filtered onto the floor and drifted into the air. Sprinkles and chocolate chips crunched underfoot, and there was so much coconut everywhere that it looked as though a condor nest had exploded overhead. But Linda was humming, Lacey was cooperating happily, and Ben stood nearby applying muscle to stiff chocolate-chip cookie batter. Georgia had a strong sense of all being right in her world.

Pressing out heart-shaped cookies, she waited until Linda turned her back to put a tray in the oven, then reached her index finger into the chocolate-chip batter and put it into her mouth.

Ben slanted her a scolding glance. "I don't think that's allowed," he cautioned quietly.

"Of course it is," she whispered. "I'm the mother."

"Isn't that abuse of authority?"

She frowned at him. "We're talking about chocolate-chip cookie dough, Ben. Marquess of Queensbury rules don't apply.'' She looked into his curious expression and guessed, ''You've never had cookie dough, have you?''

''Never had a mother who made cookies.''

Without pausing to think, Georgia ran the index finger of her left hand along the top of the dough and put it up to his mouth. The suggestive quality of what she was doing did occur to her then, but it was too late. His eyes settled on hers for one lengthy, lazy moment, then he dipped his head. She felt the slightest graze of his teeth, the barest touch of his tongue as he nipped the dough off her finger, then the soft warmth of his lips as he closed his mouth and drew away.

Struggling desperately to maintain her equanimity when her entire body reacted to that small touch of his mouth, she asked calmly, ''Well?''

He closed his eyes to consider. ''Good stuff,'' he agreed, then he opened his eyes and looked at her again, a dangerous light in their depths. ''But served that way, you could make me beg for cat food.''

It was well after eleven when the kitchen had been cleaned up and they all sat around the table sampling cookies.

''The chocolate sandwiches are the best,'' Lacey voted enthusiastically.

Georgia examined the perfectly round shape of the powdered-sugar-covered confection in her hand. ''I like the Russian tea cakes.''

''What are these called?'' Ben asked of a macaroon-like cookie he held between thumb and forefinger.

''Kisses,'' Linda replied.

Georgia could not explain the sudden tension that surrounded her. She waited, her breath caught in her throat so that she dared not bite into the tea cake. Waves of awareness emanated from Ben, though he did little more than push the plate of cookies toward her. "Try one," he suggested. "You're in for a treat."

Georgia glanced at him, saw that dangerous look still alive in his eyes and returned her attention to the tea cake she held. The girls, in discussion over whether the chocolate sandwiches needed more or less filling, noticed nothing.

"I'm stuffed, thanks," she said evenly.

He pulled the plate back toward him. "Too bad," he said. "You're missing out."

"Mom, do you think I should go for real butter in the butter cookies?" Linda nibbled at a heart-shaped cookie, then broke the point off and handed it across the table. "The added expense would mean I'd have to cut back one kind of cookie."

Lacey bit into a dark, square cookie and grimaced. "You can scratch the prune bars."

"But save the kisses," Ben said.

Georgia looked up at him, warning him with her eyes. The girls had noticed nothing yet, but they were frighteningly astute. "These are delicious, but they'll be heavenly with real butter."

"I was thinking we'd frost half and leave half plain for people wanting less sugar."

Georgia nodded approval. "I'd say you're off to a great start, Lindy."

"Wouldn't you make more money," Lacey asked, "if you just made a whole bunch of the fancy, frosted ones?"

"Maybe," Linda replied, "but it's a project for all the cooking classes, and believe it or not, there are a few guys in them. And some girls who cook like Mom.''

Georgia turned at that remark, her frown threatening. Linda laughed. ''With skill, but not a lot of enthusiasm. Anyway, bar cookies are easier for them to do, and they're usually full of stuff the guys like to eat. Drop cookies and refrigerator cookies are good for the kids who are better bakers, and those of us who love to bake will do the fancier stuff.''

''Well-thought-out plan, Linda,'' Ben said with a sincerity that brought a blush to her face. ''You'll probably be ready to compete with Mrs. Fields by the time you're out of high school.''

Lacey leaned across the corner of the table toward her sister. ''Aren't you even a little upset that you didn't get princess? I mean, you came so close. And Shelly got it.''

''It's kind of neat that I got so close,'' Linda admitted, ''but if I'd gotten it, I'd have died. For a whole week before the pageant, the princesses from each of the high schools go around to all the service clubs and give talks about Columbia River Days.'' When Lacey failed to see the cause for her relief, Linda said plainly, ''Public speaking, Lace! I hate that! You get to act like a princess the night of the pageant and the dance that opens the weekend, but all those other times I'd be scared to death. That's not for me. I'd rather bake behind the scenes.''

Lacey looked at Georgia. ''See what I mean? Weird.''

Georgia smiled fondly at both of them. ''You'd better get to bed. It's almost midnight.''

Lacey stretched. ''Tomorrow's Saturday.''

"You still have volleyball practice. And no music tonight, please. It's too late."

Lacey smiled at Ben as she stood and pushed her chair in. "The tape player sure works great, Ben. Now it's got *lots* of volume."

Linda laughed, following her sister toward the stairs. "Bad for Mom's nerves, but we love it."

Georgia waved the girls off and found herself in the suddenly silent kitchen, an arm's reach away from the man who had been making playful, suggestive remarks all evening. She tried to look severe, but her pulse was skipping. "That's dangerous," she said.

"What?" His look of innocence made her wonder if she had imagined his teasing.

"I keep my personal life very circumspect," she replied a little stiffly, angry now that she might have misunderstood. Or was she disappointed? "My girls see and hear everything and understand more than that. Teasing me about kisses is…is…"

"Dangerous," he supplied for her, and she knew suddenly that she hadn't imagined a thing. He leaned toward her on an elbow, his eyes warm and frank. "Because they might think their mother is interested in a man? Or because you might discover that you are?"

"My man is dead," she said calmly.

Ben studied her, trying to decide if that was simply a defense mechanism or if she was as sincere as she sounded. "Then, isn't it time you found another?"

For an instant, he thought he saw longing in her eyes. Then she closed them and shook her head. "No."

"Why?" He knew he was pushing. As a rule he didn't like his own space invaded and made it a point to keep at least an elbow's distance from everyone else's. But some kind of strange magnetism surrounded this woman and drew him.

"Because…" Georgia wanted to explain but couldn't find a way to state simply what had become such a complex burden. "He died unexpectedly. There was so much between us that's just—" she spread both hands in a gesture of helplessness "—unfinished, I guess."

He reached out to enclose her wrist in his fingers. "Georgia, Gary is dead. What you had is over. You can't leave the rest of your life unfinished because of that."

Her hand lay quietly under his. He had expected her to yank it away impatiently or wriggle free of his grip to make her point. She simply looked at him with a sadness so grave that he opened his hand. "I have the girls and some lovely memories," she said.

"In a couple of years," he said gently, "they'll be off to college, and if the male population of this country is in its right mind, they'll have families of their own before you know what happened. Then all you'll have will be the memories. What then?"

She pushed her chair back and gathered up cups. She gave him a look of resignation with a little laughter behind it. "Then I guess it's my shawl and my rocking chair in the sun on the porch of some convalescent home."

Exasperated but not discouraged, he helped her clean up. "I'll bet you've even forgotten what it's like," he said, putting the carton of milk back in the refrigerator.

"What?"

"Being kissed."

She turned from the sink in surprise, wet hands held away from her body as he walked toward her, a dish towel in his hands. His even, hazel gaze held hers as he stopped inches away.

"Of course I haven't. Gary was always so..." She paused, expecting the memory of being in Gary's arms to waft around her as it always did, sharp and clear and painful. But it wouldn't form. She frowned, trying to help it along. "Kisses never became perfunctory between us. They were always warm and..."

It occurred to him that this wasn't the way he wanted to kiss her. He'd read that search for the memory in her eyes and guessed by the surprise and disappointment there that she hadn't found it. It proved his point but put him in the position of being a reassurance to her rather than allowing him to play any of the other dashing, more romantic roles he had in mind. Still, he experienced a vague surprise when his mind pushed aside any disappointment he might have felt and decided that being what she needed was a place to start.

He handed her the towel and waited while she dried her hands. Then he put a hand under the short, silky hair at the back of her neck and pulled her closer, bridging the few inches that separated them. She didn't resist. Her hands flattened against his chest, not to hold him away, but as though she weren't quite sure what to do with them. Her soft, dark eyes were still confused, still unfocused, in search of a memory. He put his other arm around her and leaned down to close his mouth gently over hers.

There. That was it. Georgia gave herself over to the memory of warm, gentle lips, a hand in her hair, arms that were strong and protective. Warmth and tenderness filled her...and relief that she hadn't forgotten. Settling into the familiar comfort, feeling his flash of response, she pushed her hands up his chest and over his shoul-

ders to twine in his baby-fine hair. That was what finally alerted her. The hair in her fingers was wiry and
curly, and her arms were stretched farther than had
been required to hold Gary.

She came to full awareness with a little start, drawing her arms down and looking into Ben's now very
gold eyes in surprise. But he didn't free her and she
didn't struggle.

"Now that you know I'm not Gary," he said quietly,
"do you want to try that again?"

Georgia couldn't have said what made her raise her
arms to him a second time. There was something familiar in the tender way he held her, in every sure but
gentle move that lent a certain comfort to the promise
of excitement, a safety to the tantalizing threat of danger. Ben wasn't Gary, but he had goodness in common
with him and an appeal for her that was uniquely his.

The prideful edge of distance Ben had planned to
maintain in the kiss, to let her know he wouldn't be
mistaken for her husband a second time, melted when
she raised her arms to him. It dissolved completely
when she leaned her body against his in total trust,
parted her lips and waited for his.

Ben had never gone into a kiss with his spine like
oatmeal. He liked to have charge of a relationship, even
just an encounter, but power was the last thing on his
mind at the moment. He felt a responsibility here he
didn't entirely understand, and it made him go carefully. He sensed that Georgia needed kindness more
than passion, a reminder of what she was missing rather
than full-blown evidence.

As his mouth closed gently over hers, Georgia tasted
a hint of coffee, a suggestion of coconut and the very
distinctive flavor of man. After two years without even

a kiss, the headiness of it struck her like a blow. The tingling sensation brought on by fingers moving against her scalp, the delicious feeling of hands roving her back, brought back a host of things ignored and forgotten in the past two years. Even clinging to Ben as her senses were assaulted, she realized she was recalling not memories of Gary but memories of her own femininity, those emotional parts of her person that had been tucked away with her husband's clothes.

Though her mind was cautioning her to be careful, her body seemed to revel in its renewal, as though celebrating the restoration of its missing components. That was what this kiss felt like, she thought in wonder, a celebration.

Without understanding what was happening to her, or to himself, for that matter, Ben felt the newness. He had certainly never experienced this before—this promise of something wonderful curiously coupled with the patience to pursue it slowly. He raised his head while his body wanted more, amazed at his own restraint. He looked down into her brown eyes and smiled, pleased they were now focused—on him. "So I was wrong. You do remember."

She smiled up at him. "Ben," she said. That was all.

As he walked back to the workshop in the cool, breezy night, he knew what she meant. It had been a simple reassurance that she knew he wasn't Gary.

CHAPTER SEVEN

"HAVE YOU HAD HIM fill out a W-4 yet?" Karen asked Georgia. "Ben certainly seems to be working for you."

It was a quiet weekday afternoon, the first sunny day after a week of rain. Georgia and Karen had concluded earlier that all their customers were working in their gardens instead of shopping. The two women leaned on Georgia's counter, sipping coffee and watching the scaffolding being erected in front of the building. Through the window, they could see Ben in discussion with John Kirby and Wally Bishop.

"He's here with you every day, does all your heavy work, runs out for your lunch and coffee." Karen turned to grin at her. "Is there something developing here that I should know about?"

Georgia sighed. "This is all your husband's fault for saying in front of Bea that the girls and I shouldn't be alone. When the alternatives were moving in with her or letting Ben move in with us, the latter seemed more desirable. Now I'm not sure."

Karen toyed with a pencil on the counter, rolling it forward and back. "Is the widow's wall beginning to fall?"

Georgia glanced at her friend with a moue of disapproval. "It isn't a wall, Karen. How can I embark on a relationship when I don't know what went wrong with the other one? Or even if anything did?"

Karen ignored her dilemma and focused on the information that intrigued her. "So there is potential for a relationship here?"

Without warning or time to try to hold it back, a rosy glow climbed from Georgia's neck. Karen saw it and smiled. "What happened?" she demanded.

"Nothing momentous," Georgia lied. It shouldn't have been momentous, but it was.

"What?" Karen asked. "What?"

"He kissed me," Georgia reported simply, clearing her throat and shrugging. "That's all."

"That's all?" Karen put an arm around her shoulders and squeezed. "That's everything! You're coming back to us! Georgia…"

Taking exception, Georgia frowned at her friend. "I wasn't dead, Karen."

"No, but you had definitely retired." Karen squeezed her again. "What do the girls think of him?"

"It doesn't matter," Georgia insisted, trying to defuse Karen's excitement. "Sometime soon Ben will have to go back to Portland."

Karen recognized her evasion. "They like him, don't they?"

Georgia took the pencil from her and tossed it into her pencil cup. "He fixes breakfast every morning and they take time to eat it. He repaired the kitchen faucet, their stereo and the dishwasher. He knows a lot about volleyball." She frowned at Karen in concern. "I think they must have ordered him from God."

"Maybe God sent him," Karen suggested quietly, "because He wanted to do something nice for you. Maybe it's time to forget about how Gary died and move on."

Georgia straightened and looked levelly at Karen.

"If it had been Phil in those circumstances, could you just put it aside and get on with your life?"

Karen returned her even gaze. "If there was little chance of ever finding out the truth, I would. You have to think of yourself. Anyway, the more you hold on to that, the greater chance you have of the girls finding out." When Georgia looked at her in alarm, she said implacably, "I'm sorry, but you've got to face it. You've been lucky so far. Those few of us who know would never breathe a word, but you know how those things happen. A careless word is overheard, a kid tells another kid, someone at school thinks Linda and Lacey know and it comes out. Let it go, Georgia. Let yourself get serious about Ben Stratton."

The girls finding out the strange circumstances surrounding Gary's death was her worst nightmare. They'd worshiped him. Through their teens and as long as she could maintain it, she wanted their memory of him as the perfect, loving father to remain intact. She had held stubbornly to her own memory of him as the perfect, loving husband, though she admitted to herself in dark, private moments that she had a particle of doubt.

"Come on," Karen said bracingly. "I didn't mean to upset you. I just want you to start thinking about yourself for a change. You don't think your firm bosom and tight bottom are going to last forever, do you? Pretty soon you'll get saggy and wrinkled, and even the garbage man won't look at you twice."

Georgia glared at Karen. "Don't you have to get back to work?"

"No," Karen replied blandly. "I'm yours for as long as you need me. You're so lucky."

"Is that what you call it?"

Suddenly another figure appeared in the window, stopping to talk to the men outside. It was Phil.

"Hi," he said as he came through the door. To Karen, he added, "Thought I'd find you here."

"Don't tell me," Karen sighed. "You're not coming home tonight. A stakeout or a raid or a big bust or something."

Phil frowned in mock confusion. "I don't think there's a woman with a big bust in this town."

"Ha, ha." Karen made a face at him. "So which is it?"

"You were right the first time," he replied, hooking an arm around her. "A stakeout. I won't be home until late."

"Don't get hurt," she ordered, "or I'll kill you."

He gave her a quick kiss and turned to leave. "Bye, Georgia."

"I've got to go, too." Karen winked at Georgia. "I want to see you make something out of this."

"Out of what?" Wally Bishop asked, holding the door open for Karen to leave as he walked into the shop.

Karen merely smiled at Georgia and left.

"What are you up to?" Georgia asked, resting an arm on the cash register as she smiled at Wally. "You should be home preparing for the onslaught of the Columbia River Days Committee."

He leaned on the counter and smiled at her. "You coming?"

"I think as cochairperson of the committee, I'm expected to put in an appearance. And who in his right mind would ever turn down the opportunity to visit your place?"

He grinned and gestured over his shoulder toward

Ben, who was still talking with John Kirby. "You've been keeping kind of close company with Stratton lately. I thought you might have made other plans."

Georgia gave him a scolding look. "He's my landlord, Wally."

He quirked an eyebrow. "And I understand *you're his* landlady after hours."

Georgia sighed. Any hope she might have entertained that no one would notice was shot down in flames. "Who told you that?" she asked.

"It's common knowledge." He shrugged. "When the winsome widow takes a beau, news travels fast."

"He's acting as a sort of bodyguard since the break-in," she explained with a practiced ease that told him she wanted no smirks or smart remarks. In view of the way she reacted around Ben, the practiced ease was more difficult to project than she'd imagined.

Wally's expression was noncommittal. "He's letting you come alone tonight?"

"He offered to wait in the car." Georgia reached out to pat Wally's shoulder. "I assured him you'd be gentleman enough to invite him in. He's into restoring, too, you know. I'm sure he'd appreciate your home."

Wally rolled his eyes. "Soft soap, Georgia? You must really be smitten. All right, all right. Bring him along. I lost you to Gary when I was a sensitive youth. I guess I can live through losing you a second time now that I'm suave and mature." He smoothed his hair back with exaggerated affection.

Georgia laughed lightly, swatting at his arm. "You didn't love me in high school. You just wanted to date me because I was the only girl in the junior class who wasn't impressed with your Corvette." She sobered a little. "And you don't love me now. I'm part of your past, and you're in love with yesterday. That's all."

With a tolerant smile, Wally rested his eyes on Georgia. There was a pain behind them she didn't see. "So you have me all figured out?"

She shook her head. "No. I don't understand anything these days—or anyone."

He frowned at her. "Problems?"

She shrugged philosophically, coming around the counter and walking beside him as he headed toward the door. "My kids are growing up, and my own life is changing. I guess I can't help but be confused. Even my shop will look different."

Wally put an arm around her shoulders and gave them a friendly squeeze. "It'll look like it did at the turn of the century. You're as tied up with the past as I am. I'll bet it'll feel familiar to you even though you've never seen it the way it was."

That thought brought Georgia a little shudder of excitement. She did love this town. She wanted so much for it to prosper, but its heritage was rich and warm. She wanted nothing to change that. She felt a new thrill at having helped save the Jeremiah houses.

As KIRBY SHOOK hands with Ben, then ran across the street to his truck, Ben turned toward the door of the shop. The sight of Wally Bishop with his arm around Georgia, talking intimately as they looked up the street, checked him in his tracks. What could he get for murdering a curator? he wondered. In view of his growing feelings for Georgia, Ben decided he had sufficient cause. Still, murder was a drastic measure. He could probably have the charge reduced to manslaughter when he explained his difficult childhood. Surely the district attorney would have sympathy for how much he'd missed and his fantasy that he might still have it all, which this beautiful woman had woven in his head. He lost his faculties when he looked at her or thought about her. No doubt he could plead insanity.

Ben walked toward Georgia and Wally, ready to risk murder one and the chair. Then Wally spotted him and dropped his hand from Georgia's shoulder. "Hello, Stratton. I'd like to invite you to join us at the meeting tonight."

Wondering if Bishop knew how close he'd come to an ugly demise, Ben shook his hand. "Thank you. Georgia tells me it's a turn-of-the-century showplace."

Wally smiled affably. "I'm fortunate enough to have come from a family that saved everything. See you both tonight."

"WHAT TIME should we open the beer garden?"

"Tomorrow!"

Laughter ran through the group assembled in Wally's Victorian living room.

"Traditionally, it's been seven." Georgia sent a scolding glance to Jasper Johnson, who had answered her question. She and Karen sat side by side on a horsehair and mahogany Grecian couch. Fifteen people faced them in a semicircle of antique chairs. "But the Elks would like permission to open at five this year. With the Scandinavian Society providing sausage sandwiches to go with the beer, they think they could make it a dinner event, as well. Any objections?"

A hand went up.

Ben watched the proceedings from one end of the back row of chairs. He had long ago tuned out the discussion to watch the committee and wonder if one of them could be responsible for the vandalism in Georgia's shop and the attempt to run her down. It seemed unlikely that anyone in this collection of teachers, civil servants, merchants and attorneys could be insincere about his devotion to this project or his affection for one of its cochairs. Yet it was likely that someone was.

MacKay still hadn't been found, but Ben was less and less convinced that he was responsible. Though he'd obviously been angry at Georgia, even threatened her, Ben found it hard to believe he'd have done that if he'd intended to punish her by trashing her store. Not only did it make him the obvious suspect, it blunted the effectiveness of his destruction. Ben knew his reasons weren't necessarily scientific, but he felt sure the guilty party was someone pretending to be a friend. Still...nothing had happened while MacKay had been missing.

"Tea?"

Ben came out of his thoughts with a start to find a white-haired woman holding a flute-rimmed china cup and saucer toward him. People were up and moving around, conversation buzzing. Ben reached cautiously for the cup.

"Ladyfinger?" Another woman of the same vintage offered a silver platter of delicate strips of sponge cake. He could have eaten them all, by himself, before breakfast. He took one and placed it carefully on his saucer.

"What do you think of this place?" Georgia settled into the now vacant chair beside him, a long canvas skirt covering her small-heeled shoes as she crossed her knees. She balanced an even smaller cup with yellow roses on it and three cookies on the saucer. "Doesn't it make you want to put on your starched collar and your white suit and part your hair down the middle?''

Almost ready to agree, he balked at parting his hair in the middle. "I have a cowlick," he said.

Georgia's brown eyes turned to his hair for a moment's study, then lowered to his eyes, a smile in them that robbed him of breath. "How charming of you," she said.

He hadn't seen this mood before. She was sweet and playful and just a little reckless, as though she were testing the strength of a tether with which she'd grown impatient. Suddenly feeling as if she were as strange to him as the china cup in his hand, he nibbled on the cookie. It was sweet but airy and dissolved on his tongue in an instant. He thought longingly of Linda's chocolate-chip cookies. "So where would I be going with my stiff collar, my white suit and my hair parted in the middle?''

"We give you dispensation to part it on the side," she said, glancing at him as she nibbled thoughtfully on her ladyfinger. The tip of her tongue came out to snatch a crumb off her lips, and he tried to concentrate on getting his cup to his mouth without shattering it. "Probably into some rose garden in search of your ladylove. You'd have a nosegay and chocolates."

He smiled. "What would you be wearing?''

"Oh…" She was off in thought again, sipping from the thin china cup. "Something white and lacy…and a wide-brimmed straw hat with a few stems of lavender in the band." She smiled as she continued to unravel the fantasy. "I'm a woman with plans to travel. I might become a great actress, a dancer or possibly a doctor."

He laughed softly. "That way if you botch a surgery,

you can dance out of your patient's life and never be heard from again.''

Georgia moved her cup to her left hand and rested her right elbow on Ben's shoulder. The gesture put them eye-to-eye—hers filled with laughter, his with a kind of awe he felt but didn't understand. "I never suspected you could be this much fun," she said.

"Does that mean you might change your travel plans?"

She shook her head. Her hair swung and light rippled in it. "It means I might share the chocolates with you. Wally has invited all of us to tour the house. Would you like to?"

"Yes, of course."

Georgia put their cups on a nearby table and led the way into the elegant parlor. Groups wandered at will, one following Wally, who explained some of the older pieces and answered questions. He fairly beamed with pride in his antique possessions. Other people took off on their own, looking around with the reverence of those fascinated by history.

But Ben had difficulty concentrating on anyone but himself—Georgia had taken his hand. "You won't believe the kitchen," she said as she pulled him in that direction. He followed her, prepared to believe anything.

The kitchen was almond with dark blue accents, the tall cupboard doors bearing hand-painted illustrations of herbs and flowers. "This is the kind of kitchen Linda should have," Georgia said dreamily. "I'm sure she could become *cordon bleu* quality in this room. And under all this charm and authentic face—" she patted the counter with its long cabinets "—are a dishwasher, garbage disposal, microwave oven.'' She moved to an ornate cast-iron stove. ''And this beauty is wired.''

Ben grinned down at her, unable to resist the joke. ''And this beauty is wired, too, isn't she?''

She laughed, unoffended. ''This house makes me a little giddy. It's probably best that Wally got it rather than I. A few weeks in it and I'd be so steeped in Victorian atmosphere that I'd probably cease to function and become simply a decoration.''

''Oh, that wouldn't happen,'' Ben said, putting his arm around her shoulders. She wove her fingers in his as they wandered up the back stairs. ''You have to study all those medical texts between pirouettes.''

The back stairs were plain and narrow, but the pine shone. They deposited Ben and Georgia in a wide hallway that led to several guest bedrooms, a wonderful, book-lined, claret-carpeted library and what was apparently the master bedroom. Georgia stopped in the doorway. A large four-poster with ornate carvings dominated the room, its posts reaching almost to the high ceiling. A marble fireplace stood between two lace-paneled windows, and two spindly legged chairs were pulled up for conversation or dozing. Around the room were Chinese pots, silver candlesticks, paintings in gilded frames and thriving ferns.

''Wally's great-great-grandfather was a ship's captain. This house is filled with treasures from all over the world,'' Georgia said a little wistfully. ''I could never have done this with it.''

''Maybe if your ship comes in,'' Ben suggested, ''you could buy one of the other two.''

''Now that the grant came through, they belong to the museum,'' she said. ''Their protection was my primary concern. Wally plans to fill them with some of the overflow furniture from the basement of the museum. He'll do a superb job."

To Ben, who loved restoring old buildings to their original style and elegance but preferred space and quiet lines in his private life, this was all a bit much. But Georgia loved it so much he was able to see it from a different perspective. He wasn't sure he could ever live in a place like this, but he could appreciate its warmth and cheerful clutter. As his eyes passed over the bed and settled on the chairs pulled cozily near the fireplace, an image filled his mind, unbidden, but clear.

In his stiff collar and white suit, he sat in one of the chairs looking at Georgia, who sat in the other in her white lacy dress with its rose pinned to the collar. The rose was red rather than yellow, and her hat lay discarded at the foot of the bed. Wordlessly, as though by mutual consent, they extended hands to each other and stood. He pulled off his jacket, and she began to pull the pins from her hair.

"You're getting into this, aren't you?" Georgia asked.

Ben focused on her with a little difficulty, confused by the bright scarf around her neck and the absence of a wide-brimmed hat.

"Things from the past are seductive. It's my theory that they don't want to be relegated to uselessness, so they make us see the past when we look at them. You look at an old book or a water pitcher and wonder who held it, who used it. Then, when you're really hooked, you feel that if you buy it and have it around, it'll all come to you. You'll know what the original owner thought and felt about it." She sighed and pulled him out of the room. He followed, his heart beating fast, his mind still disoriented.

Then he gave the chairs one last glance over his shoulder, and as he dragged his eyes away, he saw the shoes standing near the closet—and something on the sole that would have been invisible except for the soft light of the oil lamp on the table near the wardrobe.

"Wait." Suddenly alert, Ben stopped Georgia and went several steps into the room to kneel beside Wally's shoes, probably hastily changed before the meeting. He reached to the sole of the shoe and extracted a piece of straw.

"What is it?" Georgia asked, leaning over his shoulder.

Straightening, he held his palm out to her, the piece of straw picking up the light.

"What…?" She began to ask him why he'd stopped for a piece of straw. Then she remembered the piece Phil had found on the floor of her shop the morning after it had been vandalized. She shook her head. "No, no. I know what you're thinking, but that's impossible. There are lots of dishes and framed photos and stuff in the basement of the museum that are packed in straw the way they were in those days. I'm sure that's where it came from."

"That could very well be," Ben said quietly. "The question is, where did the straw in your shop come from? MacKay's or the museum basement?"

The sound of laughter and footsteps coming up the stairs captured Georgia's attention. She whispered firmly, "Wally's been helping me with this all along! He's the *curator* of the museum! He wouldn't be opposed to restoring downtown and saving two historic homes. He owns one just like them and has done wonderful things with it!" She spread her hands to indicate the beautiful room.

Ben put the piece of straw in his pocket. "Don't yell at me," he whispered back. "I can't explain it either, but this is the same stuff we found on the floor of your shop."

Georgia frowned at him, turning quickly to smile as two older ladies peered into the doorway. She pulled Ben through the bedroom's other door and into the main hallway. She backed him up against the wall and frowned again. "How can you accuse me of yelling when we're whispering?" she demanded softly.

"I know a whispered yell when I hear it," he returned. "I don't want you seeing him without me, understand? Whether it's business or pleasure."

"Don't get imperious with me!" she warned.

"How can I sound imperious," he demanded, "when I'm whispering?"

Georgia closed her eyes and drew a breath for patience. "Wally and I don't see each other socially."

"He was able to make a social occasion out of looking in on you at the shop today."

Georgia's eyes widened. "What?"

The crowd was beginning to thicken upstairs. Ben took Georgia's arm and led her down the winding main staircase. At the bottom they almost collided with Karen, who was being helped into her jacket by their host. She turned to wave at Ben and Georgia as she left, her expression speculative.

Georgia hoped she looked natural. She couldn't believe that seconds ago Ben had been suggesting that her lifelong friend might be responsible for the damage done to her shop, very nearly done to her body and very surely done to her peace of mind. Guilt that she had even listened to the suggestion made her hug Wally when he turned to her.

"This place is so wonderful, Wally. Every time I go through it, I covet it more and more."

"What did you think of the place?" Wally asked Ben.

"Very elegant and very beautiful," Ben replied sincerely. He might be suspicious of his host but not of his host's ability to recreate the warm domesticity of a fascinating period.

Georgia smiled at Wally. "I've been bragging about you all evening. Thank you for opening your home to us. The upstairs is still full of people oohing and aahing over your things."

"You run a good meeting, Georgia," Wally praised, reaching to the overburdened hall tree for the canvas jacket that matched her skirt. "We have most of the details wrapped up. Patsy Butler tells me Linda was runner-up for princess. She must be disappointed."

"Actually, she's delighted," Georgia corrected as he helped her into her jacket. Her glance bounced threateningly off Ben's watchful hazel eyes as she turned to accept Wally's help. "She's been put in charge of the high school's cookie concession, and she's thrilled to death about it. She'd rather be second prettiest, not have to make the speeches and have the opportunity to bake."

"Just like her mother," Wally said, pinching her chin. "Always happier working behind the scenes. Thanks for coming."

Wally waved them off and closed the door behind them. Georgia walked silently beside Ben to his truck and waited while he unlocked the door. Because of the fullness of her long skirt, she didn't have to wait for his help to climb into the front seat.

"Don't glower at me," Ben said from behind the

wheel as he turned the key in the ignition. "I didn't put the straw on his shoes."

Folding her arms, Georgia did glower. "What was that crack about his making a social opportunity out of visiting the shop?"

The truck roared off into the night. "He had his arm around you," Ben said calmly.

"So did you fifteen minutes ago," she reminded. "What's the difference?"

"I didn't trash your shop and almost run you down."

"Neither did he."

Ben glanced at her as he made a turn. "How do you know that for certain?"

"He's my friend!" She raised her voice impatiently. "He and Gary and Karen and Rob and I all went to school together. We palled around, double-dated. He wouldn't do that to me."

"You dated him?"

"A few times in our junior year. Then Gary and I got serious."

"How did he take being jilted for Gary?"

Georgia tried to remember so she could tell Ben he'd been a paragon of maturity. But her memories were crowded with falling in love with Gary. "He wasn't jilted," she said, her voice losing its earlier conviction. "He was very popular because he was rich and fun to be with. And he had a Corvette. He had lots of girls, and I'd only gone out with him a couple of times."

"He's still in love with you," Ben said seriously.

"He's in love with the past." Georgia turned to study his impressive profile in the shadows that raced through the truck. For a moment it distracted her. Then she remembered that she was angry with him. "You're trying to tell me that he's done these things to me because I jilted him in high school?''

''No, I'm not. But he had straw on his shoes and he's…a little weird about you.''

''Weird about me?''

Ben sighed and shrugged. ''I can't explain it.''

''Because it's absurd.'' Georgia settled glumly into her corner. ''You're taking your role of bodyguard too seriously.''

''Good thing for you,'' he said. ''Or you wouldn't be here.''

Annoyed because he was right, she was tired, and it was all so unbelievable, Georgia suggested haughtily, ''Maybe it's time for you to move out.''

''No.''

At Ben's implacable reply, she turned to him and reminded, ''You're a *guest* in my house.''

Without looking away from the road, he replied, ''And Riverfront Books is a tenant in my building—without a lease, as I recall.''

As he turned into her driveway, Georgia gaped at him, wondering if she could have misunderstood the suggestion that he could evict her if he so chose. The set of his jaw convinced her that she hadn't. She accused indignantly, ''That's blackmail!''

He turned the engine off, leaned back against the upholstery and gave her an unrepentant smile. ''Yeah.''

Georgia looked into his eyes, now dark green in the shadows of the truck cab, searching for the man who only an hour ago had joined in her playful Victorian fantasy. There was nothing of the gentle sweetness she saw in him so often. He was dead serious and dangerously determined.

"How will you be able to sleep tonight?" she asked, hoping to shame him into some admission of guilt.

He laughed mirthlessly and reached his left arm out to rest his wrist on top of the steering wheel. "I haven't slept since I met you. What's one more night?"

Unsure what he meant, she said defensively, "That sofa is very comfortable."

He nodded, looking through the windshield into the night. Then he turned to her, his eyes stormy. "But my thoughts are not. I'm a little bit in love with you, Georgia."

Her anger completely derailed by that unexpected admission, she swallowed, staring at him. "Is...that possible?" she asked after a moment. "To be a little bit in love?"

He shook his head. "I don't know. I didn't think it was possible for me to fall in love at all. I've never been loved, so I've settled for being liked and respected. When I travel around to our various properties, I'm always welcomed sincerely, and since I was an orphan chucked from place to place, that's all I've ever really wanted. I've been doing fine without love. But here I am. Since I know nothing about it—except that I've never had it and don't know how to return it—I imagine I can only be a little bit in love. But it's enough to make me worry about you and be unwilling to trust anybody else with the responsibility for your safety. So humor me, will you?"

"Ben—"

"All I want to hear," he interrupted quietly, "is that you're not going to insist that I leave."

"How can I?" she demanded in exasperation. "You'd throw my bookshop out in the street. Wouldn't you?"

He considered a moment. "Possibly. I'm at least as stubborn as you are."

Georgia folded her arms and leaned back against the door. "If you stay, I won't have you making cracks about Wally."

He nodded. "I'll keep my opinions to myself."

"And I'd be careful about telling me who I can and cannot see and when."

"I don't care who you see or when," he said, "as long as I'm with you. I promised Bea I'd keep an eye on you." He inspected the fingernails on his free hand. "I suppose she could make your life difficult if you make my job difficult."

"You're very unscrupulous."

He shrugged modestly. "I've been blessed."

Suddenly very tired, she paused a moment to contemplate the long drop to the pavement. Climbing up without assistance had been one thing, vaulting down was another. Ben came around the truck to stand in front of her. "Need a hand?" he asked, smiling.

She peered down. "That, or rappeling gear." Thinking he intended to offer her his hand, Georgia extended hers. Instead, he put an arm around her back, the other under her knees, and lifted her out. "Close the door, will you please?" he asked, turning her so that she could reach it. Flustered, excited, charmed, she complied.

Looping her arms around his neck, Georgia relaxed for the brief walk to the back door. "This is probably beyond the call of your duties," she said, her heart ticking against her ribs with a strong steadiness she suspected he could feel against his chest.

He dipped under her spirea bush, then turned sideways through the gate that connected the edge of the house to the workshop. "This has nothing to do with my duties," he said quietly.

"What does it have to do with?"

"A sudden need to have my arms filled with you." The still dormant climbing roses woven in the trellis that covered the patio rustled in the night breeze. Lilac and camellia perfumed the air.

Is this really happening to me? Georgia wondered. She had only to tighten her arms to assure herself that it was. There were sturdy shoulders under her hands, strong arms supporting her, wiry hair that smelled of a man's shampoo only inches from her nose. Awareness rose in her, demanding her attention. It was the wrong time, and probably the wrong man, but something deep inside her didn't seem to care. "Because you're a little bit in love with me."

They had reached the door and he stopped, still carrying her. He looked into her eyes and nodded as though that admission disturbed as well as pleased him. "Yes."

With a small sigh, Georgia leaned her forehead against his. "This is going to be a problem for us."

He nuzzled her face aside to plant a light kiss near her ear. "It's my problem," he said. "It doesn't have to affect you. I understand the limitations of my job."

She sighed again and pulled back slightly to look into his eyes. They were dark in the shadows. "I'd like to make it that easy for you, but I can't."

He studied her a moment. "I take exception to the word 'easy,' but what do you mean?"

"I'm a little bit in love with you," she said. "So it will affect me, and I think that confuses the limitations of your job."

He seemed to be smiling and frowning at the same

time, or maybe it was a trick of the shadows. "But you were snapping at me a minute ago."

"You threatened to evict me."

He laughed throatily. "I have a unique approach to courting." He sobered suddenly and leaned down to set her on her feet. Then he took a firm grip on her shoulders and looked into her eyes. "I don't know what to do about this. I...I..." Almost daily he made decisions involving large amounts of money and people's jobs, and here he was stammering.

"I know," Georgia said quietly, remembering what he'd told her about never having had love and being unable to give it. "I'm not ready for this, either. Yet, here we are. The important thing is not to panic. This could all be a reaction to the strange circumstances. You're attracted to the damsel in distress, and I'm idolizing the storybook hero. Maybe it'll go away."

He doubted that seriously. It wasn't a troublesome itch, it was a need—almost a pain deep in his gut. He couldn't see it conveniently disappearing. "That's wishful thinking, Georgia."

"Well then, you tell me how to handle it," she said with sudden impatience. "The last time I was in love I was seventeen. I'm not a practiced hand at this."

A little surprised but also pleased by that little slip of control, Ben reminded her gently, "I thought you said the important thing was not to panic."

She tried to shake his hands off. "Well, I've changed my mind. I mean, I have two kids to think of, and Gary's...Gary's..."

He understood her love for Gary—his own respect and admiration for the man grew the longer he occupied his shop—but at the moment, he didn't want to hear about him. Retaining his hold on Georgia, he pulled her closer and stopped her worried ramblings with his lips.

Her sigh of frustration then acceptance filled his mouth. Her lips responded to his with the same eagerness and urgency he felt; her tongue toyed with his without constraint. He felt her light weight incline against him as she tried to accommodate his height. The roaming of her small hands across his back, up the sensitive ridge of his spine, up and down his sides made putty of his determination to retain control of this kiss.

Georgia felt the subtle change in his touch and his stance. She'd been held and kissed enough times to know surrender when she felt it. A part of her that wasn't occupied with delight and sensation thought how ironic that was; she'd thought she was the one surrendering. Could it be that a true battle of the sexes involved only mutual surrender and no conqueror? It was too complex a thought for a mind lost to the demands of her body.

Ben's hands were everywhere and she was too occupied with the sensations they were causing to give any thought to stopping him. Her back and shoulders were a mass of tremors, her breasts felt swollen against the armor plate of his chest, and the hips that had taken one light, brief pass of his hands wanted more. She was all nerve endings and pounding heart. She had no breath at all.

They emerged from the kiss, gasping and leaning on each other. "I'm…glad we're just a little bit in love," Georgia whispered, her voice strangled. "I don't think I could live through a grand passion."

Ben straightened and drew a ragged breath. "This could be a bigger problem than we first imagined.

You'd better get inside." He pulled the screen door open while she routed blindly in her purse for her keys. When she found them and pushed the door open, he put an arm up across the door frame to block her way. She looked up in the light filtering out from the kitchen and saw a wry smile on his face. "It also occurs to me that the rewards could be bigger." He leaned down to kiss her lightly, then turned and headed for the workshop. She flipped on the porch light to guide him, and he turned back with a wave, his smile still in place. Georgia closed the door and leaned against it for a moment, trying desperately to collect her fragmented thoughts. They refused to come. Feeling was still so strong in her heart and throughout her body that she could not recall or analyze or predict. She could only tremble and smile and know she was in trouble.

Her smile widened as one thought did take shape. Ben was in trouble, too.

CHAPTER EIGHT

DRESSED IN BATHROBE and cat-faced slippers, Georgia wandered groggily down to the kitchen, intent on putting the coffee on. Ben had been faithfully fixing breakfast for a week, but it was only 5:00 a.m. Even he wouldn't be stirring for another hour. Since sleep insisted on eluding her, she sought to thwart it completely with a jolt of caffeine. Midnight meowed at her from his comfortable perch on one of the chairs.

The shrill ring of the telephone startled her, and she scuffed toward it, frowning. "Hello?" she said.

"Georgia?"

At the shaky sound of Karen's voice, she came fully alert, afraid of what she was about to hear. "Yes, Karen. What's wrong?"

There was a small sob and Georgia's stomach tightened. "Phil's been shot!" There was another sob and Georgia unconsciously put a hand over her eyes, waiting for more. "He's all right, sort of. I mean, it was just in the leg, but I...I'm a mess."

"Where are you?"

"At Columbia Memorial."

"I'll be right there." Control asserted itself and Georgia's brain began to work. "Give me ten minutes."

In her I-function-best-in-a-crisis mode, she wasn't even surprised when Ben stepped out of the service porch, a wrench in his hand, a frown between his eyes. "What is it?" he asked.

She hung up the phone and began tearing off her robe as she headed for the stairs. "Phil's been shot," she explained over her shoulder. "Karen's at the hospital."

"I'll get my keys," he shouted up the stairs, "and wait for you in the truck."

In five minutes she was in jeans and a sweatshirt bending over Linda and shaking her lightly.

"Mmmf?" Linda asked, opening one eye, which seemed to refuse to focus.

"Honey, Mr. Hansen's had an accident and I'm going to the hospital. Can you get yourself and Lacey going in time for school if I don't get back?"

Linda propped up on an elbow, rubbing a hand over her eyes. "What happened? Is he okay?"

"I think so. I don't really know the details." Georgia kissed her forehead, pushed her back against the pillow and pulled the covers over her. "If you get a chance to call me between classes, I'll probably be able to tell you more. I've got to go."

Ben's Le Mans-style drive to the hospital had Georgia running through the emergency room doors eleven minutes after she'd hung up the telephone. Karen ran into her arms, sobbing, "I knew this would happen! Didn't I tell you this would happen?"

"How is he?" Ben asked, leading both women to the beige vinyl waiting room sofa.

Karen glanced up at him broodingly, her eyes red from crying, her cheeks puffy and blotched. "It's just a flesh wound. He's going to be fine, then I'm going to kill him."

"Right." Ben nodded. "You two sit here. I'll see if I can find out how it's going and get you some coffee."

The coffee was easy. Getting into the emergency room to try to talk to Phil was not.

"I'm a friend," he told the nurse on duty, a white-clad version of a determined Bea.

"I'm sorry. The doctor is with him."

"I have to speak with him about the case he was investigating when he was shot."

"You can do that when he's released."

"It's important that I do it now."

"The man has been shot," she said, as though to a dull child. "It's more important that his care not be interrupted."

Beyond her, Ben could see Phil propped up on a gurney while the doctor bandaged his leg. He was talking and laughing. "I'll ask the doctor if he minds." Ben started around the counter that separated the emergency room from the waiting area. The nurse stood squarely in his way. Though she was a foot shorter than he, she made up for it with a superior girth and a stare that gave him a moment's pause. She looked into his eyes, then drew a breath that raised her ample bosom a full six inches. "*I'll* ask him if he minds."

Ben smiled winningly. "Thank you."

The nurse closed her eyes and turned to do as she'd promised. She was back in a moment. "You can have five minutes."

He smiled again. "Thank you."

She gave him a withering glance and turned back to her paperwork.

"Hello, Stratton." Phil smiled as Ben approached, offering his hand.

"How do you feel?" Ben asked.

Phil laughed, then winced. "Glad to be alive. I've never been shot before. For the first few seconds the pain radiated everywhere and I thought it might be curtains. Turns out to be just a flesh wound."

"Lucky."

"Yeah."

"You were staking out MacKay's place?"

The bandage neatly in place, the doctor went to the pristine counter that ran the length of the room.

Phil nodded and spoke quietly. "We had a tip he was coming back. He pulled up behind his barn, got out of his truck, we put the lights on him and—" he shook his head "—I'm not sure what happened then. One of our lights was shot out, then I went down."

"He shot you?"

Phil shrugged, then winced again. "I don't know. I didn't see him pull a gun. But after MacKay took off, we didn't find a gun at the scene, either." He grinned. "I was smart enough to retain the bullet, though. Now we have something new to go on."

Ben laughed. "Good work. Can you go home, or do you still have to file your report?"

"The captain's sending someone to drive me and Karen home."

"Then take care. Can you arrange for me to get a copy of your report?"

Phil nodded. "Sure."

After a fellow officer put Phil and Karen into the back of his patrol car and drove off, Ben put an arm around Georgia's shoulders and wandered across the parking lot to the truck.

It was natural and comfortable for her to wrap an arm around his waist. "What were you working on in the service porch at five o'clock this morning?'' she asked.

''The drain's sluggish in the utility sink,'' he replied.

''How did you know that?''

''I was helping Linda wash off that old baker's rack Karen loaned her for the cookie concession. I think you were up in your room, working on that Pacific Pipeline book order.''

At first it amused her that Ben took notice of and retained so many of the details of her business. He could discuss it easily with her with an enthusiasm she found touching as well as helpful.

They had reached the truck and stopped, arms still around each other. ''Couldn't sleep again last night?'' she asked, turning to face him.

He shook his head as though his insomnia was a fact of life he now accepted. ''I kept thinking about this beautiful woman telling me she was a little bit in love with me. What were you doing up at five?''

She shrugged, wrapping her other arm around his waist and smiling up at him. ''Same problem. Same reason.''

He leaned down to take a small, quick kiss, lingering a moment to nuzzle the fragrant silkiness of her hair. The need that was now always just a heartbeat away rose out of his weariness, surprisingly intense. ''We could go home and take a nap. The girls'll be gone.''

''A nap?'' she asked, planting a kiss on his earlobe. She leaned back to look into his eyes. Her own were amused, confused and tired, but he could see in them that she knew exactly what he was suggesting.

''It's going to happen,'' he warned gently. ''It's just a matter of time.''

She shook her head, looking sweet but stubborn. "That's for people who are completely in love."

"How do you suppose they get that way?"

"By knowing each other, sharing the same goals, living the same dreams. Sex doesn't have anything to do with it, except that it becomes perfect because of all those other elements."

When he looked skeptical, she asked, "Have you ever been in love?"

He replied without hesitation, "No."

"Well, I have," she assured him smugly. "I know how it works."

Ben drove back to the house, Georgia leaning drowsily against his shoulder, thinking that he'd certainly gotten himself in a hell of a mess. He wanted to make love to Georgia more than he'd ever wanted anything. He wasn't sure where the need had come from or how it had developed in the short two weeks he'd known her, but it was there—demanding and real.

Georgia would not be made love to except by a man with whom she was completely in love. He already knew her well enough to know that that man would have to be completely in love with her, too. That meant it couldn't be him. A little love was all he had to give. It hadn't been offered him, developed in him as it was in most people. For the first time since he'd been old enough to understand about himself, he felt cheated rather than free.

BEN FROWNED over Phil's report. He read it after midnight that night in the workshop that now felt very much like home. The bullet the doctor removed from Phil's leg was a .38 caliber. It bore a unique circular marking identifying it as having been shot from a Harrington & Richards Defender.

Ben rubbed his eyes. He had only a very basic knowledge of weapons, but he knew enough to realize that that particular weapon was not in common use. He picked up the telephone and dialed. After David's answering machine asked him to leave a message, he said, "David, this is Ben. Would you ask Pete Carey to—"

"Ben?" David's voice interrupted.

"Hi, David. Why aren't you asleep?"

"Because you called and woke me up. Are you coming home?"

"Not yet. Look, I need you to do something for me, please."

"At this hour?"

"No, when you have time. First thing in the morning."

There was a snicker on the other end of the line. "Generous of you. What is it?"

"Tell Pete Carey I need some information about a Harrington & Richards Defender."

"What in the hell is that?"

"A gun."

"What's a plumber going to know about guns?"

"He's a weapons collector, David," Ben explained. "This thing shows up in a ballistics report, and I need to know more about it."

There was a moment's pause. "What are you doing with guns and ballistics reports? I thought Astoria was a quiet little town. You're supposed to be working on a face-lift on a building."

"I'm on top of that, David," Ben said bracingly. "You'd be delighted by how well it's going."

"I'd be more delighted if it didn't involve guns and ballistics reports. When are you coming back?"

"I don't know. But I'll explain it all when I do."

"I can hardly wait."

"Thanks, Unc."

"Sure."

"I WANT YOU to take a trip!" Bea marched into the shop, looking large and imperious in a brightly patterned fuchsia and black suit. She paused a moment to locate her prey. Rags, following slowly and with apparent reluctance, stopped just short of colliding with her.

Looking up in surprise from a complicated rack she and Ben were trying to assemble from instructions written in Swedish, Georgia groaned softly at the sight of her mother-in-law. She knew that look.

Bea covered the distance between them in a quick march and slapped a folder containing airline tickets into Georgia's hand. "You're going to Victoria." Bea glanced up at Ben. "You're going with her. The girls will stay with me." She raised her chin, waiting to crush a protest.

"Bea, I can't—"

"I don't want to hear it!" she said firmly. "Did you think I wouldn't learn about someone trying to run you down in the Dutch Cup's parking lot? Or that the policeman investigating your case was shot?" For a moment her expression of woman in control was replaced by a look of deeply injured feelings. "I'm only your mother-in-law. You don't owe me anything. But you and the girls are all I have left of my son...." There was the smallest break in the firmness of her voice, a quiver of her sturdy chin.

"Bea, stop that," Ragnar said gently, patting her shoulder. It reminded Ben of a rabbit consoling a bear. If he hadn't known that this particular rabbit had a tactic with a tennis racket that was more concentration than swinging skill but that defeated his opponent every time, he'd have thought his interference foolhardy. Instead, he watched in fascination as Bea subsided and leaned into his shoulder.

"Bea," Georgia said calmly, placatingly, "those things did happen, but Ben was with me. You can see that I'm fine. I didn't tell you because I didn't want you to get upset like this."

"I want you to take the trip," Bea insisted, though her tone had lost some of its earlier forcefulness. "I know about all the things Linda has going, but I can see that she gets to everything and I can help her with it."

Georgia hugged her. "Thanks, Bea. But I want to be with her for it. Whoever is doing this to me isn't going to cheat me out of being with my children and enjoying their successes with them. Ben never lets me out of his sight. I'll be fine. Really."

"Never?" Bea looked from Georgia to Ben, and Ben swallowed a smile. The question was as much about sleeping arrangements as about a need for confirmation that her daughter-in-law was being protected. Her next question confirmed it. "Are you still comfortable in the workshop?"

"Very," Ben replied blandly. "Thank you."

Bea looked from one to the other again, but apparently whatever she suspected, she did not consider it cause for concern—at least not yet. She focused on Georgia. "I thought you'd be stubborn about it. The tickets can be used at any time. If you have any sense, you'll use them now, tonight.''

Georgia smiled at Bea. ''I married Gary Madison. How can you accuse me of having sense?'' For a moment the two women shared a fond smile and a silent grief that bound them together and excluded Ben and Rags. The men looked at each other and wandered toward the door, ostensibly to watch the face-lift taking place outside.

''You're sure you have this under control?'' Rags asked.

''Positive,'' Ben assured him.

Rags knew it wasn't misplaced self-confidence. He'd shared the court with Ben often enough to know he was a partner you could count on. ''I love Bea. She was frantic when she heard about the Dutch Cup thing. Then Phil Hansen.''

''I know.'' Ben grinned at him. ''Try to assure her that Georgia will be safe with me.''

Rags shook his head and groaned. ''That's a hardheaded woman. And a bighearted one. She feels a responsibility for Georgia and the girls, particularly because of the way Gary... You know. Anyway, she doesn't believe in shifting her responsibilities onto someone else. Bea's letting you stay with Georgia because you could defend her physically where she couldn't. But heaven help you if you let anything happen to her.''

Ben laughed. ''That alone would be enough to make me vigilant.''

After Bea and Rags left, Georgia went back to the instructions for the rack. Working from common sense rather than the diagram, Ben put the wall mount assembly together, stealing a glance every once in a while at

Georgia as she fit brackets onto shelves. She wore that slightly withdrawn look that seemed to overtake her every time the subject of Gary came up. He remembered the impression he'd gotten shortly after meeting her, that there was more than simple grief to her memories of her husband. He recalled her saying that there had been so much "unfinished" between them. Rags had apparently presumed that Ben's proximity to Georgia had made him privileged to whatever the mystery was surrounding Gary's death. He was beginning to wish that was true. He was sure nothing permanent could come of his feelings for Georgia, but he'd like to see her free of pain before he had to walk out of her life.

BEN AND GEORGIA HEARD the screams as they pushed through her patio gate and rounded the corner. The rack had finally gone together and they were laughing about the three strange-looking pieces left over and what might happen to the rack because they were missing.

One high-pitched, hysterical scream rang across the patio, loud and long.

"Oh, my God!" Georgia cried, dropping her purse and briefcase as she ran for the back door, suddenly sure her antagonist's prey had switched from herself to her daughters. If anyone truly wanted to hurt her, that would be the sure way.

Ben caught her before she was through the screen door, not bothering to argue, simply pushing her aside and running through himself. Following him in, Georgia stopped beside him in the doorway to the kitchen, her heartbeat strangling her, her eyes unable to believe what they were seeing.

Linda was pounding Lacey. Literally. She had her

taller sister backed into the small space between the refrigerator and the microwave cart. Lacey had both arms protectively over her head and was bent over, screaming, while Linda rained punches on her back. "You idiot!" Linda was screaming. "You stupid baby! How could you have done that?"

For a moment, Georgia could only stare. Like all siblings, her daughters argued, even fought, but they hadn't come to blows since they'd been toddlers. And of the two of them, Linda would not be the one she could imagine becoming violent.

She was galvanized into action when Linda took a fistful of Lacey's hair. "Linda!" Georgia took a firm hold of her oldest's arm and pulled her out of the corner. Linda resisted, still swinging at Lacey. "Linda!" Georgia shouted, taking both the girl's arms and backing her up against the refrigerator. Linda's cheeks were purple with fury, her eyes bright with a temper her family seldom saw.

"I'm gonna kill her!" Linda shouted, turning away from Lacey, who took the opportunity to escape. "Look at my sweater! My sixty-dollar Generra sweater! The newspaper's coming to school tomorrow morning to take pictures of me and the cooking classes, and dumbo dyed her hair wearing *my best sweater!*"

Georgia's eyes flew to her younger daughter in alarm. The head sobbing into Ben's shoulder was covered with black hair—a little stiff, dull and very black hair. A small sound of horror came from Georgia's throat. "Lacey!"

Still holding on to Ben, as though for protection, still sobbing, Lacey turned to reveal the scope of the destruction to Linda's sweater and her own hair. The long, white bulky-knit sweater with its bold designer name across the chest was now slashed with several purplish-black streaks that Georgia felt sure were permanent. Lacey's thin, milky-complexioned face, usually bright and beautiful with its frame of red hair, now looked deathly pale in the overpowering cloud of dull black. It crossed Georgia's mind in a flash of gallows humor that she looked like a female vampire.

"Look at my sweater!" Linda shrieked. "I baby-sat for four weeks while everyone else went to the games and dances. I gave up onion rings after school to be able to buy that sweater!"

"You have everything, anyway!" Lacey shrieked back at her. "What's one crummy sweater? I'll pay you back."

Incensed, Linda leaped at her. Lacey ducked behind Ben as Georgia caught Linda's arm, preventing her from reaching her target. "With what?" Linda demanded, pulling against Georgia's hold. "You borrow money from me for everything!"

"Because you've always got everything!" Lacey shouted back, coming around Ben but still maintaining a healthy distance from her sister. "You save your money, you're always organized! You're the smart one! You're the pretty one! I'm always making mistakes and look like—" Lacey's face began to crumple "—like a tomato on a stick!" she blurted, then dissolved into tears again.

Georgia felt the same shock that registered on Linda's face. For a moment they both stared at Lacey as Ben wrapped his arms around her. Then Linda looked up at Georgia. "What is the *matter* with her?"

Georgia didn't know. She was feeling more and more lately as though she no longer understood or controlled anything. But for the girls' sakes, at least, she had to keep up appearances. She looked up at Ben. "Would you stay with Lacey for a few minutes, please?"

"Of course," he replied.

Georgia turned Linda toward the stairs and followed her up. Linda's room was decorated in a country style with curtains she'd made herself and artistic touches all around that reflected her interest and aptitude for all her arts and crafts electives. Georgia never walked into it without thinking how remarkable it was that this gifted child was hers, but she was too troubled now to notice.

Linda sank onto the side of her twin bed. Georgia took the small stool in front of the old dressing table that had once been hers. She tried to gather her thoughts, to find the moral of this story and explain it with the clarity her own mother always seemed able to find in a crisis. But the crises were stacking up on her these days, and she was becoming more and more convinced that she'd never be the clear thinker her mother was. The only important point in all this stood in the forefront of her mind, and she focused on it. "You have every right to be angry, Linda," she said calmly. "But you never have the right to hit."

Linda's eyes filled, fury turning into tears. She fell back onto the bed, tears sliding down onto the bedspread as she stared at the ceiling. "Everything's going wrong, Mom. I asked everybody to come over this weekend so we could get the dough made for the refrigerator cookies. It should be made a few weeks ahead of time, but everybody's busy with other stuff. Even Shelly's going to Portland, shopping with her mom. Shelly's mother ignores her every day of the week, but the one day I need her, her mom takes her off to Portland." Linda swallowed and raised a hand, then dropped it angrily to the bed. "Why didn't she take my sweater off if she was going to color her hair? I'm glad it came out looking so stupid."

"Linda."

"Well, it's true!" Linda sat up and wiped both hands across her face. "I loan her money when she's blown her allowance and doesn't want you to know it, I wash her fancy stuff when I do mine because she doesn't know how, I even help her with her homework sometimes. And then she does this to me."

"I don't think it was malicious," Georgia said gently. "I think it was just thoughtless. It doesn't make it any less wrong, I just think you should try to understand that she didn't do it purposely to hurt you. She'll pay you back every dime, I promise."

"What do I wear tomorrow?"

Georgia remembered that Shelly had been along the day Linda had bought the sweater and that she'd bought one just like it. "Doesn't Shelly have one exactly the same?"

Linda shook her head. "Yeah, but she doesn't loan her clothes."

"She borrows yours."

Linda shrugged with that curious acceptance she had for the foibles of her friend. "She doesn't think about that."

Georgia swept a hand toward the open closet bulging with clothes. "Isn't there something in there that will do? Honey, even if I could afford to buy you another sweater, there isn't time. Nothing's open tonight, and the picture's being taken tomorrow morning."

Linda nodded with grim acceptance. "I know. I just...wanted to look special."

Georgia moved to the bed to put an arm around her. "Darling, I know you won't believe this, but you always do look special. You *have* something special—a sweetness and a competence that always shows, no matter what you're wearing."

Linda gave her a disbelieving side-glance.

"Didn't you hear what Lacey said?" Georgia asked.

Linda thought and frowned. "That I always save my money and I'm always organized."

"And what else?"

Her frowned deepened. "That I was the smart one. That I was the—" she looked at Georgia and finished with a puzzled tone "—the pretty one. She's crazy! She's the one all the guys—"

"Lacey is beautiful," Georgia explained, squeezing Linda's shoulders. "Feature by feature, she's probably prettier than you are. But you have almost two years' maturity on her, and even more than that because you've always been responsible and creative, able to make things happen because you don't mind working and having to give up some things to get other things." She paused, feeling Linda relax against her. She held her a little tighter. "Now, guys at your age might not notice those things. They see the obvious. But other girls notice, adults notice, little sisters notice and become jealous."

Linda pulled back to look Georgia in the eye. "Are you saying Lacey is jealous of *me*?"

Georgia nodded. "She knows beauty isn't everything. One day she may have all the qualities you've acquired, but she doesn't have them yet. She's as envious of your maturity as you are of her looks and her hair."

"Her hair." Linda put both hands over her eyes and

shook her head. "Do you believe she did that to her hair?"

"I think she wanted to look like you."

Linda digested that in silence, then shook her head, as though having difficulty believing it. "Do you ever wonder how things get so complicated?"

Georgia laughed. "That just means you're approaching things correctly."

Linda grimaced. "Why?"

"Your father always used to say that if things seem clear to you and you always know what to do, it means that you really aren't aware of the problems involved. Living is complicated." Georgia watched the little shadow that always came with the mention of Gary fill Linda's eyes.

"Loving is complicated, too, isn't it?" Linda looked up into her eyes, almost as though searching for something. Georgia wondered if she suspected something was developing between herself and Ben. Did she disapprove?

"Yes, it is," Georgia agreed. "It's probably the most complicated thing we do in our lives. Why do you ask that?"

Linda shrugged. "I guess because sometimes things look one way and are really not like that at all."

Trying to analyze that answer and finding nothing in it clear enough to settle her maternal concern, Georgia persisted. "Like what?"

"Like Lacey being jealous of me, when she's the one who's really beautiful. Like Mrs. Gordon thinking you and Ben are having an affair because he sleeps in the workshop, and all you've ever done is kiss like a couple of freshmen."

Georgia closed her mouth before the gasp could escape. She didn't know whether to be more horrified that Linda had seen them or that she'd classified their style as "freshman." What Shelly's mother thought didn't count. Georgia tried to concentrate on the issue. "Is that what upsets you every time I mention your father? I know you said that I should find another man to be happy with, but has it just occurred to you that you'd have to accept another man in your life where Dad was?"

Linda looked into her eyes again, and Georgia looked back evenly. Whatever answer Linda sought there, Georgia needed to hear, as well. Maybe then she'd finally understand the question. Linda lowered her eyes. "No," she said.

Georgia covered Linda's hand with her own. "Then, what is it, Lindy?" she asked gently, holding her breath, praying for an honest answer.

Linda shrugged and smiled, her eyes shuttered. "I just miss him, that's all."

That wasn't it. Disappointed and feeling just a little defeated, Georgia hugged her and kissed her forehead. "Get cleaned up for dinner. But you don't have to hurry. I want to have a few words with Lacey."

Georgia heard Lacey's anguished voice before she'd reached the bottom of the stairs. "Because it's geeky!" She slowed her steps as Ben's reply followed quietly.

"Your red hair was beautiful, Lacey."

"No, it wasn't. The boys called me firecracker and carrot top, and today, Aaron Mitchell said I looked like—" there was an audible swallow "—a tomato on a stick!"

Ben made a sympathetic sound. "So you're going to change yourself because this Mitchell jerk has no taste in women?"

There was a moment's silence, and Georgia smiled in the quiet dimness of the hallway. She blessed Ben for his choice of words. She could imagine Lacey trying to decide whether to defend the reputation of the freshman class's number one hunk or bask in the glory of being considered a woman.

"I just want to look like Mom and Linda," Lacey said feebly.

"Lacey," Ben replied quietly, "they are both elegant ladies. I can see why you'd want to be like them. But, you're Lacey. You don't have to look like them to have that style and charm that I think are what you're really after."

"I do," she insisted. "I don't want red hair."

"You have it. They're beautiful because they make the best of what they have. And because each one of them thinks of other people first."

"What does that have to do with it?"

"Goodness shows."

There was a frustrated sigh from Lacey. "This is really ugly, isn't it?" Georgia could imagine her holding out a dry strand of black hair.

"No," Ben answered. "It's just not you. And it would have been smart to take the sweater off before you used that stuff."

"I didn't think about it."

"That's the plague of being young. If you want to be like your mother and your sister, that's a good place to start. Think first, then do. And apologizing when you're wrong doesn't hurt, either."

"I'm probably out sixty bucks for a new sweater."

"It's only fair."

As Ben had handled the kind and understanding part of her parental duties with skillful competence, only the dark task of the disciplinary part remained. Squaring her shoulders, Georgia walked into the kitchen to find Ben and Lacey sitting at right angles to each other at the table. Ben had made cocoa. Lacey looked chastened and calm.

"Tomorrow," Georgia said to Lacey, "you will come home right after school and take the sweater to the cleaner's. If they can't do anything with it, you owe her a new one. And you are forbidden to borrow anything of hers or mine until you can behave more responsibly. Is that clear?"

Lacey nodded and pushed away from the table. "I'll go apologize. I was thinking she could borrow the sweater you gave me for my birthday, but it would be too big for her."

Georgia patted her shoulder. "Yes, but it was a nice thought."

Lacey headed for the stairs, then stopped and turned. "If I don't come down for dinner, you'll probably find my body under her bed. I don't want a fussy funeral."

Ben got to his feet. "We'll just lay you to rest in a garbage bag," he said.

"You could say a few words, like—" she joined her hands and looked heavenward piously "—'She was stupid and she had hair like burned spaghetti.'"

"That would be memorable." Georgia pointed to the stairs. "Go."

"Mom?" Lacey's small burst of humor slipped, and she looked dolefully, pathetically, at Georgia. "I suppose I deserve to go to school like this tomorrow."

Georgia heard the unspoken plea and couldn't ignore it. "I'll take you to the beauty shop in the morning and see what they can do. I'll call your counselor and explain why you're absent."

Lacey heaved a deep sigh. "Thanks, Mom."

As the girl disappeared into the hallway and up the stairs, Georgia turned to Ben. "Thank you for talking to her," she said a little stiffly. "You said all the right things. I'm sure they made more of an impression coming from you."

She looked tired, Ben thought, wrung out—as though a large hand had taken her by the throat and shaken her. He wanted to touch her, to take her in his arms, but she looked as though she'd pull away...or slug him. He felt fairly sure that she didn't think he'd overstepped in talking to Lacey, that her gratitude was genuine. But she was deliberately keeping him at a distance. He could understand that. There were times he didn't like his space invaded, either.

"Want me to run out and get something for dinner?" he asked. Maybe practical matters would relax her.

"Thanks, but I took a casserole out of the freezer this morning." She glanced at him hopefully but still distantly as she took it out of the refrigerator and put it in the oven. "Would you put together a salad so I can check on the girls?"

"Right. Go ahead."

Listening to Georgia's footsteps on the stairs, Ben reached into a lower cupboard where she kept a large stainless steel bowl. Retrieving lettuce, spinach and cabbage from the crisper, he began to tear leaves for salad, allowing himself to feel smug for a moment. He'd handled that well. Wordlessly, she'd asked him to back off, and he'd had the sense to do it. He'd grown attached to Georgia and her girls, but that didn't allow him access to things that were none of his business. If he'd learned anything growing up an orphan, it was the importance of keeping one's place. You might be invited to share rooms and food, but that didn't necessarily entitle you to emotional intimacies. There was a lot less pain involved when you didn't presume that it did.

Suddenly, Ben remembered the look in Georgia's eyes just moments ago when she'd thanked him politely for talking to Lacey. Behind the cool manners he'd seen exhaustion, frustration, panic. He realized with startling sharpness that she'd been suppressing a cry for help. And he'd overlooked it, relieved to be able to keep his distance.

Suddenly his smugness became guilt—guilt accompanied by pain. Rinsing lettuce, he reflected grimly that sometimes you just couldn't win.

CHAPTER NINE

LIFE WAS OUT of joint. Georgia wandered through the quiet house trying to pace away an uncharacteristic rise of panic. The girls had gone upstairs early, relations still a little too strained for their nightly cocoa ritual. Ben had left for the workshop more than half an hour earlier. Georgia had noticed he'd forgotten the thermos of coffee she always sent with him, but she was feeling too grim to take it over. She didn't want to burst into tears in front of him. He should be spared that—after all, he was only a little bit in love with her.

Georgia's eyes burned and her throat closed as she fell into the big chair that had been Gary's. She felt as though she desperately needed some little touch of him, some shred of memory, some remnant of him of which the house usually seemed so full. But tonight, because she needed him, she seemed unable to tap her memories, to see anything that would wrap her in the comfort and security he'd always made her feel.

She pulled her knees up and wrapped her arms around them, telling herself bracingly that it had only been a simple argument. The girls had had them before and they would have them again—it was a fact of life. For the first time in her life, she didn't feel strong enough to face it. She'd never been one to shift her parental responsibilities onto Gary because he'd been taller and stronger and had a bigger voice. But now she found herself wishing desperately that there was someone else to whom she could turn over responsibility—if only for a day. For twenty-four hours it would be such a luxury to have a thought that didn't involve her children, her store or her personal safety.

The reality of her widowhood struck her more clearly than it ever had before. She felt the loss of her husband and the fact of her solitude with more keenness than she had the day Phil had come to tell her about Gary's accident. She was alone. Wretchedness rose to overpower her, and she turned her face into the wing of the chair and cried.

BEN WONDERED what he was doing there. He went quietly into the kitchen prepared with the excuse that he'd forgotten the thermos, but he knew that wasn't his reason for coming back to the house. He'd been remembering the look in Georgia's eyes, and suddenly, keeping a clinical distance in a relationship didn't carry the same nobility it once had.

Seeing that most of the lights were off and hearing the house's late-hour silence, he grabbed the thermos and turned to leave, presuming everyone had gone to bed. Then he heard the sound coming from the living room. He recognized it instantly as a woman in tears. It wasn't the soft sound of easy sobs, but large, tearing gulps of pain and anguish. So he hadn't been mistaken about the cry for help in Georgia's eyes.

He wanted to run away, to go back to the workshop and simply pretend he hadn't heard. He wasn't good at this. But even as the thoughts formed, his feet were moving into the living room, following the sound to the big tapestry chair he'd noticed no one ever used. Georgia was huddled in a corner of it, shoes off, knees

drawn up, heart apparently breaking. Instinctively he
knew she was looking for Gary—but Gary was gone.

He sat on the arm of the chair and put a hand to her
hair. "Georgia?"

She didn't start as he expected her to, but simply
froze for an instant, sniffed, then buried her face deeper
into the chair. "Go away," she said, her voice muffled
by the upholstery. "I'm indulging in a bout of self-
pity."

"You're certainly entitled," he said gently, stroking
her hair. "Don't let me stop you."

"I can't do it with an audience."

"Then it isn't true self-pity. That requires someone
on whom one can dump the long string of injustices
that have led to such a sorry pass. There's not much
point in telling yourself about it."

Georgia pulled her face out of the corner but didn't
turn to him, except for one swift, not entirely friendly
glance out of the corner of a red-rimmed eye. "This is
the way I always do it."

He continued to stroke her hair. "How satisfying has
it been?"

Suddenly she was out of the chair, all tension and
cool distance again. She'd changed into jeans and an
old red sweater, and she looked wonderfully disheveled
and soft as she spun on him. "Don't be charming, Ben.
I'm in an ugly, knotted-up mood." She made a fist to
express the extent of the knot. "I'm angry and confused and upset." Her voice wavered and she swallowed with difficulty. "And if you stick around you're
going to end up in the middle of a scene. I don't think
a man who's just a little in love should have to deal
with that. This kind of thing is for husbands of long

standing...." The words died on her lips, and she put a hand to her mouth as a sob erupted.

"Georgia...." He closed the distance between them and reached out for her, already resigned to playing stand-in.

But she drew back, folding her arms and shaking her head. "No," she said. "I won't keep doing that to you."

"What?"

"Turning to you because...because Gary isn't here. It isn't fair."

"Are you sure that's why you do it?" he asked. He reached out to her again, and she let herself be caught. "Maybe you're just falling in love with me—more than a little bit."

It was true. He could see it in her eyes. He knew with certainty that it was true of himself, too. He was much more than just a little bit in love. She didn't deny it, but she didn't necessarily look pleased about it, either.

"I can't let that happen," she said.

He raised an eyebrow. "Can you stop it?"

Her face began to crumple. "Apparently...not," she wept, coming toward him blindly as tears fell again.

He enveloped her in his arms and held her long enough to steady her, then swept her up and carried her to the big chair, sitting down and cradling her in his arms. Still sobbing, she shifted against him, getting comfortable, twining her arms between her chest and his, burrowing her face in his neck. Ben hooked the hassock with his toe and pulled it over, stretching his legs out to pillow hers.

She cried while the clock ticked, the refrigerator hummed and an occasional car passed outside. Ben continued to stroke her hair and rub her back while whispering reassurance. Slowly her body began to relax against his and her crying quieted.

"Ben?" Her head still nestled in his shoulder, Georgia tucked a hand around his neck.

He held her a little closer. "Yes."

"Do you want to hear about Gary?"

"Do you want to tell me?"

She sat up a little, leaning back against one wing of the chair, her hand on his chest. "I want you to understand."

He leaned into the other wing, his arms still circling her waist. He wasn't sure he wanted to hear this. It was going to be a reason why their love wouldn't work, the explanation for whatever lay "unfinished" between her and Gary. He also had many reasons why their love wouldn't work, but somehow he wasn't too interested in them at the moment. They seemed less and less real every day. But she had to talk, he knew, and he had to listen. "All right," he said.

She closed her eyes a moment, seeming to collect herself as well as her thoughts, then she opened them and focused on his chest, where she traced a shirt button with her forefinger. "We were happy," she said quietly. "We loved each other and the girls very much. Sometimes—" she lifted her shoulder, tipping her head to meet it for a moment "—I would get a little jealous of his secretary because she was pretty and smart and nice." She sighed, her hand still on his chest, her eyes raised to the ceiling. "I worked with him, too, but I took care of the schedules and the books. Sara knew every small detail of Gary's work and could discuss it all with him. He would call her at night or on weekends when he had a problem he couldn't see through himself. They had something I couldn't share. It wasn't a monumental jealousy on my part, just a nagging little wish that I could be as gorgeous and as smart as she was.''

She paused and Ben waited quietly for her to go on. ''Two years before he died, he sold out to a larger competitor who left him little choice. West Coast Haulers had bigger trucks than we had and could go longer distances for less money. The business had been in Gary's family for three generations, so he suffered a lot of guilt as well as the sense of failure that goes along with that kind of a loss. Anyway, West Coast kept Gary on as district manager, and that consoled him somewhat. But the following year they sold out to Nationwide Transportation, a conglomerate that bled all the little companies it held to feed the corporation. We went down so hard and so fast, Gary was broken-hearted.'' She closed her eyes, pale again with the remembered pain of that time.

''Gary had been out of work almost five months when he died.'' Her eyebrows drew together and she firmed her lips, as though they wanted to quiver and she refused to let them. ''We'd lost everything but the house.''

''What happened?'' he asked quietly, tightening his grip on her.

''He...was in a light plane,'' she said, her voice steady but faint. ''It went down in sudden bad weather over the Coast Range.''

''He was a pilot?''

She shook her head. ''I guess he'd hired the plane. The pilot was a friend of his.''

''To go where?''

She shook her head again, meeting his eyes this time,

her own miserable. "That's the big question. He hadn't said anything to me about taking a trip."

Ben frowned. "Where do you think he was going?"

"I really have no idea. When I feel strong and capable, I think he had some kind of business scheme going that he didn't want to mention to me because he knew I worried about everything." She said that with all apparent conviction that it was true. Then she focused on Ben, and he watched a single tear fall unchecked. "When I'm scared and don't know what to do next, I think he was leaving me."

"Georgia…" Ben began gently, prepared to scold.

"Sara died in the plane with him," Georgia added quickly, tears falling rapidly now. "There were two suitcases. Bea tried to pull strings to keep it quiet. The girls don't know, of course. What else could he have been doing, Ben? What else?"

"Had the pilot filed a flight plan?"

"He was going to Portland. Their ultimate destination could have been the Portland airport and a commercial flight. I don't know." Her voice sounded desperate.

"What about Sara's family?"

"She had no one close. Just an aunt in a nursing home in Denver, who couldn't even remember who she was."

Ben pulled her back into his shoulder, wrapping his arms tightly around her. "I don't know, Georgia. And you don't know. I suppose there could be a handful of reasons that just aren't obvious. Isn't it best to just not speculate?"

"I loved him," she insisted, her arms around Ben's neck. "I have to know if I failed him, if the marriage

I'd thought was so wonderful had all fallen apart without my noticing it.''

"How do you plan to do that?''

"I don't know that I can,'' she replied, shaking her head against him. "I just know I can't let myself love you completely unless I can find out what happened, where they were going and why.''

He held her away from him and frowned at her. "You're going to live on hold forever?''

"I have to know,'' she insisted quietly. Then she curled up against him again with a heavy sigh. "I told you this wasn't a lightweight burden.''

Ben sighed, planting a kiss on her side part. "I won't just walk away from you.''

She tightened her arms around his neck. "I don't want you to. Maybe there's a solution we just don't see right now.''

He wasn't sure he believed that, but it was better than considering the obvious alternatives. "Right. Well...'' He straightened in the chair. Reluctantly she dropped her arms from around him. "If you're going to be okay, I'd better get back to the workshop before I complicate things further.''

In the nighttime quiet of her living room, Georgia looked into the dark hazel eyes of the man who had brought such comfort and so many questions into her life, and for the first time in two years, she considered what it would be like to make love again. She noticed in vague surprise that her thoughts were not as filled with old memories as they were with all the unknown possibilities.

Ben's touch would be magic—she already knew that. His hands could calm her or excite her, his lips could offer comfort or extend a potential for pleasure she'd been unwilling to consider...until this moment. Now was not the time, but the realization that a time would come made her eyes widen and her pulse thrum.

Ben watched her gaze focus on him. Their bodies were so close that he felt her accelerated pulse, the sudden tension of her awareness. When she leaned her cheek against his, he understood what she was telling him because he felt it, too. They had moved well beyond "just a little bit in love" and were going headlong toward complete love, toward physical love. It didn't matter that both resisted and both recognized the dangers. There was a power at work here Ben had never encountered before and Georgia hadn't felt in a very long time. The intensity of it surprised them.

Ben nuzzled her cheek. "We're in trouble, aren't we?"

She sighed and kissed him quickly, sweetly. "Yes, we are," she admitted, and got to her feet, tugging him up after her. She rested her hands comfortably at his waist and smiled into his eyes, her own reflecting a new intimacy between them. "Thank you. With what happened to Phil, the blowup between the girls and my constant concern about Gary I...just sort of lost my equilibrium. But you helped even things out for me."

"Anytime. Good night, Georgia." Ben walked out of the house and across the yard to the workshop, glad she felt on an even keel again. He, on the other hand, was listing dangerously and taking on water.

"THE HARRINGTON & RICHARDS Defender was carried by postal inspectors," David said.

In the privacy of Georgia's office at the store, Ben scribbled notes on a scratch pad while keeping one eye toward the front where she was gift wrapping a book for a woman who chatted while waiting.

David continued, "They all have a five-digit serial number. They were used for eight years, then sold to a Washington, D.C., wholesaler who marketed them to dealers throughout the country." There was a pause. "That tell you anything?"

Ben frowned to himself. "I'm not sure, but it's more than we had before. Thanks, Dave. Tell Pete I'll buy him a Scotch when I get back to Portland."

"Well, he said if this information helps you, you owe him a charter fishing weekend right there on the coast."

Ben laughed. "Tell him his rates are outrageous, but I'll think about it. Thanks again, Dave."

As Ben hung up the phone and made his way to the front of the shop, rereading the notes he'd made, Georgia handed the brightly wrapped package across the counter. With a smile and a wave, her customer walked out into the late afternoon downpour.

"Did you reach your uncle?" Georgia asked, endorsing the check with her store stamp and ringing up the sale.

"Yes." Ben leaned his elbow on the counter and frowned over his notes. Georgia came to lean beside him. "He says the Harrington & Richards Defender is a fairly unique pistol that was used by the U.S. post office."

Georgia frowned at him. "I thought mailmen just carried mace."

He laughed and nudged her with his elbow. "The guns were used by postal inspectors, not mail carriers. They enforce postal regulations, investigate thefts, stuff like that. I doubt that mace would do the job for them."

"MacKay was never a postal inspector," she said seriously. "And neither was Wally."

Ben straightened and put the note in his pocket. "The post office later sold these pistols to a dealer in Washington, D.C., who distributed them to dealers around the country. Anybody could have bought one." He sighed.

"What did the police say about your piece of straw?" Georgia asked, suppressing a smile.

"Don't smirk at me," he scolded. "They sent it to the state police crime lab in Salem, apparently having more respect for my opinions than you do. Which one of us is cooking tonight?"

"Neither. I have a million phone calls to make to finalize the placement of the craft booths, and Linda's going to have cookies all over the kitchen. I thought we'd bring home Chinese or something. Ah! Here's the newspaper."

A small boy, hands inky from newsprint, slapped her paper on the counter while blowing a grape-scented bubble of frightening proportions. He snapped his gum, retracted it expertly and waved as he went on his way.

Ben shook his head in wonder, watching the boy walk away. "One day they're going to find him somewhere on his route, vacuum sealed for all eternity in a giant bubble."

Georgia opened the paper to study the front page and squealed with delight when she found Linda's smiling likeness looking back at her. At her side, looking serious and important, was Shelly. Behind the two girls in semicircular rows were the cooking classes helping with the cookie concession.

Ben leaned over her to read the short article.

Linda Jean Madison of Astoria, chairman of Astoria High's always popular cookie concession at
the Columbia River Days celebration to be held
in several weeks, amasses her troops for the big
event. Under her direction thousands of cookies
are being prepared. "The hardest part of the job,"
she says, "is preventing my staff from eating the
project." Miss Madison is also first runner-up for
Junior Class Columbia River Days Princess.

Georgia smiled at the picture. With the utilitarian
bibbed apron Linda wore, it was impossible to identify
what she had on underneath. The second-best yellow
sweater she'd finally decided to wear was practically
invisible.

"Someday," Ben said, "her photo's going to be in
the *Wall Street Journal* and the caption's going to read,
'Young Northwest entrepreneur's restaurant chain
listed on the big board.'"

Georgia folded the paper, grimly thoughtful. "She's
certainly got what it takes. She's talented, she sub-
scribes to *Bon Appétit* magazine out of her own money,
and she's not afraid of working hard. But she's not as
sure of herself as she used to be."

Ben glanced at his watch, then went to the door to
lock it and turned the Open sign to Closed. "Teenagers
are supposed to be a little self-conscious and confused,
aren't they?"

She nodded. "But it's more than that. She comes
close to telling me sometimes, then she backs away."

"I don't know her as well as you do, of course,"
Ben said, hooking an arm around her neck and bringing
her with him to the back of the store, where she kept

her jacket. "But she seems happy enough now. Over-worked but happy."

Georgia nodded and sighed. She had no doubt that the past few weeks had been a valuable experience for her daughter, but she knew it had given her an insight into the vagaries of human nature, as well. In all the time Linda had put in preparing doughs, shelling nuts, performing tasks that friends had proved too busy to do despite their promises, the only classmate to help her faithfully had been Randy Martin, the dark-haired boy in the letterman's jacket whom Ben had noticed. Busy preparing for her duties as princess, Shelly had shown up for photographs and interviews at the radio station and that was all. Except for that part of the project done at school, most of the other kids had ignored Linda's deadlines for reports and failed to come through in other ways.

"She's doing such a remarkable job against difficult odds." Ben helped Georgia into her jacket and shrugged into his own. "I'm sure once the project is over, once her adviser sees what she's done and she realizes it herself, she'll feel the boost to her self-confidence. Cheer up." Ben started toward the front door. "While you're making your million phone calls, I'll probably be drafted to crack nuts. We still have fifteen pounds to go."

Georgia smiled at him with genuine affection, re-membering how he'd spent several hours Sunday after-noon with a nutcracker and a mound of walnuts. "Why didn't you buy them already shelled?" Lacey had grumbled while picking the nuts out of the shell.

"Because I saved all kinds of money buying them unshelled from Julie Johnson's grandfather in the valley. Not only are they less expensive this way, but he gave us a deal.''

Georgia, also picking nuts out of shells, had looked up at Ben and seen the fond, respectful smile he'd given Linda.

Georgia let Ben out of the shop before her and turned to lock the door. ''I'll bet you never thought you'd be spending your time as a bodyguard cum kitchen helper when you decided to buy a building in Astoria.''

He put his arm around her with a laugh and snapped open a folding umbrella. ''No, I didn't.'' He held her close with one arm and the umbrella over them with the other. Rain pelted furiously against the taut nylon as they rounded the corner and left the shelter the scaffolding provided.

''Sorry?'' she asked, running beside him.

They stopped at the corner for a red light. Ben looked down at her, the lazy humor gone out of his eyes. Every time he looked at her now, there was a deeper intensity to his gaze, a longing that both humbled and frightened her. ''No,'' he whispered. Street and pedestrian traffic forgotten, he leaned down to kiss her slowly, lengthily. When he raised his head her breath was gone and his was ragged. ''No,'' he said again.

CHAPTER TEN

"YOU'RE GOING TO LEAVE US here cracking nuts and *you're* going to Shelly's?" Lacey glowered up at her sister from her lotus position on the living room carpet. Then she cast a wry glance at Ben, who sat on the other side of the spread-out newspapers covered with walnut shells. "Do you think that's fair?"

"Shelly's having a problem with her cookie gun," Linda explained again, pulling on her jacket. "I'll just be a couple of minutes."

"You need a ride?" Ben asked.

Linda shook her head. "It's just through the backyard and four houses over."

Lacey snorted. "I'll bet the problem is that she hasn't made the batter to put in the gun yet."

With a smile at Ben and an ugly face at her sister, Linda headed for the back door.

"My, my, what an industrious pair you are." Georgia peered into the living room from the kitchen, a steno pad in her hands, a pencil behind her ear and horn-rimmed glasses halfway down her nose. "How's it going?"

Ben and Lacey exchanged a dark glance. "Only twelve pounds to go," Ben replied. "How are you doing?"

"Only seven hundred and twenty thousand calls left to make. I have to get one of the posters out of the garage. Then I'll make cocoa and we can raid some of Linda's test cookies." She blew them a kiss and disappeared.

Lacey glanced at Ben. "Who do you think that was meant for?"

"What?" he asked without looking up.

"The kiss."

He concentrated on his task, wondering if she was simply interested or upset about his developing relationship with her mother. "I think blown kisses are up for grabs."

"I'll take it, then," Lacey said. "You get the better kind anyway, don'tcha?"

Ben raised his eyes at that and found amusement and a kind of comfortable acceptance in Lacey's gaze that worried as well as pleased him. "Been snooping?"

"No, but I live here. I see stuff. You love Mom?"

Ben had found that conversation with Lacey was good for one's character; she left so little room for evasion.

"Yes," he replied. "That all right with you?"

Lacey studied him a moment, then nodded. "Yeah. You living here is a little like having Dad around again. Not exactly the same 'cause he couldn't cook. I think you're a little better at fixing stuff than he was, too. But it felt good when he was there sitting in the chair or talking with Mom in the kitchen. When he died, it felt like there was something missing in the house." She looked Ben in the eye and her sincerity struck him like a sledge. "It doesn't feel like that anymore. Linda's noticed it, too."

Ben was flattered and touched by Lacey's honesty, but in view of the imprecise nature and direction of his relationship with Georgia, it gave him cause for concern. Still, he found himself unable to say anything to dampen her feelings. "I'm glad," he said. "It's been important to me to be part of this family for a little while."

"You said when we had pizza that you didn't want to get married because your work keeps you traveling around a lot."

"Yes."

"I don't think Mom would ever want to leave here."

He had to admire the child's skill at cutting to the heart of the matter. "We're not sure at this point it was meant to be permanent," he said honestly. "But if it is, I'm sure we'll find a way to work that out."

Lacey nodded thoughtfully as she picked at the contents of half of a walnut shell. "I'd hate to go to another school, but a bigger city means more boys!"

GEORGIA PULLED the door closed that led from the service porch into the garage. The garage wasn't heated and she always preached to the girls to keep the precious warmth confined to the house. She flipped the light switch on and started across the garage to where she had stored the boxes from the printer's. But the light didn't go on. Moving blindly toward the boxes, silently cursing the house's old wiring, Georgia wasn't alarmed until she heard the noise.

It was the smallest of sounds—a breath drawn in, a rustle of fabric or a faint disturbance of air—but it raised the gooseflesh on her arms and scalp and made her realize with sudden sharpness how vulnerable she was. She did a slow turn in the complete darkness, trying to home in on the sound before her accelerating heartbeat rendered her unconscious from fright.

"Who's there?" she demanded in a voice that wouldn't have threatened a mouse.

How many times had she watched a heroine on television or in a movie ask that question to a darkened room? How many times had the heroine gotten an answer? Stupid, she told herself. Who would give themselves away like that?

When the deep, low voice spoke from immediately behind her—between her and the door—it came as a horrifying surprise. "Me, Georgia."

Fear enveloped her like an ice-water shower. She opened her mouth to scream and a hand clamped over it, hard and smelling strongly of fish. An arm snaked around her waist and held her fast to a tall, muscular body. The odors of fish, game and unwashed man assailed her nostrils. "You've gone too far this time!" the voice whispered harshly in her ear. "I want to know why you did it."

Her mouth covered, she had no opportunity to reply—not that the person holding her seemed to expect one. "Damned bleeding heart! You aren't happy with saving every Victorian house in Astoria, you accuse *me* of trashing your store and running you down just because I think we could do with a few less."

MacKay! Her gasp of surprise escaped even the hand over her mouth.

"I ought to go up for twenty years," MacKay said, giving her a shake, "for *not* having thought of it! You're coming with me, Georgia, and you know if you make it hard for me, I'll make it hard for you."

Georgia tried desperately to think. With the door closed, Ben would never hear her even if she was able to scream. Her only recourse was to get away from MacKay and trust that, in the dark, her knowledge of the garage would allow her to make it to the house before MacKay could catch her.

As MacKay dragged her toward the large garage door, Georgia opened her mouth wide beneath his hand and bit down with all her might on the fleshy pads at the base of his fingers. His scream mingled with hers as his hand fell away and the door leading from the house flew open.

"Georgia!" Ben shouted, light filtering into the dark garage from the service porch behind him.

"Ben!" Georgia ran for the light, but a big hand caught a fistful of the back of her sweater and yanked her backward.

This time the hand closed around her throat rather than her mouth. MacKay held his other hand up as Ben skidded to a halt several feet from them. "Stop!" MacKay shouted. "Or I'll cheerfully throttle her to death, so help me."

Ben, his heart in his throat, adrenaline rushing through his body, was momentarily distracted by the fact that MacKay didn't appear to have a weapon. And the threat to throttle Georgia sounded more like dire frustration than willingness to murder. He took a second look at the man holding Georgia captive. He was wearing camouflage pants and shirt, high black boots and a cotton boonie hat hung with fishing flies. The pants, shirt and boots could have passed for effective though dramatic wear for clandestine work. But the hat and the fact that the man reeked of fish were contradictory notes. Ben was fairly sure MacKay's intentions were innocent.

"Why don't you let her go and we'll talk about this over a cup of coffee?"

Georgia's eyes widened in stunned surprise, and MacKay looked at him suspiciously.

"You didn't come to hurt her, did you?" Ben asked.

MacKay looked down at Georgia with a disgruntled growl, then shoved her at Ben. "No, I came to take her to the police with me, to make her tell them the truth."

Georgia landed against Ben's chest, then turned in his arms, eyes blazing. "Truth!" she shrieked at MacKay, terror and relief expressing themselves in anger. "Everything pointed to you, but I tried to tell them you didn't do it! Then you come in here and frighten me out of my wits!" She took several steps toward him as her anger grew, but Ben pulled her back.

"I didn't do it!" he bellowed at her. "I went away to spend a couple weeks in the mountains after you ruined a beautiful business deal and came home to find a friend warning me to lie low and telling me there's a warrant out on me for vandalism and two counts of attempted murder!"

For a moment, silence hung heavily in the garage. Then Georgia asked, "Do you own a gun?"

"A handgun and a rifle," he replied. "I've got a 300 Savage in the trunk right now. If *I'd* shot Hansen, he'd be dead. And I'd have more creative ways of getting rid of you than running you down with a mint Camaro. A good Camaro's worth a few thousand bucks."

Georgia ignored his estimate of her value. "You don't own a Harrington & Richards Supporter?"

MacKay raised an eyebrow at her. "You think I shot him with a jock strap?"

"A Harrington & Richards *Defender*," Ben corrected.

MacKay shook his head. "What the hell is that?"

Ben pushed Georgia toward the house and invited MacKay to follow. "A handgun. Come on inside. You look like you could use a drink."

Lacey stood in the garage doorway, pale and holding a ten-inch skillet with both hands. Georgia put an arm around her and led her back to the kitchen. "What's going on?" Lacey asked, eyeing Rob MacKay suspiciously. "Why were you all shouting? Did he try to hurt you?"

"It was kind of a misunderstanding," Georgia said, putting the skillet back on the stove. "Would you go upstairs for a little while so we can talk to Mr. MacKay?"

"Why?" Lacey asked. "What's wrong?"

"Nothing serious. We just need privacy."

Lacey looked at Ben, who was pouring coffee. "Please, Lace," he said.

She blew out a disgruntled breath. "Okay. But somebody'll have to explain to Linda why all the nuts aren't cracked."

Ben put three cups of coffee on the table, then added a shot of brandy to each. Georgia sat quietly while Ben questioned MacKay about where he'd been and what he'd done. His story was simple enough to be completely believable. "I've been on a little lake in the Strawberry Mountains in eastern Oregon for ten days. I'd arranged to meet a friend at Upper Big Creek outside of town here for two days, and he tells me the cops are looking for me. I tried to sneak home the other night and find the police at my place. Then somebody starts shooting! I've been skulking around town ever since waiting for a chance to talk to you without your bodyguard." He slid Ben a wry glance. "Never far away, are you?"

Ben ignored the question. "Any thoughts on who could be doing this? Did you see anybody?"

MacKay expelled a deep breath and shook his head. "No. Far as I know, I'm the only person in Astoria with a commercially progressive thought in his head. Everybody else loves the little house hugger."

"Progress," Georgia said quietly, "does not have to require destruction."

"How many old houses do we need?" MacKay demanded impatiently.

"How many fast-food restaurants do we need?" Georgia countered.

"I know that's an important issue to both of you," Ben interrupted calmly, "but it's not the problem here. If I were you, MacKay, I'd let the police know I was back."

"That's what I intended to do," he said with a glare at Georgia, "as soon as I got Georgia to come to the station with me."

"The statement she gave the police says she doesn't believe you did it," Ben said, pointing significantly to the phone. "Prove it to all of us by calling your attorney, then the police."

When MacKay hung up after making both calls, he downed the rest of his coffee and shook his head balefully. "The police are sending a car for me. Who the hell is going to believe I've spent the last two weeks fishing?"

"Anyone who gets downwind of you," Georgia replied.

MacKay pinned her with a glance, then sighed and

turned to Ben. "When they find the guy who's harassing her, I want to shake his hand."

LINDA CAME HOME more than an hour after the excitement was over. "What were you doing there so late?" Georgia asked. After filling Linda in on what she had missed. Her voice was high and slightly sharp, the imprint of her frightening few minutes in the garage still in evidence.

"Shelly needed some help," Linda said evasively.

"Did you fix the problem?" Ben asked.

Linda, sipping cocoa, nodded grimly. "Yeah."

"I was right, wasn't I?" Lacey pushed the plate of cookies toward her sister. "She only called you because she wanted you to help her make the batter."

"No." Linda selected a butter cookie and studied it, mentally contemplating the calories. Then she bit an edge off aggressively. "She also wanted me to help her write her speech for the service clubs she has to visit."

"And I suppose you did it."

"Of course. I don't want Astoria High to look bad. All she was going to do was talk about where the river starts and how wide it is, the stuff we already know. There's so much interesting stuff in Lewis and Clark's journals, and what happens on the Columbia today is kind of exciting."

"You should have gotten princess," Lacey said with a rare display of loyalty. She loved her sister, Georgia knew, it just seemed against some code for her to allow Linda to see any evidence of it.

Linda shook her head. "She'll do a better job."

"You had to tell her what to say!"

Linda shrugged. "She'll say it better. I should get to

bed.'' She stood and looked curiously around the kitchen. ''Who cleaned up for me?''

''Ben did,'' Lacey replied. ''But we didn't get the nuts done because of all the excitement.''

Linda smiled at him. ''Thank you.'' Then she put her arms around Georgia's neck. ''I'm sorry you had such a fright, Mom. But if Mr. MacKay isn't the one who trashed the store, tried to run you down and shot Mr. Hansen, who did?''

Georgia stood and began to clear away cups. ''I don't know, but whoever it is has been quiet lately. Maybe he's given up and gone away.''

Linda frowned at Ben. ''Do you think so?''

''It's possible.'' He tried to sound convincing, but he could see as she leaned down to hug him good-night that she didn't believe it, either. He caught her hand and held her back a moment. ''I'll take good care of your mom. I promise.''

She nodded, her eyes still troubled. ''I know that. But now I'm worried about who's going to take care of *you*. 'Night, Ben. Good night, Mom.''

His elbow resting on the back of his chair, Ben watched moodily as the girls disappeared. ''It's a heavy responsibility,'' he said, ''knowing a child is worried about you.''

''Love is filled with heavy responsibilities,'' she replied, putting the cups in the dishwasher. ''You now have three women concerned about your safety. If you're going to run, you'd better do it now.''

He couldn't deny to himself that running had occurred to him, but he felt safe enough in denying it to her because he knew he wouldn't do it. And it was more than Georgia's safety that kept him here. He went to the counter, caught her chin between his thumb and forefinger and lifted it until he could look down into her eyes. "Storybook heroes never run," he said, leaning down to seal the promise with a kiss.

Georgia watched him walk out to the workshop, thinking that her dependence on him in big and little ways, her own personal need for him, were growing stronger every day. She knew she'd gone beyond the point where she could watch him walk out of her life with any philosophical acceptance. It would hurt. She closed her eyes for a moment and longed for the dull but relatively uncomplicated life she'd led before he came to Astoria. She'd still had her concern about Gary's death, but finding an answer hadn't been so important then. Now, a solution was critical if she was ever to let herself love Ben completely—and she had no idea how she would find one.

SOMEHOW, DESPITE the undercurrent of danger and the pressures of preparation for Columbia River Days, life went on at a quieter pitch.

The police questioned MacKay and released him. The bullet taken from Phil matched nothing MacKay owned. The man from whom he'd rented a boat in the Strawberry Mountains verified that he'd been in the area, though he hadn't seen him on either of the days in question. It wasn't inconceivable that MacKay had driven back to Astoria, but it wasn't likely. The police concluded that there wasn't sufficient evidence to hold him.

The face-lift on the Roberts Building moved forward at a heartening rate as warm, sunny days began to outnumber rainy ones.

"Culture is important in your lives." Bea, corseted, bejeweled and elegantly dressed in lavender lace,

shooed Linda and Lacey toward the front door and the
car where Ragnar waited. "You should be made aware
that there is music that is actually pleasant on your ears,
music with lyrics that invite you to be happy and to
love someone rather than encourage you to violence.
You're going to love the concert."

Georgia followed her mother-in-law and her girls out
into the hot, sunny May afternoon. It was unseasonably
warm for Astoria, and Lacey pleaded in a whisper,
"Please, Mom! We could be going to the *beach*!"

"Stop it," she whispered back firmly. "Grandma
wants to share something she loves with you. That's
important."

Linda and Lacey, looking as though they were being
taken to Siberia, carried overnight bags and schoolbooks. "We won't be back at my place until after midnight." Bea bustled the girls into the car and turned to
hug Georgia. "Don't worry about a thing."

"But are you sure you want to keep them overnight?" Georgia asked. "Monday mornings are pretty
ugly."

"We'll be fine. You just relax and enjoy your Sunday."

CHAPTER ELEVEN

GEORGIA TURNED BACK to the house, the beautiful weather already beginning to chase away the concerns that so filled her mind lately. Ben stood in the doorway, waiting for her, a hand across the portal. He didn't lower it when she approached. She looked at him questioningly and he grinned. "This is now the location of a very covert operation. What's the code word?"

"Vasectomy," she said.

He blinked.

"You said a covert opera—"

Ben but a hand over her mouth and closed his eyes, obviously summoning patience. "Not that kind of an operation." When he opened his eyes they were filled with lazy laughter. "I'll give you one more chance."

"Okay." Infected with the playful mood of his game, she asked, "Can I ask for clues?"

"Only two."

"How many syllables?"

"One."

"One." She frowned thoughtfully. "How many letters?"

He grinned expectantly. "None."

That confused her for only a moment. Then she read the message in his eyes, green this morning as they reflected the color all around them, and put it together with the bizarre clues. She had her answer. Rising on tiptoe, she looped her arms around his neck and pulled his head down. "The code word is..." She kissed him, the freedom of this beautiful afternoon divesting her of all the inhibitions that usually confined her. Bea had the girls today, and the store was closed. She wasn't mother or shopkeeper, but simply woman. That was a part of her person she couldn't indulge very often, and she accepted the opportunity with an enthusiasm that left Ben surprised and shaken.

His hand wound in her hair, he pulled her head back and looked into her bright eyes, his own darkening dangerously. "I...didn't hear you," he said.

Georgia rose again to meet his lips, parting her own as his tongue teased them. Hers parried then began to explore. She forgot that they stood on the doorstep until he lifted her bodily, their mouths still connected, and pulled her inside. His leg shifted and the door slammed closed. The quiet shadows of the house enveloped them, and Georgia drank from Ben's mouth, seeking to slake a thirst so desperate she felt as though she might die if he pulled away. His hand went under the back of her sweatshirt, fingers spread and mobile as they worked their way up. It occurred to Georgia that her back hadn't been touched in two years. She'd never thought of it as an erogenous zone, yet the touch of his warm hand between her shoulder blades made every nerve ending in her body come alive. Her breath caught, and she was sure she could feel the thick, languid movement of her blood.

Ben had never felt like this. He'd known passion, but he'd never felt this blazing awareness in every particle of his being. He'd made love to women with enthusiasm and satisfaction, but pleasure had never roared over him during a simple kiss. Kisses were meant to presage pleasure, to simply heighten anticipation. Yet, here he stood, his skin flushed, his heart pounding, his spine feeling as though whatever kept it aligned and connected had been removed. He didn't want to consider what was happening elsewhere.

He held Georgia away from him and took a breath. "Get changed," he said.

She tried to emerge from the intoxicating effects of his kiss. "Where are we going?"

He took a step back and opened the door again. "I don't know."

"Maybe we'd better decide so I'll know what to wear."

That made sense. He was glad something did. "Right. Why don't we spend the afternoon at the beach, then I'll take you to dinner?"

Georgia hadn't lain on the beach in years. She smiled, delighted with the idea. "Really? Shall I pack a lunch?"

"Just bring a couple of cans of something cold. Save your appetite for tonight." He looked down into her happy grin and felt his heart turn over. "Meet you at the truck in fifteen minutes."

"THE CLOUD COVER is tricky. It looks and feels as though you're not getting any sun, then you come home looking like red patent leather." Georgia slathered suntan lotion on Ben's back as he lay on an old plaid blanket she'd brought.

Ben tried desperately to concentrate on what she was saying rather than what she was doing. "That wouldn't go with my stiff collar, my white suit and my hair parted down the middle."

She turned to sit beside him and spread the lotion

on her legs. He didn't watch. "I told you you could part it on the side. I'm a little disappointed that you didn't bring your red-and-green striped knee-length swimsuit." She glanced at the brief black trunks covering his neat, tight bottom, then turned back to her suntan lotion. "'Course, there are no cabanas here to really set the mood."

"And you'd have to wear bloomers and a scarf over your head." Ben glanced at her nearly bare back and the high-cut sides of her suit, then put his head back on his arms. "The Victorians knew how to dress ladies for the garden, but their idea of beachwear could have killed the reproductive drive altogether."

"But it didn't." She dropped the tube in her large tote and settled down beside him on her back, wriggling her shoulders to get comfortable. "It just proves what I'm always telling the girls. Love doesn't notice what you're wearing. It counts on what's inside a person."

There was a moment's silence. A warm wind blew. Ben felt sand drift across his back and a strand of Georgia's hair tickle his elbow. "So, how did such a nice guy, inside and out—" Georgia shielded her eyes from the sun and turned to grin at him "—escape a nice woman? Or even a bad one?"

"Have I escaped?"

She glared at him, and he raised his head to meet her eyes. "That isn't clear yet," she said scoldingly. "I meant before you came to Astoria."

He laid his head down again. "I just never made myself available."

Eyes closed, Georgia smiled at the sun. "According to Linda, this is the nineties. Women go after what they want. Certainly some woman must have tried to force your attention?''

''No,'' he said simply.

There was another brief silence, then Georgia turned to lie on her side, bracing her head on her hand. Her hair was tied back from her face with a white bandeau, and he thought how charming she looked, even as he knew she was about to ask him questions he didn't want to answer. ''What happened to your parents, Ben? Can you tell me about it?''

''I guess,'' he said reluctantly. ''It's nothing very dramatic. I'm sure the same thing has happened to more kids than you care to think about.'' He braced himself on both elbows, dusting sand from his shoulders, trying, Georgia suspected, to appear unaffected by what he was about to say.

''Tell me,'' she insisted gently.

He gathered a handful of sand and let it sift through his fingers, catching it with his other hand and sifting it again. ''My parents died when I was six. I think I was happy until then—I'm not really sure. I just have this vague memory of warmth and comfort. My mind keeps trying to reach back for it, but I can't quite catch it. I don't know if it was really there or if I just want it to be there.''

Georgia waited while he dusted his hands off and focused on the grassy bank that separated them from the parking lot. ''I lived with my maternal grandmother for a year. She was kind but crotchety.'' He smiled, staring ahead. ''I remember being hugged and held. Then she died suddenly and I spent the next few years going from relative to relative, fitting nowhere, unwanted. In their defense I have to say that I didn't make much of an effort. I'd become proud. I certainly had no reason to be, but every time I moved in with another family, I could read the reluctance under their superficial welcome. I decided if they didn't want me, I wasn't going to stay." He turned to give Georgia a self-deprecating shake of his head. "I had no idea I was asking the impossible. By then I was an eleven-year-old boy with a chip on his shoulder, a bad mouth and a list of demands God Himself probably couldn't have met. At twelve I stole a car to go to Arizona."

Georgia laughed at his audacity. "Did you make it?"

He, too, laughed. "Of course not."

"You wrecked the car?"

He looked offended by the suggestion. "No, I had no money for gas. I made it as far as Salem. I sputtered to a stop on the freeway and was pushed to the side by a very helpful state policeman who took me to Children's Services. Obviously the uncle I'd been staying with didn't want me back. I'd worked my way through all the relatives on both sides of my family, so I went into foster care. My teen years were interminable and fairly ugly."

Georgia shifted closer and linked an arm through his. "But what about your Uncle David?"

"We're not related by blood. He was my last foster parent. I was fifteen then. He was hard as nails, never gave me an inch and made me more miserable then I'd been in all the years before." He shook his head and expelled a breath. "He made me study, he made me take and keep a part-time job, he made me do chores around the house, and once, when I called him something foul, he slammed me up against the wall and told me if that word ever came out of my mouth again I'd need false teeth. I believed him. I couldn't wait to move out of his house. When I was sixteen, he helped me declare myself an emancipated minor. It wasn't until I was alone in my own apartment that I realized how much I missed him.''

"What did you do about school?''

"I finished in the army. I looked David up when I came out. He gave me a loan to go to college, I graduated, paid him back, and we've been partners ever since.''

Georgia kissed his shoulder. "It's a sad story, Ben, but it came out well, considering.''

He nodded agreement. "I've learned to deal with people. I know that being honest and hardworking makes you friends in business and outside of it.'' He turned to her, his hazel eyes iridescent in the bright sun. "But I've never lived anywhere or with anyone longer than two years. I don't know that I have what it takes to establish a family and sustain it for a lifetime.'' He brought her hand to his lips and kissed her knuckles. "To keep a woman happy until she's old.''

"Nobody reaches maturity knowing how to do that, Ben.'' Georgia leaned her head against his shoulder and kissed it again. "It's something you learn to do, day by day. When you start loving someone, the part of you that gives becomes more noble and good than anything you ever thought you had in you. It can put up with more and offer more without wanting anything back but that same kindness in return. It's more instinctive than you think it is, Ben. You're probably filled with those qualities—you've just never used them.''

He looked at her doubtfully. "It just always seemed safer not to take the chance. I don't want to mess myself up again, but more than that, I don't want to ruin somebody else's life.''

"I can understand that, I guess." Georgia sighed, rubbing her cheek against his shoulder. "I think I could be a good wife again, but not until I know what Gary was doing the day he died. That would always be in the way. And a man and a woman have to be able to be as close as the pages in a book to make it." She sighed and fell onto her back beside him, smiling into his eyes. "I wonder if we'd met at the turn of the century without all the stuff we're carrying around inside us, if I'd be the lady you'd be looking for in the garden."

He leaned over her, his head blotting out the sun. His eyes were dark green and grave. "Without a doubt. But would you hide from me or come running to me?"

A slow smile formed on her lips as she reached up to encircle his neck. "I'd probably shout 'Yoo-hoo!' in a very undignified fashion and wave my hat until I caught your attention."

He didn't smile as she expected, but continued to look into her eyes. "I love you, Georgia," he said, a quiet element of wonder in his voice. "God, I *love* you."

She knew that shouldn't fill her with joy and warm satisfaction, but it did. It would eventually be trouble— a lot of trouble. But right now being loved by Ben was a miracle, a blessing, a delicious and unexpected gift.

"I love you, too, Ben." She pulled him down to her, holding him fast against her, forgetting the potential danger and considering only how wonderful the knowledge was—for now. "I love you, too."

He could die of this, Ben thought, feeling a burst of joy deep inside so exquisite he could hardly believe it was happening to him. He didn't feel things with intensity. He was mellow, calm, steady. He got angry but never lost his head. When he was happy, he was never deliriously so. But at this moment he was all feeling, all warmth, all glow. Georgia had done a number on his psyche.

"We're going swimming," he said suddenly, springing to his feet and pulling her with him.

She tugged at the back of her suit as he towed her toward the water. "You certainly pick your moments," she complained, her expression amused and perplexed.

He stopped her at the water's edge and pulled her into the cold shallows, his eyes just beginning to catch the laughter in hers. "Without my immediate immersion in cold water," he said significantly, "you'd find yourself in an embarrassing position."

She giggled wickedly. "Really."

"And since you're the cause of my discomfort—" he swept her up into his arms and strode into the water over her protesting squeals "—you get dunked first."

They played in the water for more than an hour, splashing, laughing, dunking, kissing. Each was aware of a dangerous energy, of a force closing in over which there was no control. Ben was leery because he'd never experienced it before. Georgia held back because she knew its power.

"Where are you taking me for dinner?" Georgia asked as they started to fold the plaid blanket. The sparkling path of the sun on the water grew wide as the afternoon waned.

"The way I've been treated this afternoon, you deserve a sardine sandwich." Ben folded together the two ends he held and waited for Georgia to fold her half.

Instead, she frowned at him. "Who dunked who first?" She shook sand off the blanket, causing Ben to lose the end he held.

He bent forward to retrieve it, giving her a dangerous glance as he picked it up. "Which time? I'm sure you got me four to one."

She looked at her nails as he stepped away to tauten the blanket and join the ends once more. "You're supposed to be alert," she reminded. "You're a bodyguard, remember? Do you think we could get this blanket folded sometime this afternoon? I'd like to be home by morning."

"If you'd quit snapping it..." he said, starting to come toward her to make the second fold.

But she shook it again, snapping it out of his hands. "Like that, you mean?" she asked, her expression all sweetness and exaggerated innocence.

Ben considered her for one long, deliberate moment. She'd pulled white shorts and a yellow T-shirt on over her bathing suit. Her hair was sandy and tousled despite the bandeau, her cheeks and limbs pink from the afternoon in the sun. He felt weak with tenderness.

Georgia watched Ben take several slow steps toward her and backed away giggling, still holding the blanket. "What are you doing?" she demanded. Shirtless, his jeans snug over his wet trunks, he advanced. He looked wonderful, she thought absently, ensnared by the dangerous teasing in his eyes. The strength and the humor that always worked in concert in him were a provocative combination at that moment.

"I'm going to teach you," he threatened quietly, "what happens to a woman who lures a man with Victorian charm and sweetness, then turns on him with the ruthlessness of a nineties woman."

He had picked up the other end of the blanket and gathered the slack in his hands as he spoke, still advancing.

She continued to back away. "It's not ruthlessness," she said quickly as he closed the distance between them. "It's determination and a...a...forcefulness equal to any man's!"

The last was spoken on a shriek as she stepped into a hole and fell backward. Ben pounced, throwing the blanket over her, rolling her until she was completely covered, then lifting her and tossing her over his shoulder.

"Ben!" she screamed, laughing. Confined by the blanket, she couldn't pummel him, but she could kick. He was striding purposefully and she bounced along, demanding to be let go. "My bag!" she cried.

"Pipe down, I have it," he assured her.

"The towels!"

"You already put them in the bag."

She subsided. "Well, at least I know we have the blanket. As I recall, Cleopatra traveled this way."

"That was a carpet."

"You must look cute carrying my tote bag. Did you notice that it has a teddy bear on it?"

"It's attracting no less attention than you are. Did you realize that the soles of your feet are sunburned?"

"Wait'll I get you home, Stratton," she threatened. "I'm going to knot *your* feet together! Ben, it's getting hot in here."

"Be still," he said, "I'm trying to unlock the trunk."

"Do I ride in the front as a passenger or in the back as freight?"

"Depends on your attitude when I set you free."

Georgia heard the sound of the truck door opening, then felt her feet connect with the parking lot pavement. Suddenly the blanket was whipped off her and tossed into the bed of the truck. She squinted up into Ben's laughing eyes.

"So who do I take home?" he asked, hands loosely on his hips. "The sweet Victorian miss or the nineties termagant?"

She spread her arms gracefully. "I'm afraid we are one and the same. Which one of us you draw out," she said, "is up to you. I can be a sweet Victorian, but then she'd never take the initiative and kiss you the way you're longing to be kissed at this moment. The termagant would do it—" she gave him a seductive arch of her brow "—but then she'd want to drive home."

He put a hand over his eyes, wondering if he was winning this encounter or losing it. "You mean that to get the kiss I have to let you behind the wheel of my precious truck?"

"You're very astute, Stratton."

He appeared to consider. "I paid a lot for that truck. It's like my child."

Georgia rolled her eyes. "I promise not to kill it."

He sighed. "All right. But it better be some kiss." He reached for her, but she pulled away.

"It will be," she promised over her shoulder as she walked around the truck. "So I can't do it here." She pulled the driver's door open. Under normal circumstances the height of the truck made it difficult for her to climb up to the seat. Without her shoes, she found it impossible. She smiled winningly at Ben across the front seat. "Could you help me in?"

With exaggerated exasperation, he complied, then started in alarm when he rounded the truck to the passenger side as she turned on the ignition and revved the powerful engine. "Hurry up!" Georgia called. "She's raring to go!"

"This is going to feel a little different than your station wagon...." Ben cautioned, just having time to close his door before she pulled out of the parking space. He had a close encounter with the dashboard before he could get the ends of his seat belt connected. "Ever drive a stick before?" he asked, a slight edge of sarcasm to his voice.

She didn't notice. "In high school. Hold on, this might be a little bumpy."

An eternity later, Georgia pulled into her driveway. "There," she said with satisfaction. "That wasn't so bad, was it?"

His eyes covered with one hand, Ben shook his head. "I don't know. After you ran the red light in Warrenton and passed the bus on the Young's Bay Bridge, I stopped looking."

"When you have to shift and work the clutch," Georgia said airily, "there's so much to think about. I sort of didn't notice the light. You coming, or are you going to dinner like that?"

She was out of the truck, her tote bag slung over her shoulder as she headed for the house.

"Just a minute," he called, closing the garden gate behind him as she stopped inquiringly in the middle of the patio. "You seem to have forgotten something."

Georgia shook her head at him. "Don't tell me you rub the truck down after a hard ride...."

He stopped inches from her and folded his arms. "I refer to the deal we made so that you could drive my truck—if that is indeed what you call what you did."

"Ah, yes." She looped her arm in his and drew him to the back door, then stopped to delve for her keys.

He could have had his out in an instant, but instead he leaned against the door frame and watched her rout through the tote. He wanted her with a desire so strong it was almost painful.

"You probably lost my key in the sand when you were doing your Neanderthal routine," she babbled, a subtle change had taken place in her behavior. Something had driven her most of the afternoon, but Ben hadn't questioned it because something he didn't want to analyze too closely was growing at the heart of him, too. She was nervous. He could see it in the way she kept her eyes averted, the way she kept grumbling. She knew what was happening, he thought, and she was afraid.

"Neanderthals didn't have blankets," he said.

Producing the key, she gave him what was supposed to be a dry look, but he could see the hectic light in her eyes. "Well, they probably wrapped their women in banana leaves and carried them off the same way."

"I'll bet they didn't let them drive the mastodon home."

Georgia laughed, pushing her way into the cool and shadowy service porch. "I suppose not. That was generous of you." She dropped her tote bag into a corner and went into the kitchen. She turned in the middle of the room, arms extended in an attitude of surrender. "Take your kiss. You have it coming."

He approached her shaking his head. "The agreement was not that I would take it but that you would give it."

"You're such a stickler." She brought her arms together and took a step closer to him so she could put them around his neck, but he made no move to touch her, sensing the hesitation in her, thinking he understood her shift in mood.

He felt her fingers caress the hair at the back of his neck, trying to elicit a response from him so that he would initiate the kiss or at least provoke her into finally offering it. But he remained still. "You can't do it, can you?" he asked finally.

"What?" she asked innocently.

"Give me another play kiss," he replied quietly.

She dropped her arms and shook her head, not entirely surprised that he'd read her mind so closely. "No, I can't."

He put his hands on her arms then, stroking gently with his thumbs. "That isn't bad, Georgia. It just means our love is growing and that the bond between us is strengthening."

She looked up at him, her eyes dark and bright, filled with love and some concern he couldn't quite identify. He put a hand to the side of her face. "You're thinking about Gary."

Her eyes reflected surprise and genuine denial. "No. But he was the only lover I've had, Ben. I went to him as a bride, committed to our love and our future." She turned her hands to touch his arms. "That's the only way I know how to do this. You'd probably like a no-strings, no-promises affair so you don't feel obligated to anything. That's fine. I'm not asking anything of you. I just want you to understand why I'm doing it. Because I love you, because I need you in my life. If I could find a way to start all over again, it would be with you. That's what you're getting into, Ben. If you're having second thoughts, this is the place to stop."

Ben enfolded her in his arms, closing his eyes and

letting himself feel the magic of what he held. All the love he'd never had in his life, all the love he'd been so sure could never be his, had just been handed him with humbling honesty. "If I had any second thoughts," he said softly, "they would be that you should wait for someone better than I. But I don't know if I can be that generous. I love you, too, Georgia, and I love your girls, and if I were sure I could be the perfect husband and father, I'd give you that promise in a minute. I just don't want to do it and then fail you. But now and for as long as I can be what you need, I love you."

Her arms around him, she leaned back to look into his eyes. "I guess that's a lot for two haunted people to find. Come upstairs."

Her bedroom door was open, the jeans and sweat-shirt she'd changed out of to go to the beach lying across the arm of the small upholstered chair near the window. For a moment, she wished desperately that there was someplace else to do this. She had that feeling of being a stranger again, even now, when she was bringing a man into this room to make love with him.

While she hesitated on the threshold, Ben took several steps into the room, then stood at the foot of the bed to look around. "This is so much like you," he said, smiling as he touched the quilt folded on the bed. "Sweetness, cheer, lace in one corner and—" he pointed to the far corner of the room where her small desk stood, piled with paperwork from the store and all the little details of Columbia River Days "—the no-nonsense of business in the other." He reached a hand out to her as though he were the host and she the guest.

She took it and let him draw her to the foot of the

bed. She began to smile, touched by his unhurried tenderness.

"I suppose for true romance," she said, settling her head against his shoulder, "this room should have a fire, a fur throw and maybe a canopy."

He kissed her temple. "No. All we need for true romance is us."

Wrapped in his arms, Georgia felt restraint fall away.

The setting sun filled the room with long shadows. A light breeze stirred the lace curtains and wafted around them with the fragrance of roses and honeysuckle. Ben's hand moving beneath Georgia's shirt had the same effect on her it had earlier. Sensation bumped the flesh on her arms and along her scalp so that she felt like something struck by lightning, ionized. He gathered the shirt up, and she raised her arms to allow its removal. He leaned down to kiss her lips lightly, then trace a path along her neck to her shoulder. A taunting heat rose in the wake of his lips, sending sensation to her fingertips and the tips of her toes.

His hand went to the back of her suit. "No zipper?" he asked.

She laughed softly, the sound a little tremulous. "No. I slither into it and peel it off."

He waggled an eyebrow wickedly. "'Slither.' 'Peel.' Provocative talk, lady." He lowered one strap, then the other, then with a sudden gravity that stopped her breath, he peeled the suit down to her waist. Her small breasts, porcelain white and sprinkled with sand, seemed to swell under his eyes, aching with the need to be touched. His hands closed over them and Georgia closed her eyes, wondering if he was trembling or if she was. Had anything ever felt so perfect? she wondered. Sensation concentrated there, right over her heart, building with the movement of his thumbs across her nipples. She drew in a breath and wrapped her arms around his waist. He enfolded her against him, bare, beaded breasts against his naked chest, and she knew suddenly this was going to be more than she'd suspected, more than she'd known before. She kissed his collarbone and whispered, "Oh, Ben."

Ben heard the surrender in the sound. He struggled against racing desire with gentle, careful movements. Lifting her in his arms, he laid her on the middle of the bedspread, pulled off the white shorts and tossed them aside. The suit clung to her like snakeskin and he peeled it down slowly, afraid the sand that clung to her would rasp her skin. The small waist, flat stomach and jutting hipbones that were slowly revealed humbled him with their beauty and scrambled the sense of reality he clung to with desperation.

He tossed the damp, sandy suit aside and grinned at her. "I'll get a towel. You look a little like a sand dab."

She pointed to a door behind him, amazed she could think with sufficient coherence to form a word. "Bathroom."

He was back in an instant, a thick, light blue hand towel balled in his fingers. Kneeling on one knee on the bed, he brushed gently at the sand on her breasts, then where it was trapped beneath them. He brushed at the hollow of her waist, across her stomach and where it adhered to the juncture of her thigh. He leaned over her to plant a kiss between her breasts. "There. More comfortable?"

She caught his shoulders and pulled until he fell down beside her, laughing. "God, don't tell me the termagant is back?"

She knelt over him, unbuttoning and unzipping his jeans. "No," she said, leaning down to kiss the hollow under his ribs. "It's just me. Loving you."

He reached out to cup her face in one hand, running a thumb lightly over her bottom lip. "Do you have any idea," he asked seriously, "how happy that makes me?"

She turned her face to kiss his palm. "Yes, I think so. I see what I feel reflected in your eyes." As she peeled the snug jeans off, his damp trunks came with them. She dropped them on the floor and picked up the towel. She worked up from his knees but didn't get far at all before he sat up to take hold of her arms and pull her down beside him. He took her lips in a kiss that drew every emotion to the surface, making her want to laugh and cry, leaving her longing for him with a power that was frightening.

Ben wondered if a man could die of going slowly. He felt like lit dynamite in a can of gasoline, as though he would fly apart at any moment, completely destroyed. Georgia lay easily in his arms, unafraid, even eager. He wanted to touch her gently, but every time she responded, he came close to losing his mind. He'd never known this complete loss of control, this tyranny of emotion.

When her small hands began to move on him, he took it as an indication that she was as ready as he was. She raised her head from his shoulder and looked into his eyes, confirming it. *Think,* he cautioned himself. *Take time to think of her.* He swept a hand down the silky skin of her breasts and stomach, then lifted her thigh and stroked it, feeling the muscles tremble in response. A sigh caught in her throat, and she turned her face into his shoulder again, her body, her entire being poised for him.

His touch was exquisite. Georgia could think of no other way to describe it—and she tried to do that only as a way of maintaining sanity. Feeling roared through her body, sharpening her senses, flaying every nerve ending. Ben's hand moved and she felt herself rise against it, wanting, waiting. He stroked and teased until she was mindless with need, uttering small cries of delicious distress. The pleasure broke over her and she lay still to absorb it, marveling at its newness, sure this was something she'd never experienced before.

The miracle of it awakened her to the man who had created it, and she looked up at him with new insight, new understanding. Pushing gently against him, she rolled him onto his back and knelt astride him, nibbling, stroking, kissing her way through the wiry hair across his pectorals, over the sharp angles of his ribs, into the hollow at his waist and downward. She had wanted to linger over him, to give him the same slow, delightful torture to which he'd subjected her, but he couldn't allow her the time. He pulled her back to the pillow, rose over her and filled her. For a moment the utter rightness of their two bodies joined surmounted even the pleasure. It was so perfect Georgia knew that when they drew apart again she would be different than she'd been before, and she would never feel complete again without him.

Then Ben dropped his head to her shoulder, pleasure overrode them, and they went together beyond thought or reason.

They lay in the darkened room, arms and legs entangled. Ben buried his lips in Georgia's hair and frowned. His body was still trembling. Hell, his mind was trembling. He was in love, no doubt about it. And he was *loved*, which might even be worse. Avoiding it for most of his life had been painful and left holes where his memories should be, but it had been safer than trying it and discovering that the people who'd rejected him all his life had been right—that there'd been nothing in Bennett Stratton to love. What did he do now? he wondered. Try to accept love and give it back and pray that he could do it? Or walk away before irreparable damage was done to both of them?

Half-asleep, Georgia stirred in his arms, hers firmly wrapped around his neck. She kissed the lobe of his ear and snuggled against him, content. He accepted without reservation that walking away was simply not an option.

"DEFINITELY ONE of my better ideas," Ben said into Georgia's ear.

She leaned back against him, nibbling on a sour cream and onion potato chip. "Mmm," she agreed dryly. "Explain to me again how the promise of dinner and dancing turned into sitting on the hood of your truck and eating hero sandwiches from a minimart. Chip?" She offered the bag. He reached into it.

"I forget sometimes that I'm not in Portland, where you can get dinner any hour of the night. Anyway, you're the one responsible for keeping me distracted all evening until it was too late to find a restaurant that was open. 'Course, who'd want to be inside when you could be watching that?" When they had realized the restaurant Ben had chosen had stopped serving dinner, they'd picked up sandwiches and driven to the pier, where the lightship *Columbia* and the Coast Guard cutter *Resolute* were moored. Climbing onto the hood of the truck, they'd picnicked and watched the lights of the fishing boats waltz past. Now a freighter went by, lit up and every bit as inviting as if they were on a dinner cruise on the Seine.

Ben leaned back against the windshield, bringing Georgia with him. They were wrapped in the sandy blanket they'd taken to the beach. He closed the wings of it around her against the midnight wind. "I know what you're thinking," he said.

She rested her head on his shoulder. "What?"

"That we're a couple of Victorian kids who've just graduated with honors, and we're about to take our 'grand tour.' That ship's going to take us to Tangier."

She smiled into the darkness, enjoying the fantasy. "Do you have the Dramamine?"

"Has it been invented yet?"

"Hmm. We'll probably have to rely on chamomile tea."

"Do you have your bloomers?"

Georgia turned her head, trying to focus on him in the darkness. "A lady doesn't travel without them, but that's a personal question, sir."

"I meant," he explained patiently, "your swimming bloomers."

"No." She settled back against him. "I've decided to embark on a life of debauchery. Now that I have my doctor's degree, an impressive list of acting credentials and am dancing *en pointe*, I feel a need to be free of the strictures of society. I intend to skinny-dip."

"You'll have to wait till we get to the Riviera. I think in Tangier you even have to cover your face."

Georgia bit down noisily on a chip. "Well, that's it, then. You'll just have to speak to the captain and change our destination to the Riviera. You do have influence, don't you?''

''Indeed. I come from a long line of soldiers and barristers. You're lucky to have landed me—I'm quite a catch.'' Ben sighed moodily. ''It's almost one-thirty. I should take you home.''

She snuggled closer. ''Not yet,'' she wheedled.

In their sandy cocoon they sipped wine and watched the lights of the ship diminish until they were pinpricks in the night, then finally disappeared. Georgia waited one more moment as a feeling of melancholy threatened her happiness. She was acting like a child, she thought, loath to let go of a beautiful day. Tomorrow was Monday and everything would be back to normal. She would go to the store, the girls would come home, and the woman who'd been so indulged today would have to slip into the background again and settle for life's smaller satisfactions.

Ben rubbed a hand gently down her arm, planting a kiss at her ear. There was a proprietary quality to his touch now, a look in his eye, a note in his voice that spoke of the intimacy they'd shared. She smiled to herself. Perhaps things wouldn't be *quite* the same.

CHAPTER TWELVE

GEORGIA DIDN'T KNOW what had awakened her. Startled without knowing why, she tried to sit up, to clear the sleep from her mind and bring the darkness into focus. But there were warm, strong arms around her, and her attempt to move was futile. Ben. She forgot her alarm and reveled in contentment and security.

But Ben's hand closed over her mouth, and she became aware of the tension in the arms that held her. The smallest of sounds came from downstairs. He put his lips to her ear and said quietly, "Stay here."

She tried to stop him as he moved quietly out of bed, fear for him bursting on her, full-blown. He pushed her back against the pillow, repeating in a whisper in her ear, the words separated for emphasis, "Stay...here."

Ben crept noiselessly into the hall, listening. He heard only the faint rustling of something indistinguishable, then a very distinct click. Not the loud cocking mechanism of a gun or the subtle flip of a switch—something else. Moving stealthily along the wall, he stopped at the top of the stairs. A sudden rush of sound came from somewhere beyond the kitchen, followed by an ominous crackling. The instant Ben heard the sound of hurried footsteps, he launched himself down the stairs. A shadowy figure raced through the open back door and Ben ran in pursuit, straining his eyes to see in the darkness, straining his memory to remember the lay of Georgia's patio. Near the gate, he collided with a clay strawberry pot he remembered was filled with herbs. He cursed, lost stride, then caught himself, but the pause was enough to give his prey time to disappear into another backyard or around the corner.

Ben turned to hobble back to the house, when Georgia, armed with a broom, collided with him. "Who was it?" she demanded. "Did you see him?" She held the broom, handle forward, as though it were a rifle.

"What were you going to do with that?" he asked, turning her back toward the house. "Fill him full of twigshot? I thought I told you to stay upstairs?"

"I thought you might need me," she said seriously.

He put an arm around her shoulders and hugged her to him. "I thought your weapon was a squeegee." At the doorway he stopped suddenly, his nostrils filling with the acrid smell of smoke. Suddenly he remembered the whoosh of sound and the crackling noise he'd heard before the intruder ran away.

"Fire!" Georgia cried.

Ben ran as far as the living room doorway, flipping lights on as he went. A fire already blazed three or four feet high in the middle of the living room carpet. He pushed Georgia toward the service porch. "Get the beach blanket!" he ordered.

Ben shoved an overstuffed chair threatened by the fire into the farthest corner of the room, then walked around to pull a coffee table out of reach of the greedy flames. He took the blanket from Georgia and threw it over the fire, jumping on it before he remembered he was barefoot. He leaped off of it again as Georgia began to pound on the blanket with the handle of the broom. The flames were smothered quickly, and smoke rose, thick and murky, from the now black and holey blanket. Ben took the broom from Georgia and pushed the blanket aside, getting down on his haunches to see what had been used for fuel. He pinned a corner of thick yellow paper with the end of the broom handle and pulled it out.

"The Columbia River Days posters," Georgia said, kneeling down beside the paper. She shook her head at the stack that was now a pile of ashes with bright yellow corners. "All of them."

BALANCED ON CRUTCHES, Phil Hansen looked down at the pile of ashes in the middle of Georgia's living room carpet and shook his head. "You don't need a bodyguard, kiddo, you need your own personal police force."

Several officers were milling around, one poking through the ashes with a stick, another talking on the telephone to the station. Georgia had pulled on a robe and pushed her tousled hair back. "Ben almost caught him but was felled by my strawberry pot. What are you doing here, anyway? I thought you wouldn't be back on duty for another week."

"Heard it on the scanner. Thought I'd better check on you."

Georgia drew him toward the kitchen, where a hastily made pot of coffee gurgled that it was ready. She filled two mugs and offered him one, then realized he had no free hand with which to take it. She placed both mugs on the table and held his crutches while he fell into a chair. "So what time did this all start?" Phil asked.

While Georgia repeated the story she'd already told the police on duty, Ben came into the kitchen from the service porch, where the doorknob was being dusted and taped for fingerprints. He poured himself a cup of coffee and joined them at the table. Phil turned to him.

"Could you make out anything about him? Tall, short, fat, limping?"

"Not very tall, and slender," Ben replied. "No fingerprints on the doorknob and no forced entry, either. No open or broken windows."

Phil frowned at Georgia. "You leave the door unlocked?"

"Of course not," she denied, then tried to think back. It had been very late, and Ben had been kissing her when they walked in the door. Her mind had been on other things. "At least I don't think I did."

Ben shook his head. "You didn't. I checked before we went to bed."

It was such a simple statement, Georgia thought, sipping at her coffee. It could easily have meant before they went to bed separately. But it didn't, and Phil was good at what he did because he didn't miss anything. He gave Ben a level look that Ben returned. Then he nodded. "So how'd he get in?"

Ben leaned back in his chair. "My guess would be a key."

"What?" Georgia demanded. "That's crazy."

Phil shook his head. "No, it's not. I was coming to that conclusion myself. This is someone who knows you well, Georgia. And he's pretty desperate to make his point if he'd come into your home—particularly with Ben here. Everybody knows he's living in the workshop. I hate to think of what could have happened if Ben hadn't been in the house with you."

Georgia put a hand to her forehead. "I can't believe

someone in Astoria actually wants to kill me. For what?''

Ben reached out to rub the back of her neck.

"I don't know that killing you is what he had in mind,'' Phil said. "It's almost as though he didn't really want to hurt you—just let you know he could get to you if he wanted to. But with fire, you never know what could happen. Particularly in an old place like this. It's somebody who's upset about the old houses on Duane, but I sincerely don't believe it's MacKay. So who else could it be? Was anyone else planning anything for that spot?''

Georgia shook her head. "Not that I know of.''

"What do you know about Bishop?'' Ben asked Phil.

"Wally doesn't have anything to do with this!'' Georgia turned to Ben impatiently. "He couldn't. He's worked with me to have the houses restored. He tried to get the grant once *himself*.''

"What happened?''

She shrugged. "I'm not sure. Grants are tricky. A request has to have all the elements they're looking for. He just didn't quite do it.''

"Or didn't really want to,'' Ben said.

"That's crazy.''

"This whole thing is crazy. And getting more and more dangerous. Does he have a key?''

"Of course he doesn't have…'' she began to deny, then remembered she'd given him one about a year previously when he'd delivered a chair he'd recaned for her. "He gave it back to me,'' she said grumpily, ignoring the obvious possibility that a copy could have been made.

Ben focused on Phil again. "Can you humor me and ask for a check on him?"

"Sure," Phil replied. "But I doubt seriously that we'll find anything. He really is a squeaky clean, pillar-of-the-community type."

"Whoever I chased out the back door," Ben said, "didn't fall over the strawberry pot."

Georgia sighed and rolled her eyes. "Which proves only that he was more coordinated than you are."

He cast her a quelling glance before turning back to Phil. "Which proves that it's someone who's been here before, probably more than once. The thing's right by the gate. To miss it in the dark, he'd have had to know it was there."

"You knew it was there," Georgia reminded, "and fell over it anyway. It doesn't compute."

"I was half-asleep and worried about you." He looked at her steadily. "He, on the other hand, was cold-blooded enough to come into your home and take time to set a fire. He knew exactly what he was doing."

Georgia subsided, unconvinced, but out of arguments.

"Any leads on the owner of a Harrington & Richards Defender?" Ben pulled Phil's chair out of the way as he struggled to his feet with the crutches.

Phil shook his head. "No. There isn't one registered around here." He raised an eyebrow. "That doesn't mean somebody doesn't have one. I checked with the postal service and there was a postal inspector in this county who was issued a Defender, but he passed away seven years ago. He had no family. Presuming he still had the gun and it didn't go back to the postal service to be sold off with the others, it could be anywhere. Sold at an auction, packed away in a trunk.... Georgia, are you sure you don't want to leave town for a while?''

"Do you want to take over as cochair of Columbia River Days?'' Georgia asked. ''Do you want to explain to my daughter why she has to leave town eleven days before the event she's baked cookies for for weeks?''

Phil grinned at Ben. ''Go figure a woman's mind. Carrying out her duties and seeing that her daughter gets to carry out hers becomes more important than her skin.''

Ben folded his arms. ''I just live here. I don't pretend to understand.''

The moment the last policeman was out the door, Georgia turned to Ben. She was strung out and tired, frustrated beyond endurance by whoever was doing this to her, and she was annoyed by Ben's continued harping on Wally. And in the gloomy dawn of a Monday morning, her Sunday dreams seemed painfully naive. ''You live in the workshop,'' she said.

Ben returned her cool, even gaze. He, too, couldn't quite believe he'd let yesterday happen. Her wary look came as no surprise. Hadn't he been certain she'd have second thoughts? Still, her safety was at stake and he was getting a little tired of this whole business. ''Not anymore,'' he said firmly. ''Now I live on the sofa— at least at night.''

IN FRONT OF THE BOOKSTORE, Ben watched in satisfaction as the finishing touches were put on Georgia's new bay window. It reduced her window display space but added a charm to the exterior that transformed it from plainly commercial to invitingly quaint. He was anxious for Georgia to see it. She had had to run some errands, and Phil, still on sick leave, was happy to act as bodyguard so that Ben could watch the shop.

Ben was distracted from rubbernecking when a car screeched up to the curb. He turned to watch Bea alight, slam the door, then march toward him as the car sped away, its driver obviously in a temper. Frowning, Ben watched its dust. That had been Rags at the wheel—calm, conventional, forty-five-miles-per-hour-in-a-fifty-miles-per-hour-zone Rags.

"I'd like to have a word with you," Bea said imperiously.

Puzzled, Ben ushered her inside. She went as far as the counter, then turned to face him. She was not her usual pulled-together self this morning, he noticed. She wore slacks and a sweater over a cotton blouse, unusual garb for a woman he'd never seen without stockings and a gloves-and-picture-hat air. When a quick glance around the shop told her they were alone, she began. "By now you know that I'm a woman who believes in being direct."

Ben knew she wouldn't understand it if he smiled. "I've noticed, yes."

"I have something to ask you that is none of my business directly." She straightened and cleared her throat as though uncomfortable. "Except…that I consider everything about my daughter-in-law and my granddaughters to be my business. I know you and Georgia are close."

Ben braced himself. "Yes."

"Has she told you about Gary—about his death?"

"She has."

She sighed, her bosom heaving. Apparently that afforded her some relief. "I don't believe he was leaving them," she said, lifting her chin. Her voice wavered for just a moment and she paused. "But…he'd been under a lot of pressure, and as much as I loved him and thought I knew him—" she sighed heavily "—there are parts of ourselves we keep to ourselves. And the way this all happened, I'm afraid there is no way I will ever know for certain. I've always loved Georgia and the girls, but I've felt a special responsibility to them since then. Gary was broke when he died, and Georgia had nothing for herself and the girls. With a loan from me, and one from the bank, she made this store happen. She's worked herself to a nub to make it a success while still being a full-time mother. I admire her as well as love her and—" she sighed again, a touch of sadness in the sound this time "—I will never leave her…unless I know she's being taken care of."

"Bea…"

"I have to know," she said over him, "what your intentions are toward my daughter-in-law."

The urge to smile came over him again, not because he was amused by Bea's bold request but because he found it touching and comforting that someone cared about Georgia so much. Knowing that made whatever came of his relationship with her easier to face. But he held the smile back because under the tough facade, Bea looked as though she might burst into tears at any moment.

Ben took her arm and pulled her around the counter to the chair. He handed her a box of tissues from one of the cubbyholes under the counter. "Does this have something to do with the way Rags raced off this morning?"

Bea pressed a tissue to her mouth for a moment, then drew in a ragged breath as one solitary tear fell. She wiped it away impatiently. "I love that man, but he has a head like a mule hidden in that lanky, charming, easygoing exterior.''

Ben did smile at that. ''You mean he won't let you push him around.''

She gave him a grim glance as she tossed the tissue into the wastebasket and snatched another. ''I mean he wants me to marry him and move to Portland.''

Ben leaned back against the counter. ''Do you want to?''

''That isn't the problem.''

''You feel obligated to stay here and be available to Georgia and the girls.''

''I know they have their own lives and that I'm also entitled to mine....'' Then she looked up at Ben with a misery in her eyes that made him drop to one knee beside her chair and take her hand. ''If...if my son *was* leaving them, I have to try to make up for that.''

Ben squeezed her hand. ''You know what Georgia would say to that.''

Bea nodded, sniffing and pressing a fresh tissue to her nose. ''She'd send me on my way, but that's Georgia. Somebody's got to protect her from herself. She'd work herself to death being everything to everybody and end up all alone and lonely.'' She leveled that determined gaze on him again. ''So what are your intentions?''

''To love her,'' he said frankly, ''but how long she'll let me do that is uncertain at this point. The way Gary died has left her with her own burden of responsibility. She doesn't feel she can commit herself to another man until she can be sure she hadn't failed your son.''

Bea gasped indignantly, straightening in her chair. ''That doesn't make sense. She was a perfect wife to him.''

He smiled gently, getting to his feet. "It makes as much sense as you assuming his responsibilities. I think you both carry these burdens around as a way of keeping him with you." When she looked up at him in hurt surprise, he shrugged and smiled again. "Can't blame you for that. It seems he was the perfect son and husband. But I think he'd hate to see the two of you do this to yourselves. You're entitled to have Rags, and Georgia's entitled to start over. I think he'd want both of you to do it."

Tears fell freely down her face now. "I have to know," she said stubbornly, "that she'll be all right."

The bells over the door rang wildly as Ragnar pushed his way into the shop. "Is she here?" he demanded, stopping at the counter to peer into the back. His frown deepened when he failed to spot the object of his search. "I dropped her here fifteen minutes ago. Where could she have gone? Did you see—"

"She's here, Rags." Ben put a quieting hand on his arm and pointed behind the counter. Bea stood up, her purse over her arm, her chin in the air. Her eyes were dry, but the line of her mouth was dangerously uncertain.

"Where did you think I'd be?" she asked coolly. "Dropped me here is an appropriate choice of words. Georgia's freight is treated with more care."

Ragnar sighed and ran a hand over his face. "I was angry," he explained simply. "I'm sorry."

"For dumping me out of the car like a mail bag or for trying to force me into a decision I'm not ready to make?"

Rags closed his eyes for a moment, and Ben realized for the first time that frustration with a woman wasn't limited to men of his age group. "For hurting you," he said patiently. "As for dropping you off without ceremony, I plead just cause. You can't expect to say what you think and behave like a major hurricane and expect everyone to make way for you. I have a master's degree in naval science, I've been a ship's master for thirty-eight years, and I've piloted this river for twenty-two. I had a good marriage that lasted thirty years, and I have three great kids. I know a little about life and living. I have a thought or two on things *you* might learn something from if you'd take the time to listen." He shifted his weight, and his voice and his eyes softened. "As for forcing you into making a decision, that wasn't fair and I apologize. I know how much your family means to you. I love you, too. I'd like us to enjoy the rest of our lives together."

Bea's lips quivered as she came around the counter.

"But I'll settle for whatever you're willing to give me," he said. "At least until this problem Georgia's having is over. Then we *have* to talk about it." He opened his arms, and Bea walked into them, dissolving into noisy tears. Rags held her to him for a moment, then tucked her under his arm and started for the door. Ben opened it for them. Wordlessly, Bea reached out for Ben's hand and grasped it briefly, then let Ragnar lead her out to the car.

Ben watched them drive away, thinking grimly that Bea, too, had a question for which there seemed to be no answer.

CHAPTER THIRTEEN

BEN AND GEORGIA PICKED the girls up at school after closing the shop. Linda sat quietly while Lacey held forth at length about the classical concert they'd attended with their grandmother and Ragnar.

"I expected it to be totally gross," Lacey admitted, passing a vending-machine-size bag of potato chips to her mother, then when she refused it, to Ben. Glancing away from the road, he dipped into the bag. "But it was kind of nice in a weird sort of way. I mean, it wasn't anything you could *dance* to, but it was all right for just listening. I like words, though, myself."

"Did you enjoy it, Lindy?" Georgia asked.

Linda sat next to the door, appearing completely removed from the conversation. She turned to Georgia. "I'm sorry, Mom. What?"

"I asked if you enjoyed the concert."

She nodded. "It was nice." Then she turned back to her study of the road ahead, already disassociated from her companions in the truck.

"Grandma and Rags had a fight this morning," Lacey reported, offering the bag of chips to Linda. When her sister didn't even notice, she pulled it back and helped herself to another. "Then he came back to Grandma's this morning to take us to school."

Georgia frowned. "What about?"

Lacey shrugged. "I'm not sure, but I heard your

name mentioned. Grandma told Rags he didn't know what he was talking about, and he told Grandma she acted like a dowager with the grout.''

"Grout," Georgia repeated thoughtfully, trying to make sense of the remark.

"Gout, maybe?" Ben suggested.

"That was it," Lacey said. "Gout. What is that?"

"A sore foot," Georgia replied. "Makes people cranky."

"Anyway, I've never heard Rags yell before. Grandma didn't yell, she just got that look." Lacey mimicked Bea's chin-in-the-air, raised-eyebrow expression of imperious command.

"Like a queen with the gout." Ben laughed.

Lacey laughed with him. Georgia frowned at the road, considering various topics over which they might have argued that would have included her name.

CHANGED INTO JEANS and a pink sweatshirt, Georgia checked the noodle casserole in the oven. The top was just beginning to brown. She looked up at Lacey, who was setting the table. "Would you tell Linda dinner's ready, please?"

"She's outside," Lacey said.

Georgia lifted the lid on the steamer. "Outside?" A poke of her fork proved the broccoli was tender. She lowered the lid and looked out at the sunny early evening. It was a nice time to be outside, but Linda usually had so many personal chores to do before dinner.

Pouring coffee at the counter, Ben peered through the window. "I don't see her. I'll run out. I left something I need in the truck, anyway."

As Ben pushed his way out the screen door, Lacey came up behind Georgia and put an arm around her shoulders. "So what happened in the middle of the living room floor, Mom? You and Ben have a hot love scene there?"

BEN WALKED ACROSS the empty patio to the truck, retrieved his briefcase and frowned when he saw no sign of Linda. He walked around the front of the house, then back to the patio to check the tiny potting shed and the small garden between the back of the workshop and the fence. Still no sign of Linda. Convinced Lacey must have been mistaken, Ben went into the workshop, placed the case on the sofa and turned back toward the door. It was then that he spotted her. She was sitting on a trunk near the workbench, something cradled in her arms. She looked up at him with surprise and what he could have sworn was guilt. "Hi," she said, but her manner suggested a desire to be left alone.

Something in her voice reminded him of her mother's cry for help, and he changed direction, walking toward her. "Your mom sent me to find you and tell you dinner's ready," he said. As he got closer, he saw that what she held in her arms was the photo of her and her sister with their mother and father. She wore the same distant expression she'd had when they'd picked her up at school. He stopped within a few feet of her, straddling one of the kitchen chairs he'd repaired. "You okay?"

She sighed, staring at her lap. "Shelly has the flu," she said. "At least that's what she told Mrs. Butler. She has to give her first speech as princess tomorrow night and she's scared."

"She pretending to be sick," Ben guessed.

"I think so. Mrs. Butler wants me to give all the speeches this week in her place."

Knowing how relieved Linda had been that Shelly had won the honor and therefore the duties, he said quietly, "That's a lot to ask."

She looked at him. "The junior class selected a princess. They have a right to be represented. I was their second choice." Her eyes clouded and she shook her head. "But I hate to do that kind of thing. I always feel...dumb and ugly when I stand up in front of people."

"I don't understand why, Linda. You're a bright and pretty girl."

Linda lowered her hands until the photo rested on their palms in her lap. "My father used to say that." She smiled at the photo, touching his likeness with her index finger. Then a frown suddenly pleated her brow. "I'm not sure he meant it, though."

Quiet descended on the small room, but Ben got the impression of a turmoil of enormous proportions centered in the small, slender body facing him. He could see the toughness of her grandmother in her and the gentle, unfailing strength of her mother. And something of the good guy who had been her father.

"Why wouldn't he have meant it?" he asked cautiously.

She looked up at him again, dark eyes filled with pain and confusion, cheeks pale. "He was leaving us when he died," she said matter-of-factly. "My mother doesn't know, but Lacey and I do. We overheard Mrs. Hansen talking to Grandma right after it happened. Mom was making funeral arrangements. Grandma told Mrs. Hansen that it wasn't true, but maybe it was. Almost everybody's father leaves."

"Linda..." he began.

"He was with another woman," Linda said heavily. "His secretary. Shelly's father did the same thing."

His first instinct was to shout for Georgia. This was something that should be handled carefully—a confidence in which he really had no place. Then it struck him like a sledge that this child had carried an agonizing burden for two years, unable to share it because she thought her mother didn't know, unwilling to share it and cause her mother pain. Yet she had chosen to tell him. The responsibility that placed on him shocked him almost as much as the fact that she trusted him with it.

Ben stood, pushed his chair aside and sat beside her on the trunk. The calm, efficient junior class dynamo was now a frightened, disillusioned child. He put an arm around her, praying that instinct would guide him. "I've heard that story," he said gently. "And I don't believe it."

"You have?" She looked up at him in surprise. "Who told you? Only Grandma knows."

He shook his head. "You mother knows, Linda. She told me."

"No," Linda denied quickly. "She tells me and Lacey everything. It's like we're all in this together, you know? She tells us how the business is doing and when money's tight and how she's feeling. She tells us... everything." Her voice died in uncertainty on the last word.

"I imagine she didn't tell you about your father," he said gently, "because she didn't want you to worry about it. She had no real way to prove that it wasn't what it looked like, and she didn't want you to have doubts about his love for you."

"But he was with—"

"I know. A young and pretty woman. But she was also his secretary. They could have been going on some kind of business together."

Linda shook her head, obviously reluctant to reject the ray of hope he offered. "My dad had lost his job six months before that. They weren't working together anymore."

Ben made every effort to sound firm, "Linda, I don't know where he was going or what he was doing, but the important thing to ask yourself is, Did my father ever lie to me?"

She didn't hesitate. "No." She glanced at him with a wry twist of her lips. "Except to tell me I was pretty."

Ben laughed softly, squeezing her shoulder. "That isn't a lie." Then he said gravely, "Only a sneak and a liar would leave his family that way. Do you have any reason to believe he was either of those things?"

Linda's lip quivered and she bit it, blinking rapidly. "No," she whispered. She swallowed with difficulty. "But Shelly's dad—"

"Linda, we're not talking about Shelly's dad." He pointed to the photo she still clutched with white knuckles. "We're talking about this man—*your* father. When I first moved into this workshop, it was filled with things he'd been fixing. A man who doesn't care about his family doesn't bother with things like that. And that picture has always hung right over his workbench, hasn't it?" She nodded. "Where he could see it all the time. Your mom has the wonderful warmth of a woman who's been loved, and so do you and Lacey."

The picture clutched to her small breasts, she leaned into his shoulder and began to sob. He wrapped both arms around her and rocked gently. "You have every reason to believe in him, Linda. To believe everything he ever told you—that you're smart and pretty and that he loved you. He wasn't leaving you. You might never know exactly where he was going or what he was doing, but he wasn't leaving you. I believe that."

GEORGIA WALKED THROUGH the half-open workshop door, hoping to see that Ben had found Linda. A nagging little worry that something might have happened to her daughter had begun to plague her when Ben hadn't returned. At the sight of them sitting together near the workbench, she put a hand to her heart in relief. She had a teasing remark on the tip of her tongue about dinner burning, then she noticed that they were holding each other and heard Linda's painful sobs. Ben's quiet voice drifted back to her. "To believe everything he ever told you—that you're smart and pretty and that he loved you. He wasn't leaving you. You might never know exactly where he was going or what he was doing, but he wasn't leaving you. I believe that."

Linda knew. Georgia's worst nightmare had become reality. She went toward her daughter, her own anguish over Gary's death doubled because now Linda knew. At the sound of her footsteps, Ben and Linda looked up. Linda rose and flew into her arms, still sobbing. "I didn't think you knew, Mom," Linda wept. "I'm sorry, I didn't think you knew!"

"Who told you?" Georgia asked grimly.

Linda explained what she had overheard at Bea's after the crash. Georgia held her away, looking into her anguished brown eyes, unable to believe what that suggested. "Do you mean you've known since Daddy died—for two years—and you never said anything?"

Mistakenly presuming her mother was angry, Linda clutched the arms that held her and went on hurriedly, "We thought if you knew, you'd have told us. When you didn't—" Linda shrugged helplessly "—I couldn't tell you. You cried all the time at night. I knew you missed him even more than we did. We made a pact never to tell you."

"We? Lacey knows?"

"Where *is* everybody?" Lacey appeared in the workshop doorway in her ever present shorts and shirt and with a dish towel over her shoulder. "The noodles are burning, the broccoli smells like—" She stopped in her tracks at the sight of her mother and sister in tears. "What's the matter?" she demanded, then instead of going toward them, she took a step back, as though instinct told her what was happening. "You told her?" she asked Linda accusingly.

"I knew, baby." Georgia put a hand out to her. "Come here."

Lacey hesitated, her eyes filling with tears, unwilling to subject herself to the pain admission would bring. Ben went to put an arm around her and draw her toward her mother and sister. He understood how she felt. He wasn't even involved—at least he hadn't known Gary—and he could hardly bear their grief and their courage.

He had intended to leave them to their tears and recollections, to give them privacy. But before he could move away, Linda, still holding her mother, put an arm around his waist. When Lacey didn't let go, either, he was pulled into their communal hug as tears flowed, reassurances were murmured and confidences were finally shared with relief. He held them without stopping to wonder whose role he played—his own or Gary's. In this tight little knot of family in which he'd doubted his place just a few moments ago, he was being clung to like a lifeline.

"SO SHE WANTS ME to give all the speeches this week, and I'm scared, Mom." Linda sat in her twin bed propped against her pillows, the sheet pulled up to her waist, Garfield's face on her nightshirt visible above it. Her cheeks were still red and puffy but her eyes were clear, Georgia was pleased to note. "Actually, I'm terrified."

"You wrote the whole speech," Lacey said, lying across the foot of the bed, her head propped on her hand. "It'll be easy for you."

Sitting on the edge of the bed, Georgia tried to encourage without prodding. "I think you'd do a better job than Shelly because you understand and love Astoria's history. And that would go a long way toward convincing the service clubs to support us."

"I'm supposed to wear a dress and heels." Linda sighed. "The first speech is at the Toastmasters meeting tomorrow night at seven-thirty. If I do it, will you and Ben come with me?"

"Of course."

"The Wednesday one's at the Kiwanis Club at noon. There's no way you could leave the shop, is there?"

"Maybe Grandma would watch it for me."

Linda caught Georgia's eye, her own reflecting a sudden return to the issue of her father. "Where do you think Dad was going, Mom?"

"I honestly don't know, Lindy," Georgia replied. "I just know he wasn't leaving us."

Linda nodded, tracing the quilted pattern on the bedspread. "Ben says he feels like he's gotten to know
Daddy since he's been staying in the workshop."

"Oh?"

Linda smiled at her. "He said you've got the 'wonderful warmth of a woman who's been loved,'" she
quoted. "That Daddy wouldn't have bothered with all
the repair projects he was working on if he hadn't cared
about us, and that he had our picture over the workbench so he'd be able to see it all the time." She
sighed. "It makes me feel better to think about that. It
makes me feel better to know that you know about
Daddy and that you believe he still loved us."

"Of course he did." Georgia leaned down to hug
her. "You and Lacey were the most important things
in his life. When are you supposed to call Mrs. Butler
and tell her your decision?"

"First thing in the morning. I guess I should do it."

"I think it would be a good experience for you."

Lacey headed off to her own room but stopped in
the doorway to warn her sister. "When parents say
things are a 'good experience,' it usually means it's
hard and you're going to hate it."

"Go to bed," Georgia said with mock severity.

Smiling, Lacey disappeared across the hall.

Georgia looked down at Linda, letting herself feel
the enormity of the sacrifice her daughters had made
for her. As the oldest and the most sensitive, Linda had
made the decision. She brushed her hair back and
pulled the sheet up as Linda settled down into the bed.
"Are you all right now?" she asked.

Linda smiled. "I think so. I worried about it for so
long, it feels strange now that I don't have to worry
about it anymore. Shelly's dad left her and her mom

that way—with his secretary. I guess because it had happened to her, I thought it might have happened to me. I mean, I still loved Dad and everything, but sometimes I felt ugly and stupid and—well, you know. Sometimes you feel like such a jerk you wonder that anyone could love you. He was always telling me how smart and pretty I was, but if he and Sara *had* run off together, then it was like his loving us had been a lie. I felt guilty that I doubted him, but it happened to Shelly. It seemed like it could have happened to me.''

"But it didn't.''

Linda smiled again. "I know. That's what Ben said. It might have happened to Shelly, but it didn't happen to me.''

Georgia hugged her again and turned out the light. She found Lacey kneeling on her bed, looking out the window.

"Where's Ben?'' she asked. "I can always see the lights on in the shop when I go to bed.''

"He's sleeping in the living room tonight,'' Georgia explained, prodding her back against the pillow and pulling up the blanket.

"'Cause of the fire last night.''

"Yes.''

Lacey folded her arms. "Are you worried about that?''

Georgia shook her head. "I'm more worried about you and Linda. Are you okay with…all this about your father?''

"Oh, yeah. I didn't worry about it like Linda did. She thinks too much, you know? I figured if he was going to leave us, we'd have heard you fighting before. And you always know everything, even the stuff you don't see. I just didn't think something like that would happen and you wouldn't know all about it."

Georgia hugged Lacey, reminded of how young her tall and elegant youngest really was. She still believed in her mother's omnipotence. "He loved you," Georgia said.

"I know." Lacey's voice was filled with confidence.

Alone in her room, Georgia fell onto the bed, her heart heavy, her mind atumble, her body weary. God, she wondered desperately, would life ever even out again? She thought about Linda carrying that terrible burden for two years and was consumed with guilt. Had she been a better mother, had she made more time for her daughters during her own grief, would Linda have tried to talk to her about it and been saved such pain? Where *had* Gary been going, and had he thought about them as the plane plunged?

Tears swelled in Georgia as she went into the bathroom to take a shower, brush her teeth, comb her hair. For a woman who'd held off grief for two long years, she had certainly lost the knack, she thought as she pulled on her flannel nightgown.

She turned the light off, groped blindly for the top of the spread and blankets and tossed them back. Ben's scent, woodsy and clean, rose out of the bedclothes to assail her with memories of their beautiful Sunday. Had that been only yesterday?

Tied in an emotional knot, she knew she wouldn't even close her eyes tonight. Tense and restless, answering a need she seemed unable to ever satisfy, she padded silently into the hall and down the stairs, heading for the one place where she always felt steady and hopeful.

The living room was dark and still. As she ap-

proached the sofa quietly, wondering if Ben was awake
or asleep, his warm hand reached out to clasp her wrist.
She sat on the edge of the sofa, able to see his features
now as he lay on his back, one hand pillowing his head.
"The girls okay?" he asked quietly.

She closed her free hand over his, absorbing its
warmth and the strength with which it held her. "Yes."

"But you're not," he guessed.

"Linda kept that to herself," she whispered, the
emotion rising in her as she expressed the thought
aloud, making her soft voice crack. "For two years!"

Ben tossed the inside corner of the blanket aside.
"Come on. Climb over me." He sat up, helping her
climb onto the sofa and settle against the back cushions. He put an arm around her and drew her back with
him to the pillow, pulling the blanket up over her
shoulder.

"You're going to fall off," Georgia warned, trying
to flatten herself against the cushions to make room for
him.

"Not if you hold on to me, I won't." Ben held her
close and she freed one arm to wrap around his waist.

The tension left her almost immediately. The guilt
she felt over Linda was more stubborn. "Why didn't
she tell me that she knew?" she asked into his shoulder.

"She explained that." His hand gently stroked her
hair. "Because she didn't think you knew, and she
couldn't hurt you like that."

"She was only fourteen," Georgia said, the hand she
had around his waist unconsciously clutching at the
T-shirt he wore. "That was too big a sacrifice for a
child. She mustn't have felt she could talk to me. She
mustn't have thought I—"

"Stop that." Ben put a finger to her lips. "There's
no guilt in this for anyone. Can't you just accept that
you've raised two girls as caring and giving as you are?
It *was* a big thing for two little kids to do, but it wasn't
a failing in you that prompted it—it was courage in
them."

Georgia relaxed against him, trying to accept that.
She sighed, weariness beginning to overtake her. "Can
I just stay here for a while?"

"Why not?" He settled them more comfortably,
rubbing soothing patterns along her spine. "This is
where you belong."

THE AUDIENCE in the small hospitality room over the
bank numbered less than thirty. But Georgia, sitting
with Ben and Lacey in the back row of folding chairs,
could see that Linda was suffering. Hands folded
tightly, she waited with the other princesses, next in
line to speak. As a perky little blonde from the senior
class talked about the Indians along the river, Georgia
studied her daughter with new respect. She'd always
loved both her girls more than her own life. She'd tried
to respect their thoughts and wishes, tried to deal firmly
but kindly with their transgressions and always tried to
remember that the person inside the child was not a
copy of herself but someone in her own right. She'd
never felt that more strongly than at this moment. In a
berry-blue dress with a long, flared skirt, her dark hair
caught up at the sides, her shoulders squared, Linda
looked like a young woman, a stranger with familiar
features. Georgia felt a panicky moment of disassoci-
ation.

"There she goes," Ben whispered. Georgia watched
as Linda stepped up to the podium. She began to speak,

her first few words were indistinguishable. Linda
cleared her throat, hesitated a moment, then smiled at
the audience. "Please excuse me," she said ingenu-
ously. "I'm terrified."

There was a ripple of laughter, a smattering of applause, and Linda began again. "Tradition says that
Fort Astoria was John Jacob Astor's only financial failure," she said in a firm voice. "It's so hard for me to
look at our beautiful, green corner of the world and
think of it as any kind of a failure...." In a moment it
was clear to all who listened that Linda found her subject exciting. Georgia thought with what she considered
objectivity that Linda spoke without the stilted,
learned-by-rote delivery of several of the girls. She
didn't stumble or giggle or try to get by on "cute."
She simply shared what she knew with warmth and
enthusiasm.

It wasn't until Linda had finished that Georgia realized her fingers were laced with Ben's and that they'd
agonized over her daughter's traumatic first public appearance together.

"GOD, I'M GLAD that's over!" In the back seat of the
station wagon on the way home, Linda kicked off her
shoes and groaned.

"You have to do two tomorrow," Lacey reminded,
"and one every day till Sunday."

Linda groaned again.

Ben smiled into the rearview mirror. "You did beautifully. You'll do as well tomorrow."

"I was so scared!"

"You behaved like a lady, with warmth and mod-
esty." Georgia grinned at her over her shoulder.
"That'll get you through every time."

"You sounded smart, too," Lacey said. "That was scary. How do you know all that?"

Linda laughed. "It's in the library."

Lacey blinked. "But what made you want to find it?"

"Part of it was a class assignment last term. I just got interested and wanted to know more about it, so I looked it up."

Lacey studied her sister for a moment, then caught Ben's eye in the mirror. "That's *really* scary."

In the house, the girls hugged Georgia good-night, then Ben, and ran upstairs. Georgia turned to Ben, looping her arms around his neck. "You sleeping on the sofa again tonight?" she asked.

He circled her waist and pulled her closer. "You want to join me?"

"I wish I could," Georgia admitted with a sigh. "But with the girls around, it's too dangerous. What time did you carry me upstairs this morning?"

"About five." He kissed her cheek and then her ear. "You didn't even stir."

"I know." Georgia gave herself a moment to enjoy the sensations he was arousing in her. "I've slept better the past two nights with you than I've slept in two years. You've spoiled me for my lonely bed." She smiled into his eyes as he pulled away to look down at her. "When you move back to Portland, you'll have to commute so that you can come back at night and sleep with me."

He studied her gravely for a moment, wondering if she was opening up the future for discussion. Afraid of shattering the sweet peace, he ignored the possibility. "There must be a better solution than that. Meanwhile—'' he put her firmly away from him ''—don't torture me. Good night.''

Delighted with the personal stride her daughter had made, personally pleased that Ben considered her closeness torture, she put her arms around him once again. ''I wasn't finished.''

''Georgia...''

''Thank you for coming with us tonight,'' she said, standing on tiptoe to kiss him lightly. ''It meant a lot to Linda.''

''Yeah...well...'' He shifted his weight, careful to keep his hands away from her. ''Linda means a lot to me.''

She toyed with the hair behind his ear. ''Lacey loves you too, you know.''

He hunched his shoulder and turned his head to break the contact. ''I'm fond of Lacey.''

Georgia held his head steady. ''You love Lacey.''

He looked into her dark eyes, unable to take issue with her statement, but suspicious of the point she was making. ''I love Lacey.''

Her hands still looped around his neck, she said. ''Linda, Lacey and I are a family.''

He looked at the ceiling, then back at her. ''You're sharp tonight. What's your point, Georgia?''

Georgia stood on tiptoe to kiss him on the mouth with creativity and fervor. She hoped the memory of it would keep him awake for a good long time. She turned away to the stairs. ''Think about it,'' she said, then blew him a kiss and ran up the stairs.

CHAPTER FOURTEEN

"I CAN'T BELIEVE IT." The last sections of scaffolding were being loaded onto the painter's truck, and Georgia backed up to the edge of the sidewalk to take in the beauty of the Roberts Building's face-lift. The day smelled of hot pavement, fresh paint, the river and the perfume of spring.

Ben couldn't take his eyes off Georgia.

It had been two days since he'd had an opportunity to touch her, two days since she'd made a point of telling him she and her daughters were a family, then kissed him and suggested that he "think about it." In those two days he'd accompanied Georgia to all of Linda's speeches, done his usual duty at the store and spent most of his free time with Georgia and the girls, frosting and decorating cookies—and he'd thought about it.

The conclusion was unsettling. He was in love with the entire family. But his life was in Portland, and theirs was here. And he doubted his durability as husband and father. Just to make matters more interesting, he was in competition with a man whose durability in both roles had survived his death. "Good going, Gary," he murmured to himself. "Even I like you, but you sure messed up my life."

"I can't believe it," Georgia said again, glancing at Ben with a smile. "Do you believe it?"

He forced his attention to the new lines of the building. The bakery was a mirror image of the bookstore, small-paned windows steamed up in the shake-shingled bay, and the board and batten face of the building was stained a grayish blue and accented with sharp white trim. Wally had found an anchor from one of the many ships lost on the bar in the early days, and it was propped against the corner of Georgia's bay, invisibly secured for safety. Over her door was an old coach lantern. A slatted bench under a flowering tree encouraged shoppers to sit, relax and, hopefully, consider more purchases.

"I can't believe it's really happened," Georgia said, clutching Ben's arm in her two as she stared up at it in wonder. "Have you ever seen anything more beautiful?"

Ben looked down at the sparkle in her eyes, the smile on her lips and the ripple of sunlight in her hair, and he shook his head. "No. Never."

"We don't have the arty appeal of Cannon Beach or the midwaylike attractions of Seaside, but we have something so much richer."

"History."

"And the river." She turned away to walk the few feet to the corner, where the Columbia River was visible a block away. Sunlight embroidered it with silver, and across its four-mile width, the hills of Washington shone green and clear under a bright blue sky. "I never look at it without feeling connected to the past. God, we're lucky to be here." She looked at him suddenly, her eyes gentle. "Your uncle called you this morning, didn't he?"

Ben raised an eyebrow in surprise. "Yes. Were you eavesdropping?"

"Yes." She did not appear contrite. "He needs you back in Portland."

"I'm not leaving," he said, "until I know you're safe."

That wasn't quite what she wanted to hear. She started slowly back toward the store. "I was talking to Lacey this morning about the argument Bea and Ragnar had Monday. She said she heard Bea say she was going to talk to you that morning."

Ben looked blandly innocent.

"Well, what did she tell you?" Georgia made no effort to be subtle. "Does their problem have something to do with me?"

Evasively, Ben replied, "Mostly, she cried and I handed her tissues."

She ignored that. "Rags wants to get married, doesn't he? He wants her to move to Portland." When Ben said nothing, she added, "And she'd like to go with him, but she's worried about me and the girls."

Ben went to the new bench and sat, pulling her down beside him. "She feels responsible for you. She wants to know you're safe before she makes a new life for herself."

"That's silly!" Georgia bristled with indignation. She tried to stand, apparently ready to run into the shop, call Bea and give her a piece of her mind.

Ben held her back. "You can't argue her out of it. The best thing you can do is assure her that you're ready to start over, that you've put the past behind you."

She looked at him grimly, suddenly smiled to exchange a greeting with a passerby, then focused on Ben once again. "I've explained to you how I feel about that."

"Linda was able to do it," Ben said.

Georgia made a small sound of pain. "That isn't fair. All right, what if I said I could start over again with you, that I could finally put my memories of Gary away if you could love me completely?"

He looked back at her silently for a moment, his heart accepting that he had little choice in the matter.

She mistook his hesitation for refusal. "Not so easy when *you're* being pushed, is it?" She tried to stand again, and he held her back again. Looking into her eyes, he asked, "Will you marry me?"

She uttered a small gasp, her expression one of complete surprise. "What?"

"Will you marry me? Will you put Gary away and love me? Simple question."

"Those are not simple questions!" Georgia shouted, then suddenly remembering where they were, she looked around furtively and whispered, "You are not going to bully me into discussing this on a bench on Commercial Street." She tried to stand and he pulled her back for the third time. She turned to him with a murderous look.

"I am," he said, "going to bully you into discussing it sometime. When?"

"At home."

"When?"

She sighed. "Tonight."

"We have to take Linda to the Anchor Club meeting tonight."

She rolled her eyes at his persistence. "After the meeting. What brought this on, anyway? You just told me you were going back to Portland as soon as this mess is over."

He nodded. "I am. But I never intended to go

alone." He stood and started into the store. Looking back over his shoulder as she continued to sit, he asked, "Coming?"

GEORGIA AND BEN HURRIEDLY cleared away dinner dishes while Linda dressed for the meeting. Lacey, pressed into service to wrap and box the plain cookies, was standing at the kitchen table measuring lengths of foil when the doorbell rang. She ran to answer it and returned in a moment, a storm cloud on her beautiful features. Behind her was Shelly Gordon in a pink sweater and pants. Her hair was beautifully groomed, her makeup perfect. She did not look like a child who'd been deathly ill for the past few days. "Hi, Mrs. Madison," she said brightly. "Is Linda here?"

Before Georgia could answer, Lacey snapped, "She's upstairs, getting ready to give your speech to the Anchor Club."

Unimpressed with or not noticing Lacey's sarcasm, she smiled. "Is it all right if I run up and talk to her?" she asked Georgia.

"Yes, of course."

Georgia, Ben and Lacey stopped to watch the girl run up the stairs. "What do you bet she's come to tell Linda she's well enough to be princess at the dance tomorrow." Lacey looked at Georgia, her eyes distressed as well as angry. "And what do you bet dorky Linda lets her do it? After she's done all Shelly's dirty work."

The injustice of it bit into Georgia, as well, and she fought her maternal instinct to interfere. But she tried to will her daughter to tell Shelly where she could go Friday night.

Lacey started off for the stairs in a huff. "I'm gonna—"

Georgia caught her shoulder and pulled her back. "No, you're not. Linda will handle it."

Shelly ran lightly down the stairs a few moments later, Linda's high-heeled white shoes held together in one hand. She smiled at the three in the kitchen. "Thanks. Bye." She waved and saw herself out as though she hadn't a care in the world.

Lacey turned to Georgia, her face almost purple with anger. "Do you believe that! She came to borrow Linda's shoes for tomorrow night!"

Ben went to the phone. "I'm calling the school."

Georgia caught his arm. "There's no one there."

"Then I'm calling Mrs. What's-her-name. The one who's coordinating the pageant."

Georgia took the receiver from his hand and hung it up. "She's at a meeting with Karen and Wally tonight."

Hands on his hips, Ben glared down at Georgia. "That little brat is not going to do this to Linda."

"I'll call Mrs. Butler in the morning," Georgia assured him. "Though—"

"Nobody's going to call anybody." Linda appeared in the kitchen in a ruffled floral skirt and a matching blouse. Her hair was swept up and caught at the crown with a simple white bow. She had a large mesh purse on her shoulder and a sweater in her hands. She frowned at Ben and Georgia. "You guys don't look ready."

Ben looked into the girl's calm eyes and saw the disappointment. Anger forced him to wait a minute before speaking. "Linda, she has no right to take the title from you so that she can act like a wheel tomorrow.

You did all the work, and a hundred times better than she could have, I'm sure. Let your mom call—''

Linda shook her head firmly. "She was elected. It's all right, really. It would have been fun, but I'm really not that upset." She sighed, giving them a small, genuine smile. "I had fun this week. I expected to hate it, but I had fun. I learned something. I can talk to a group of people and not feel like an idiot. That's what this stuff is all about, isn't it?"

Georgia put her arms around her, wondering what she'd ever done to deserve this child. "Lindy, you don't have to just accept this."

"Mom, I'm fine," Linda insisted. "If you two don't hurry, I'll be late."

"It's interesting," Ben said, taking Linda's face in his hands, "that Shelly was well enough to come over to get the shoes but not well enough to give the speech tonight."

Linda laughed, just a hint of sadness at her friend's betrayal hidden beside the disappointment. "That's Shelly."

Ben leaned down to kiss her cheek. "She might have the crown," he said, "but you're the princess."

"SAY THE WORD," Lacey advised darkly as they walked upstairs to their rooms after the meeting, "and I'll booby-trap her locker."

"Just forget it," Linda said firmly. "We're going to be too busy packaging cookies to…"

Ben and Georgia faced each other in the middle of the kitchen. "Where do you want to talk?" he asked without preamble.

She glanced at the stairs. The girls would be chatting and laughing for some time. This was going to be a showdown of sorts, Georgia knew, and she didn't want the girls to overhear. "Maybe the workshop would be best."

Ben opened the back door and ushered her through.

Gary's workshop was like a room she'd seen in a dream, Georgia thought as she walked into it and Ben closed the door behind her. For a year and a half after Gary's death, she'd avoided it, afraid of the memories there. Now, though everything in it was familiar, it held no trauma for her. Had Gary's death been less mysterious, she guessed she'd be at a point where she was through grieving and ready to begin again. But it had been mysterious, and despite all she'd said to Linda to encourage her, she admitted to herself that she, personally, needed to know *for sure*.

She walked around the room, getting reacquainted with it, stalling for time. In a far corner she found a lineup of items that had sat in this room for years, awaiting repair—and was not entirely surprised to discover that many of them had been fixed.

Ben wandered over to point to a small, battered table overturned on a cardboard box. Two of its legs were broken. "I think Gary's intention must have been to replace all the legs with these new ones." He pointed to a cardboard box with four turned, unstained legs in it. "I can't find anything else in here these would have fit."

Georgia picked up one of the legs and turned it over in her hands, smiling reflectively. "These were intended for that table. I chose them one Saturday afternoon when I went with Gary to the hardware store to buy paint."

Ben walked away from her to the room's only window. It was high, curtained with a faded piece of calico and looked out onto the driveway. He could see Georgia's station wagon and his truck parked behind it. Midnight, the cat, was asleep on his hood. Loneliness more painful than any he could remember from his childhood filled his being and spilled out of him to darken what he could see of the days ahead. "How long are you going to live with him, Georgia?"

Georgia passed behind him and sat in a corner of the sofa, her feet tucked under her. She heard the pain in his voice and felt an answering pain inside her. "I don't live with him anymore, Ben. I love you."

He turned away from the window to walk toward her, stopping at the worktable that filled the middle of the room. He leaned a hip on it and looked down at her, somehow knowing that despite her statement, this was not going to turn out the way he hoped. "So you're coming to Portland with me?" he prodded mercilessly.

She looked at him a moment, her eyes miserable. Then she drew a steadying breath. "I can't leave here because I don't want to disrupt my children, because I have a business in which I find great personal fulfillment, and because I grew up here. Despite all that's happened, I love it here." She looked into his eyes. "You're afraid of that, aren't you? That's why you won't consider staying."

He tried not to react to that. "My work is in Portland."

"I thought your work was all over the Oregon map?"

"With headquarters in Portland."

"Would it be impossible to move your headquarters here?"

"Georgia," he said impatiently, "my partner lives

in Portland. He's also the only person who's ever meant anything to me since I was six years old. Until I came here.''

Calmly, Georgia shook her head at him. "That isn't it. You don't want to move here because you'd find yourself all tied up in what you've spent most of your life avoiding. The girls and I, our lives here, have gotten a grip on you, and you're afraid you're going to strangle. You're not afraid that you don't have the staying power for marriage—you're afraid you couldn't hold us that long.'' Georgia saw the reaction in his eyes, the flare of surprise before the shutter came down to close her out. She was right, she realized in amazement. This talented, giving, wonderful man still harbored the fears of his childhood, the notion that he was unlovable. "Ben.'' She stood and crossed the small distance that separated them.

He straightened as she approached him. His arms were folded across his chest to keep her at a distance.

"Don't you know how much we love you?'' she asked gently. "You are everything a woman could want in a man—everything. You were shunted around as a child because people wouldn't make room in their lives for you—not because there was any failing in you.''

He looked down at her, unmoved. "Yet it's happening again. You're telling me I can't have you unless I have you here, where you can cling to what you had with Gary.'' He paced back to the window, sighing. "He's dead, Georgia, and he means more to you than I do.''

She followed him, grabbing his arm and yanking him around. "That isn't true! I explained—''

"You're afraid to go on,'' he interrupted angrily. "I

don't think it has anything to do with the way he died. You had a marriage that was magic, and you're not sure it can happen again. You don't know if he made the magic or you did. With another man, you might just be an ordinary woman. It's safer to remain the widow everyone loves and admires.''

"Don't blame me,'' she said hotly. "You're just looking for an excuse to walk away and insisting that I leave here when you know I can't do that for you.''

"You can't because you don't love me enough.''

"How much would ever be enough, Ben?'' she demanded. "How much love would make up for your loveless childhood? Do I have to make up for every person in your past who let you down? Don't I have the right to consider what I need in this relationship?''

"You need Gary!'' he shouted at her. "And I can't give him to you. Nobody,'' he said, enunciating, "can get him back for you, Georgia.''

"I don't need him back!'' she screamed. "I just need to know where he was going!''

Ben's voice quieted. "You told Linda she had to believe in herself. You have to do that, too, Georgia. You have to accept that you have to get on with the rest of your life without knowing what he was doing that day.''

Georgia turned to him, wondering how one could ever expect to explain feelings in words. It was like speaking French to a Russian. The effort was made, but communication failed. "I can't, Ben,'' she said patiently. "That's all I can tell you.''

He turned from her, ran a hand over his face, then turned back, his voice quiet. "You're telling me that you would marry me if I moved here, but not if it means you'd have to move away with me. That doesn't make sense. Either you can go on without knowing or you can't. What does it matter where you are?''

"If I'm here," she said quietly, "I can still hope to find out what happened."

That was what finally made Ben see that it was hopeless. If he moved here, she would put the past aside, but not behind her. "I will not use *our* marriage," he said grimly, "to figure out what happened to your marriage to Gary. I think the worry is a waste of time. I think the guy loved you, and I think you should believe that. Curious," he said, walking toward the door because he needed to get outside, to breathe deeply to prevent himself from screaming, "that I have more faith in him than you do."

CHAPTER FIFTEEN

THE NEXT MORNING, Georgia felt as though she'd died. Life went on around her, but all the things Ben brought into her life were missing. There was no laughter, no excitement, no fun—no hope that one day she would regain everything she had lost when Gary died.

It was a kind of suicide. She had done it to herself. Ben accompanied her to the shop as usual but there was no light in him, and he'd become such an important part of Georgia's life that she, too, was thrown into darkness.

The only bright spot appeared that afternoon when Linda walked into the shop right after lunch, several hours before school would be out. Georgia's first reaction was concern that she was ill. Then she saw her face.

"Guess what?" Linda demanded, her eyes glowing, her cheeks pink, a giggle escaping as she hugged her mother. Ben wandered up from the back of the store, where he was building storage shelves. Linda hugged him, too. "Ben, guess what?"

"The famous Spago in Los Angeles is opening a restaurant in Astoria," he guessed, "and Wolfgang Puck wants you to be the chef?"

Linda giggled again. "No, silly. Mrs. Butler found out about Shelly, and she called a meeting of the junior class officers—" her eyes widened as she went on with her story "—and they voted that *I* should retain the title of princess. Me!" She frowned at Ben suddenly. "Did you tell her? Lacey told me you wanted to call her last night."

"I wanted to, but your mother wouldn't let me," he said. "She wanted to let you handle it."

Linda turned to Georgia, frowning. "Then you didn't, either?"

"No."

Linda's face cleared as suddenly as it had clouded. "Well, anyway, she let me come home early to get myself together for tonight. The only bad part—" her face clouded again "—is that Shelly still has the crown. I have to go get it."

"Did she go to school today?"

Linda shook her head. "I think that was one of the things that decided the officers. That and the fact that Judy Grosvenor, the vice president, saw Shelly downtown last night when I was giving her speech."

Georgia frowned in wonder. "How did she think she was going to get away with that?"

Linda shrugged. "She knew I wouldn't tell. But she should have been smarter than to go downtown. Somebody you know is *always* there."

"I'll go to Shelly's with you after I close the shop. Just in case she gives you any trouble. I'm surprised her mother hasn't stepped in before this."

"They don't talk very much. Her mom kind of…you know…runs around a lot. Sometimes she tries to make up for it by buying her stuff, but Shelly knows she doesn't really care. She wasn't even excited that Shelly was chosen princess. She probably doesn't even know Shelly was faking about having the flu."

Georgia felt sympathy for the child, but she wasn't

going to let it affect her own daughter's night of glory—not when she'd worked so hard.

"I guess I can wear the dress I wore for the Valentine's dance...." She put a hand under her hair and held it to the top of her head. "What'll I do with my hair, though?"

Georgia went behind the counter for her purse. "I think you should have your hair done. Run over to Shear Magic and tell Jerry you want the works."

"I think you should have a new dress." Ben handed Linda several bills. She looked at them, then up at him, then at her mother, wordlessly holding them out for her inspection.

"Ben..." Georgia began to protest. She could probably buy a mink with that amount of money.

"Get something really special," Ben advised, ignoring Georgia as he turned Linda toward the door.

"Mom...?" Linda asked, excited but startled by the value of the gift.

Georgia shrugged. "Have a ball, Linda. Then come back here and we'll take you to Shelly's." She turned to Ben the moment the door closed behind Linda. "Thank you, but you didn't have to do that."

He sat on the windowsill and watched Linda disappear down the street. "I've learned a little about teenage girls since living with you," he said. "And I'll bet you could count on the fingers of one hand those who'd volunteer to wear a dress they've worn before—particularly on such an occasion." He gave Georgia a wry look as he stood. "If she were my daughter, I'd send her to Europe for the summer, buy her a Porsche when she came home and enroll her in the best culinary arts school in the country. And no man would come near her until I was sure half of him was as sterling as she is and the other half tough enough to make sure nothing ever hurts her.'' His eyes were filled with a regret Georgia had to turn away from. Swallowing painfully, she heard him walk to the back of the store.

Linda came in just before five, her hair loosely curled and styled with casual flyaway ease. Chattering, she hung a long plastic sleeve by its hanger on the end of a book rack and unzipped it. Inside was a black silk dress with spaghetti straps, three inches of lacy white ruffle at the hem and a wide white organza bow that covered the back of the waist. Its ribbons fell to the hem.

Ben looked at Georgia doubtfully, obviously concerned. "Black?" he asked.

Georgia smiled. "Black and white is the fashion statement this spring. It's no longer reserved for widows and sophisticated ladies at cocktail parties."

"You don't like it?" Linda asked him, obviously willing to reconsider if he didn't approve.

"It's beautiful," he reassured her quickly. "I just thought you might be…a little…young for black. But if your mom approves, I think it's great."

That remark was so parental that Georgia was alternately touched and charmed. Then she felt guilty that she'd made it impossible for Ben and Linda to ever know each other as father and daughter.

Linda ran back to pay for the dress and returned as Georgia was getting ready to lock the doors. Ben was at the back of the store. She handed him a fistful of bills. "Thanks, Ben. It didn't even take half of what you gave me."

He handed it back to her. "Keep it," he said. "You and Lacey can go shopping for a couple of things for the summer."

Then, with startling insight, Linda curled her arm in his and pulled him to a stop as he reached for his jacket. Her dark eyes concerned, she asked, "You're not getting ready to…to leave, or anything?"

Trapped between an unwillingness to lie to her and an unwillingness to tell her the truth, Ben evaded the question. "I'll have to go back to Portland sometime."

"Why?"

Why, indeed. "I just stayed here to keep an eye on your mom. Pretty soon Phil will find whoever's been harassing her."

Linda looked from him to Georgia, who waited for them by the door. "Mom will *always* need someone to keep an eye on her, whether someone's harassing her or not." Then, on the chance that hadn't been clear enough, she added. "I don't want you to go. Lacey doesn't, either. And we've always had our say in what goes on in this family."

Ben grabbed his jacket and put an arm around her shoulders, leading her toward the door. "Well, I'm not going anywhere for a while yet. Right now, we should be thinking about how great you're going to look tonight."

Linda looked up at him another moment, obviously considering whether or not to let him sidestep the issue. She finally relented and put her arm around his waist. Ben felt himself relax. Then she said as they walked to the truck, "There's a special dance tonight for the princesses and their fathers. Will you dance with me?"

Relaxation fled and he realized there would be no clean and easy way out of his relationship with the Madison women. He loved them all and they loved him. He had to clear his throat before the reply would come out. "I'd be honored."

GEORGIA PRESSED the doorbell and waited with Linda in front of Shelly's door while Ben sat in the truck. Linda looked grim and subdued.

"I know you consider her your friend," Georgia said softly, "but she has used you, she's been selfish, and she faked an illness so that someone else would do the hard part of her job for her. Then she wanted the job back when it was time for the fun. You have no reason to feel guilty about this."

Linda nodded, but before she could speak, the door opened and Shelly stood there in jeans and a plain white T-shirt. Her eyes and the tip of her nose were red. In the two years Shelly and Linda had been friends, Georgia had never seen the other girl without makeup. Her hair was always perfectly groomed, and her clothes were the envy of every girl in school. But now it was as though she were someone else—a *real* teenager, though a distinctly unhappy one. Georgia felt a pang of sadness for her, then pushed it away.

"Hi, Shelly," Linda said. "I…"

"Come on in." Shelly stepped back to let them into the living room, then closed the door. It was a beautiful room, Georgia noted, though littered with schoolbooks and clothes and generally unkempt. In the middle of the coffee table was an empty pizza carton. Shelly looked at Linda without animosity, but Georgia seemed to make her uncomfortable. "I'll get the crown and your shoes."

Shelly was halfway up the stairs when the telephone rang. "I'll get it," Linda said, running to the kitchen. Georgia wandered after her as a kettle whistled. She turned the burner off. On the counter beside it was a cup with what smelled like a cocoa mixture in it. Georgia noted that the wastebasket near the end of the counter was filled with bags from various hamburger chains, a carryout chicken box and another flat pizza carton. She frowned. Shelly's mother obviously didn't make sure that well-balanced meals counteracted the negative effects of fast food.

Georgia turned away from the counter when there was a long pause on the telephone. "Wouldn't you like to tell her yourself, Mrs. Gordon?" Linda glanced at Georgia with a pained expression. "She'll be down… Yes, all right. Sure, I'll tell her." Linda hung up the phone. She sat at the small round table in the middle of the room, pulling a yellow paper napkin out of a holder shaped like a daisy. "That was Shelly's mom," she said, opening the napkin and studying it as though it were something unique. "She's in Cannon Beach with her boyfriend. She's been there since Tuesday."

Georgia pulled a chair out and sat across from Linda.

"She called to tell Shelly she's not coming home for the dance." She held the napkin where the fold lines crossed in the center and shook it as though it were a hankie. "She doesn't even know Shelly's not going to be princess. She thinks she still is, and she's only half an hour away, and she's not coming back to see if she's chosen queen. Does that stink, or what?"

Shelly walked into the kitchen, a glittering rhinestone crown in one hand and Linda's white dress heels in the other. She put the shoes on the table and the crown on Linda's head, stepping back to evaluate the effect. "Your hair looks beautiful," she said, her face composed, her eyes so hurt Georgia had difficulty looking into them.

"I had it done this afternoon," Linda said. Her voice was small.

"Be sure you wear the crown a little forward,"

Shelly said, reaching out again to adjust it. "Everybody tilts it back, but it looks better forward." She fluffed Linda's bangs. "There."

"That was your mom," Linda said quietly. "She…she's staying in Cannon Beach for a few more days."

There was only a second of surprise, a kind of disbelief that a dark suspicion had been confirmed. Then Shelly shrugged as though it didn't matter. She picked up one of the shoes she had placed in front of Linda and shook her head over it. "I couldn't believe you were going to let me borrow these."

Linda pulled the crown from her head and swallowed. "You're my friend, Shelly."

Shelly looked at Linda, tears brimming in her eyes. Then she blinked them back and tossed her head. It wasn't as much control, Georgia thought, as the reaction of a child who simply wasn't used to having anyone around to dry her tears.

"Look." Linda became brisk, handing the shoes and crown to Georgia and turning Shelly toward the living room. "I didn't come here for the crown and the shoes. God, I'm glad you're better. I can't wait to get rid of all this princess stuff and get behind the cookie table, where I belong. I thought maybe you'd want to bring your stuff and get ready at my house. Then you can spend the night…."

Shelly resisted Linda's efforts to push her through the doorway. "I wasn't sick," she insisted. "I let you do the hard stuff and—"

"I know," Linda interrupted impatiently. "Being stupid is kind of like being sick. But you're well now, aren't you?"

Shelly looked at Linda, then nodded firmly. "Yes. I'm well."

Linda pushed her toward the stairs. "Then you've got to be princess. I've hated it. You owe me this, Shelly."

Shelly glanced at Georgia, her eyes uncertain. Georgia swallowed with difficulty. "Get your things. There's a ride waiting for us."

Ben raised an eyebrow as Shelly and Linda piled into the truck after Georgia. Georgia whispered under the girls' giggles, "If you were her father and you'd witnessed what just went on in there, you'd have probably bought her the Hope diamond."

LACEY WAS INCREDULOUS. "What do you mean she's letting Shelly keep the title?" She followed her mother from the counter to the table, where Georgia placed a plate of cold cuts. Linda and Shelly were upstairs. "The junior class council voted! Mrs. Butler was glad I..."

Georgia turned to look at her. Ben looked up from slicing cheese. Lacey glanced defensively from one to the other before folding her arms and staring at the table. "Well, somebody had to tell her! If either of you guys had done it, you'd have broken faith or something. With me, it's just her stupid little sister doing everything wrong." She shrugged. "Everybody was *glad* Mrs. Butler thought Linda should keep the title. The whole school's been talking about how well she did with those talks. And they know how hard she's worked on the cookies." Lacey shook her head in disbelief. "And now she's blown it."

Georgia hugged her. "She hasn't blown it, Lace." Briefly, she explained about the call from Shelly's mother and Shelly's admission of guilt to Linda. "She felt sorry for her, and she wanted to do something for her. Thank you for calling Mrs. Butler. I'm glad you cared so much."

"*You* called?" Dressed in sweat bottoms and a T-shirt, her hair wrapped in a towel, Linda walked up to her sister. She wore a frown and Lacey took a discreet step back, her chin angled up.

"Yeah. You got a problem with that?"

"It was my business."

"Your business is to play Mother Teresa to everybody, and some people don't deserve it." Lacey raised both arms despairingly. "Why did you let her keep the title when she did that to you?"

"Because," Linda said quietly, "the title is *all* she has." She looked from Georgia to Ben and back to Lacey, sincere affection in her eyes. "I have lots. I figure I can afford to be generous. Can she borrow your white shoes?"

Lacey put a despairing hand to her forehead. "Sure. Why not?"

"Where are they? I can't find them."

Lacey started for the stairs, then turned back to Georgia as Linda ran up ahead of her. "She is so *weird*!" she said.

Georgia dried her hands on her apron and went to the counter to put rolls in a basket. Ben walked up beside her and passed her his handkerchief. "I don't suppose you'd let me leave you here," he asked, "and take them to Portland with me?"

Georgia dabbed at the tears running down her cheeks. "No," she said firmly. "They're the best part of me. When you go back to Portland, I want it to be hard for you. I want you to miss them as well as me, and you will, you know." She sniffed and pulled herself together. "You'll be miserable without us, Ben."

He leaned against the counter and looked down at her, nodding. "Very probably. But I'll be comforted by the knowledge that you'll have terminal insomnia."

"You'll have tenants no one is trying to kill," she predicted grimly, "and all the excitement will go out of your life."

"But I'll know that you're going to work without breakfast and that when you come home, there'll be no one around to help you with dinner."

She squared her shoulders and turned to face him fully. "You'll be safe from love," she said.

He straightened to his full height and nodded, as though the joke were really on her. "And you'll be safe from living."

EVERYONE WAS at the dance. Music blared from a live orchestra, miles of streamers were strung from corner to corner across the high school gymnasium, and, on the crowded floor, Georgia looked up at Ben, against whom she was pressed like a sardine in a can. The imprint of his body against hers was making her consider moving to Portland or kidnapping him so that he would be unable to return.

Bea danced by with Phil, who managed to look graceful despite his hobble, and Ragnar with Karen. "Have you noticed," Ben asked, "That Bea and Ragnar look happy?"

Georgia glanced at them with a smile, trying to distract herself from her own problems. "I told her we were serious about each other," she said lightly. "I think there'll be a wedding announcement one day soon."

"Them or us?"

She looked at him scoldingly.

He shrugged. "I just wondered how far you were willing to carry the lie. Why didn't you just tell her to live her own life—that you can handle yours?"

She looked at him as though he were simple. "Where do you think Linda gets her passion for taking care of everyone? Bea won't be happy until I walk down the aisle again. But she'll move to Portland with Ragnar, thinking it's imminent. I'll explain later that it didn't work out. Then it'll be too late for her."

"That's deceitful," he accused.

She dismissed all guilt with a shrug. "All's fair... Have you seen Linda?"

"Yes." Ben's smile was fond and amused. "That young man who's traded his letterman's jacket for a suit tonight has kept her dancing in that corner behind the band for the past hour. She's glowing."

"Where?" Georgia stopped and stood on tiptoe to try to see beyond the dancers to her daughter.

"Stop, you'll embarrass her." With an arm around her waist, Ben pulled her aside as the music changed tempo. "Do you tango?" he asked.

"No," she admitted, "but I've always wanted to be dipped within an inch of the floor."

Without hesitation or warning, Ben swung her backward, his hand catching her waist to stop her a hairbreadth from the gym floor. She swallowed a little cry of momentary alarm, hanging on to his shoulder for all she was worth.

"Like that?" he asked.

She giggled, trusting him completely despite her precarious position. When he righted her, her heart was pounding and she guessed it had as much to do with the look in his eye as the scare.

"Sort of," she replied, wrapping her arm around his waist as he led her off the floor. "Except that my dress doesn't have enough ruffles, and you're supposed to be dressed like Jose Greco."

"You mean I can't tango in my white suit with my hair parted down the middle?" They stopped at the punch table and he filled a paper cup for her.

"Wrong image altogether," she said, sipping while he poured himself a cup. "One's guarded control, and one's passion."

They found a spot against the wall and stopped there to watch the brave couples on the floor. Among them were Wally and Mrs. Butler and the Johnsons. "You're presuming to know what's in the Victorian gentleman's heart," Ben said. "You don't really think he's pursuing the lady into the garden to talk about flowers, do you?"

She raised an eyebrow over the rim of her cup. "I think he chose the lady in the garden to fall in love with because she was safe. She had career plans, remember? He might feel passion for her, but it's superficial. He can easily put it aside when it's over."

Georgia wasn't sure what was driving her. She was fooling no one with her little fantasy couple. The futility of their love for each other was breaking her heart, yet she felt powerless to do anything about it. So blaming Ben came easily. She couldn't help their situation, but certainly he could, if he wanted to.

"Come here." His voice was quiet and companionable as he put an arm around her shoulders and led her farther along the wall. She saw Karen beyond the door, and she presumed he was working his way toward her to say hello. She went along docilely. But instead of passing the doors, Ben went through them into the night, pulling her with him.

"What are we...?" she began to ask, but he didn't appear to be listening. Towing her along, he turned away from the sea of cars in the parking lot and went through the covered walk into the courtyard. It was dark and empty and smelled of new-mown grass. He backed her up against a post, a hand on each side of her head imprisoning her.

"Superficial?" he asked, one tight, biting word.

Her heart was in her throat. It wasn't fear of him but fear of what she felt for him—fear that the love she'd controlled through lighthearted banter and careless allusions would finally rise up to have the last laugh. Her breath seemed to stop, every nerve was alert and waiting. *You can't pretend it doesn't exist,* her body seemed to say. *Or that you don't care. I am raw with longing, desperate for his touch.*

"Superficial?" he repeated, his voice rising a note and a decibel. "I'll show you superficial."

He wove the fingers of both hands into her hair. She put her hands against his chest, self-preservation demanding that she stop him. She hadn't breath to speak, but as he lowered his head, she tried to dodge him, pushing against his chest. His hands in her hair wouldn't allow her to turn her face, and her hands pushing against him did nothing but remind the sensors in her fingertips of his warmth, his muscle and the strong steadiness of his heartbeat. She uttered a helpless little sigh of resignation as his mouth closed over hers.

Warmth filled her instantly. From hair to thin-strapped high-heeled sandals she was reminded of everything Ben had brought back into her life. She leaned against him, wrapped her arms around his middle and felt the security, the stalwart support, the paradoxical strength of his tenderness. Everything came right with her again. She wasn't a woman who had lost so much but one who had found everything. She wasn't a woman with dark questions unanswered but one with miracles revealed.

Then Ben's hands began to move on her, down her back and over her hips, and the warmth turned to fire. Everything she had regained of her womanhood that wonderful Sunday afternoon came to life like a bouquet from a magician's coat. Tingling sensation ran the length of her spine, along her limbs, to settle at the heart of her being and make her wonder why she'd ever decided to turn away from the future to settle the past.

He'd made a mistake. The minute Ben's mouth closed over Georgia's, the moment his hands traced the curve of her hips and he swallowed her little breath of pleasure, he realized this little lesson would probably teach him more than it would teach her. He wanted her to know that she could choose to live her life without him, but she couldn't blame him for her decision. His love for her ran deeper than anything he'd ever known, and he wouldn't let her make their eventual separation easy on herself by making him responsible.

God! He'd forgotten the point of the whole thing. Tenderness and passion raged side by side in him, and he couldn't find his way out of the confusion. Tenderness was a soft thing, something sweet and light. Yet when she went limp in his arms, he felt it with an intensity that was debilitating. And beside it, heat flared, demanding action and satisfaction. His hands trembled, his spine went soft, yet this frightening fire raged, incompatible with his inclination to be tender.

For the first time ever, in a life in which he'd made his own decisions since he'd been sixteen, he didn't know what to do.

With her lips clinging to his, her hands roaming his back, her body delighting in his, he couldn't leave her. Yet, if he stayed, he'd have to sift through the past with her, and he didn't want to do that.

"Ben? Mom?" He heard the voice as though from far away. It belonged to Linda. Georgia stirred against him, and he took a step back from her, needing air, needing space.

"There you are!" Linda appeared beside them in the shadows of the courtyard, rubbing her hands along her bare arms. "Mrs. Hansen said she saw you come out here. What are you doing?"

When Ben said nothing, Georgia replied a little breathlessly, "Talking."

Linda chided softly, "That's not what it looked like."

Ben pinched Linda's chin. "It's a form of lip-reading. What did you want?"

She took his hand. "It's time for the father-daughter dance, and Mrs. Butler wants me to join the princesses. She got Mr. Parrish to dance with Shelly. Can you come?"

"Of course."

Georgia trailed behind as Linda led Ben at a run back to the gym. Apparently Ben's absence had held up the dance, and there was a smattering of teasing applause as he followed Linda to the circle in the middle of the floor. He'd made a lot of friends since his arrival in Astoria, and he returned their good-natured ribbing with a smile and a wave. Then he turned his attention to Linda as the orchestra struck up something mellow and nostalgic.

Georgia couldn't decide who looked more proud, Linda or Ben. Linda beamed, her face alight with the same affection and adoration she'd once shown Gary. Ben, his long arms cradling her daughter, was all protective tenderness, a love and respect for her in his demeanor that twisted a knife in Georgia's middle.

Suddenly, an arm came around Georgia and a tissue was pressed into her hands. Karen squeezed her shoulders and whispered, "If you let him go, you're a jerk."

Georgia heaved a ragged sigh and glanced wryly at her friend. "You're a pal, Karen."

Karen nodded, accepting the praise. "I'm here for you, Georgie."

CHAPTER SIXTEEN

ASTORIA HAD GONE wild. Traffic was bumper-to-bumper on the highway in front of the high school and swarms of people moved across the lawn and into the gym, where booths were set up. As Georgia tried to reach the cookie booth with the last batch of chocolate chips, macaroons and shortbreads, she began to doubt that she would make it. While she stood helpless in the middle of the crowd, she smiled to herself at the thought that, despite the press of people, it would be impossible to faint. Not only could one not fall down, but the aromas of the Swedish meatballs, Norwegian *lefse*—a kind of tortilla covered with cinnamon sugar—Danish *abelskiver* and Finnish biscuit, kept up one's hope that sustenance was just a shove away.

"Georgia!"

Unable to turn her body, Georgia turned her head toward the angry shout of her name. Ben wedged his way between two teenage boys beside her who were munching on cookies. His eyes looked exactly as his voice had sounded, dark and stormy. "Where have you been?" he demanded.

She accepted the confrontation with a sigh, wondering how he'd found her in this crush of bodies. "I went back home to get Linda's last batch of cookies."

"You were supposed to wait for me."

"You took too long."

He reacted to her flip reply with the annoyance she knew it would cause. Still, he made an obvious effort to keep a grip on his temper. "Look," he said quietly, "this is not the time to start getting careless. You might think nothing could happen to you in this crowd of people, but I think you're more vulnerable. You've put up with me this long, certainly you can take it for a little while longer."

The truth was, she couldn't. After last night, she found it impossible to be in the same room with him, much less pressed against him by a crowd of thousands. This morning, despite the girls' excited chatter, breakfast had been an ordeal. She'd even ridden to the school in the back of the station wagon with Linda on the pretext of going over her price list for the cookies. Sitting in the front, Lacey had talked Ben's ear off. When Linda had run low on cookies earlier than expected and Ben had been under the counter, trying to see what was wrong with the electrical outlet into which the coffeepot was plugged, Georgia had taken the opportunity to escape. Her emotional stability had become more important than her physical safety.

Ben looked into her eyes, waiting for another smart remark. He could cheerfully throttle her for going off and leaving him to worry for an interminable thirty minutes that whatever lunatic was after her had finally found her alone. Then he saw all the misery he was feeling reflected in her eyes, and he relaxed a little. She was a victim of the same memories that tortured him. There was something comforting in that.

"If you do that again," he threatened with a grim smile, reaching forward to push through the crowd, "I'll sic Bea on you."

They emerged in front of the Scandinavian Women's

booth, which had various examples of ethnic embroidery hung from a line stretched across its top. An older woman customer was haggling with Bea over the price of a tea towel. With customary diplomacy, Bea pulled the towel away from the woman and turned to wait on someone else.

"Hey, you two!" Behind Bea, Ragnar sipped from a paper cup. "I hope that's more cookies. I've almost bought them out." Ragnar pointed to the high school's cookie booth on the other side of the wall. Young people and adults waited five-deep the entire length of the counter. Georgia stood on tiptoe and saw Linda, flushed with the closeness of the room and the frantic pace she'd kept since arriving this morning, looking despairingly into an empty box.

"Linda!" she shouted.

Linda's head came up to scan the crowd. Georgia handed the box to Ben, who held it over his head and forced his way forward. Linda reached way up to take it from him. "Thanks, Ben. Wait." Ben stopped at Linda's command, and she reached into the box, took out a chocolate-chip cookie as large in circumference as a dessert plate and handed it to him over the heads of those waiting in line.

"Hey!" Jasper Johnson complained laughingly.

Ben blew Linda a kiss, then shrugged at Jasper. "I'm a friend of the family."

Georgia raised an eyebrow at Ben. "I'm the one who went for the cookies, and *you* accept the reward."

Ben snapped the cookie into two pieces and handed her one. "Life is filled with inequities. You have to learn to be philosophical about it."

Georgia snatched his piece away from him and took a bite out of it. "Be philosophical about that," she advised, and turned to try to make her way across the floor.

He spun her around, all the anger gone from him. There was a hint of laughter in his eyes. She tried not to notice that it was overridden by sadness. He took her unbitten piece of cookie and held it up. "This one has more chocolate chips than the other half. I was trying to be generous, but now you've got the dinky piece. Cheaters never prosper."

She looked up at him with wide dark eyes, filled with an inability to believe that the warmth they always felt in each other's presence couldn't lead to something permanent. Her cheeks were pink, her lips parted. Ben could take it no longer. He leaned down and kissed her gently, lovingly, trying desperately to remember where they were. He felt himself about to ignite. He lifted his head, and Georgia gave him a half smile. "Who says?" she asked.

GEORGIA AND KAREN shared the five to seven shift in the Downtown Enrichment Association booth. They sold Astoria T-shirts, sweatshirts and pennants. The crowd thinned a little during the dinner hour, but for the most part, the pace remained hectic. During the brief respite in the surge of customers, Karen restocked the counter from a cardboard box beneath it and sighed. "Do you realize that in Paris at this hour men are visiting their mistresses?"

Georgia looked at her in surprise. "Do we care?"

Karen unfolded a baby-size shirt and hung it up to replace one that had been sold. "I was just thinking how much more civilized it is than this commercial ritual."

"Cheating on one's wife is not civilized."

"Well, maybe not that part. But they're probably having champagne and little pâté sandwiches and listening to Mozart."

"The French are earthier than Mozart."

"Well, then, they're doing the cancan. Anyway, they're having fun."

"Aren't you having fun?"

"No," Karen denied instantly. "I'd rather be out there shopping and eating." Then she looked at her friend in sudden seriousness. "Are you having fun?"

It should be fun, Georgia thought. She loved being part of this hardworking, fun-loving community. But until she settled things with Ben, she could find little pleasure in anything.

She looked up from the shirts she was storing by size to see Ben and her daughters several booths over buying *lefse*. Lacey was an avowed addict of the stuff. He led the girls on to the next booth, an arm around each of them to protect them from the crowd, and they leaned into him, laughing.

Since Gary had died, she'd lived her entire life with the girls' needs uppermost in her mind. And they'd been good children, responsive and obedient. The thought of hurting them by sending Ben out of their lives was almost more than she could bear. But starting over would leave her own life with that dark doubt that would never be eased.

Without responding to Karen's question, Georgia slapped a stack of shirts down and opened the side panel of the booth to let herself out.

Karen reached out to catch her arm. "Where are you going? Ben said you're supposed to—"

Georgia rolled her eyes. "Can I go to the bathroom?"

Karen studied Georgia for a moment, then released her arm and glanced at the clock over the basketball hoop. "You have five minutes."

Shaking her head in exasperation, Georgia pushed her way through the exit door behind the booths and walked the long corridor to the rest rooms. A few moments later she wandered lazily down the corridor in the other direction, toward the open door at the back of the gym. The sweet smells of late spring filled the air. She took several steps outside, putting her hands at the back of her waist and stretching her back, enjoying the quiet. A tall chain link fence separated the school from the hillside, and not a soul was visible in the neighborhood beyond. She smiled at the thought. Everyone in town was in the gym.

The sudden sound behind her didn't startle her. Certain it was just another vendor out for a breath of air, she turned with a smile, determined to lighten her mood with a little friendly conversation. Instead, she caught the barest glimpse of a burly figure before something was thrown over her and the beautiful afternoon was blotted out.

She'd never understood until that moment how anyone could be immobilized by fear. She'd been unable to believe that sheer annoyance over being manhandled wouldn't galvanize a victim into a vicious reaction. She hadn't counted on the debilitating effect of the first few moments of complete disbelief. Even after the nasty attacks on her home, her business and her person, her reaction to being bundled into an old blanket and tossed over someone's shoulder was total surprise. She heard the squeal of brakes and was grabbed roughly by other hands, then pulled into a vehicle and forced to lie down before the shock diminished enough to allow her to react.

Enshrouded as she was, probably in the back of a closed car, her awakening brain told her screaming would be useless. Her hands were trapped by the blanket over her—a moldy woolen one, she began to notice—but her feet were free. She felt the opposite side of the seat with them and pushed with all she was worth, wriggling at the same time, struggling to free her hands enough to claw at the blanket.

There was an oath, a shout and the squeal of brakes again. Rough hands pinned her ankles painfully, and a familiar voice said quietly, "Keep driving, Luke. Everything's under control." The arms holding the blanket around her remained gentle, and she suddenly understood why. Ben had been right. "Be still, my love," Wally said, patting her shoulder. "This discomfort will be over in a moment."

Shock immobilized her once again. She tried desperately to think, to analyze, to conclude, but she couldn't. It didn't make sense. Wally had been behind the incompetent, or perhaps distracted, attempt on her life, the vandalism of her store and the fire in her living room. But, why? He was a pillar of the community, her lifelong friend. Confusion became stronger than fear. Almost.

After a few moments, she felt the car stop. "Now." Wally's voice remained quiet but with a new, higher note in it she guessed was nervousness or desperation. She lay still and waited for him to go on. "I'm going to take the blanket off of you, you're going to sit up, and you and I and my friend here are going to walk into your shop." He paused a moment and she felt his hand stroke gently along her shoulder. Under the blanket, she closed her eyes against the touch as a shudder ran through her. "I would never hurt you, Georgia," he went on, "but my friend doesn't share my affection for you. He's tried to frighten you several times without the slightest remorse—he wouldn't hesitate to stop you from screaming or running away or whatever else is crossing your mind at this moment. Do you understand?"

She nodded and the blanket came off. She sat up and found herself on Wally's knees in the back of his Cadillac on the side street near her shop. She looked into his eyes in search of her childhood friend, her co-worker in so many community activities since she'd become an adult, her partner in the effort to obtain funding for the restoration of the Jeremiah houses. He wasn't there. In his place was a man with identical features but with a look in his eyes that was alarmingly remote and chillingly deadly.

Another shudder touched every vertebra in her spine. Until Ben had walked into her life, she'd refused to betray fear to anyone. Now she tried to recall that discarded trait and deny her terror. She spread both hands and shrugged. "Unfortunately, you failed to abduct my purse. No keys."

Wally smiled, a cold gesture that made her wonder if just a little bit of fear wasn't called for. "How do you think Carl got in the day he and his friends trashed your shop?"

Georgia turned to Carl sitting beside Wally and saw the rest of the face she'd caught just a glimpse of when the blanket was thrown over her. Snarl would have been a better name for him. He was probably not much older than Linda, but his head was shaved, his eyes were hard, and his mouth looked as though it hadn't curved up in years. He was built like a wrestler. Perhaps even considerable fear was called for, she thought.

"He walked through the bricks," she guessed.

Wally smiled again. Carl didn't.

"Underground, of course." Georgia pointed to the parking lot of the now vacant department store visible beyond the car window. "One of the easiest entrances in town is right beyond that bush." A stubborn weed-like bush grew tall and full at the corner of a railing that separated the sloping parking lot from the sidewalk. It made the entrance almost invisible to anyone passing by quickly. She added affably, "All the crooks and lowlifes use it."

Carl made a subhuman sound deep in his throat. Wally put a quelling hand on him. "The tunnels are the basis of our whole operation," he said to Georgia. "I want you to see it before we go.... Drive on home, Luke. We'll meet you there."

Operation? Go where? Questions nudged aside the fear and confusion as Georgia was led to the tunnel opening. Wally kept a light grip on her arm, and Carl walked behind them. Downtown was virtually deserted. Almost everyone in the county was at the high school, and all the shops were closed, except the supermarket across the street. Everyone going in and out of the market was too preoccupied with thoughts of dinner to notice two men and a woman disappearing into the tunnels under the street.

"MOM'S SHIFT IS OVER in ten minutes." Lacey tossed her head back to catch the last drop of soda, then slapped her paper cup on the picnic table. She smiled at Ben, who sat across from her. "Then I think we should all go out to dinner to celebrate. On you, of course.''

He raised an eyebrow, thinking how much he would miss her wonderful silliness. ''Celebrate what?''

Lacey leaned toward Linda, who sat beside her, and put an arm around her shoulders. ''Linda's superb job with the cookies. I mean, never in the history of the high school's cookie booth have they had such great cookies, made so much money and run out of stuff to sell by midafternoon! Then, of course, there's her moment of almost royalty.''

Linda flicked at Lacey as though she were a bug. ''You're touching me, peasant,'' she said grandly.

Lacey ignored her. ''Then there's Mom's excellent job as cochairperson of this thing. The whole thing's made more money than ever, and everyone says it's run smoother than ever.''

Ben nodded consideringly. ''So we'd be celebrating your sister's and your mother's accomplishments. Does that mean *you* can't come?''

Lacey dismissed that possibility with a careless wave of her free hand. ''Who do you think made them what they are today?''

''Are you suggesting you did?''

''Of course. All the trouble I cause builds character. Because they can live with me, they think they can do anything. And they go out and prove it.'' She smiled winningly. ''Chinese food. What do you say?''

''Italian,'' Linda said, grimacing. ''I never want to see another cookie, even a fortune cookie.''

''Linda, Lacey!'' Ragnar emerged from the crowd with a short, round man his age. ''Your grandmother says it's time for your shift in *her* booth.''

"I forgot!" Linda scrambled to her feet, pulling Lacey with her. "Come on."

"There's nothing to eat in their booth," Lacey complained as Linda pushed her into the crowd.

"Can we join you?" Ragnar asked Ben. "This is Arne Rytsala, a friend of mine. Arne, Ben Stratton."

Ben stood to shake hands. "Sure. I'd like the company. I have another half hour to kill before Georgia's free."

"Arne and I went to school together," Ragnar explained. "He probably knows everyone in this room."

Ben couldn't suppress the temptation to ask, "Would you know anything about a postal inspector who lived in this county? Passed away seven years ago."

Ben stared in disbelief when Arne nodded instantly. "Yes. That would be Ned Johnson. Lived in an old house on Franklin. Good man."

"Ben! Ben..." Phil, breathless, slipped onto the bench beside Ben.

"Hi, Phil. Wait." He turned his attention back to Arne. "I understand Johnson had no family."

Arne thought back. "That's right. His wife died when she was very young. She was a Simonsen from across the river. Her father—"

Ben put his hand on Arne's arm to stop his relation of the family history. "You wouldn't know what happened to his things when he died."

"Ben..." Phil tried to interrupt.

"Phil, please," Ben said. "I'm onto something here. What happened to his stuff, Arne?"

"Well, you see, the funny thing," Arne said, clearing his throat, then adjusting his glasses, "was that Ned's father was postmaster of Ashville at the other end of the county. When they added a wing to the post office and made a new office for the new postmaster, they let Ned have all his father's stuff from the old one. Oak desk and files, hand-painted oil lamp, maps from—''

"Arne," Ben said forcefully to call him back. "What happened to it?"

"The museum got it all. Ned left it to them."

Ben's heart gave a lurch and he felt Phil stiffen beside him. "Which museum?"

"The Columbia River Pioneers Museum. Right here in Astoria, on the hill."

Ben turned to Phil. "That's too much of a coincidence."

Phil was already struggling off the bench, Ben following. "It's not a coincidence at all. I came to tell you I just got the report from the state police crime lab on the straw. Both pieces—from Georgia's shop and from Wally's house—have no detectable traces of herbicides or pesticides and no moisture."

"Meaning they're old."

"Very old."

"Ben!" Karen appeared between the two men, her face pale, her eyes a little wild. "I can't find Georgia anywhere. I…'' Distracted by the sight of her husband, she threw her arms around him, almost smiling, but not quite. "Oh, honey! I just tried to call you. You've got to find her. She was—''

"How long's she been missing?" Ben demanded, wondering why he'd been stupid enough to think she was safe in a booth only twenty feet away from him.

"She left about twenty minutes ago to go to the bathroom and—''

"Twenty minutes ago!" Ben roared, his worst fear taking form despite all his efforts to remain calm.

"I know, I know!" Karen closed her eyes against his anger, putting both hands to her mouth in distress. "She just took off and I was swamped with customers after she left. Before I had time to realize she hadn't come back, fifteen minutes had passed. Then my relief person came and I ran to the rest room, but she wasn't there." A little sob rose in her voice. "I'm sorry."

"I'm going to radio for backup, Ben," Phil said, hobbling away as he spoke. "Meet me at Bishop's."

Ben turned to Karen. "Will you ask Bea to stay with the girls until she hears from me?"

"Of course."

"Rags, will you come with me?"

"Try to stop me."

"Mr. Rytsala—" Ben looked down at the older man "—I owe you."

The man smiled. "I won't forget to collect."

THE TUNNELS smelled of urine, decay and standing water. They were high enough and wide enough to house a small subway, Georgia thought, fascinated despite her predicament. With little traffic overhead, it was eerily quiet, and as they passed the remnant of an old shop window and a faded sign on a decaying wall advertising pipes, she almost smiled, enjoying this subterranean glimpse of the past far more than her present companions.

They stopped at a door Georgia had seen from this side more times than she cared to count this year— every time she'd had to repair or rehang or reseal it after her shop had been broken into. Wally pulled Georgia aside and gestured Carl forward. Bracing herself to watch her door with its new double bolt be destroyed by the behemoth, she gasped in disbelief when Carl simply turned the knob and the door opened.

Wally laughed at her expression. "Yesterday, when I came by the shop to pick up your master list of participating groups and organizations, I took a moment to run down into the basement and unbolt the door."

"Yesterday?" Vaguely she remembered the confusion when her shipment had arrived at the same moment that Wally had appeared to get the list. She'd sent him back to her office for it while Ben was helping a customer carry a large purchase out to her car.

"I've been planning this for some time, Georgia," he explained. "And I've had an eye on you all day, waiting for my chance. I'd have gotten you when you went home for the cookies, except that Jasper chose that moment to tell me in great detail what an excellent job I'm doing with the new exhibit at the museum. Come on."

For an instant she was relieved to find herself in the basement of her shop. The familiarity of the empty stock boxes and the table she worked on with her pricing tools diminished her sense of having crossed into another, meaner dimension—until she saw Carl, with that eager-to-smash-her look on his face on one side of her, and Wally, wide-eyed and a little mad looking on the other. He pointed to the steps. "Upstairs."

Georgia did as he asked, trying desperately to formulate a plan. Pleading for mercy was all she could think of, and that simply went against the grain. At the top of the stairs, Wally gestured her toward the shop. "We're going to the safe to get your cash drawer out, then we're coming back here to your office. Stay along the wall, out of sight of the windows."

"The only thing in the safe is my cash advance of one hundred dollars," she explained, talking to him over her shoulder as they formed a small parade to the front of the store. "You know I deposit every night."

Wally watched her open the safe, remove the drawer, then close the safe again, all the while keeping an eye on the windows. He pushed her before him toward the back room and her office. "I don't care about the money. I just want it to look as though you got rid of all the evidence and ran away with me."

In her office, Georgia turned to him in confusion. "Evidence of what?"

He removed a bank bag from his pocket and handed it to her. "Put the money in here. Evidence of embezzlement."

She forced her brain to function. "Wally, why would I have stolen from myself?"

He shrugged. "You decided to leave with me instead of paying back Bea and the bank."

Fear was becoming terror. Still, she made herself think. "No one who knows me, and that's almost everyone in Astoria, would believe for a minute that I ran off without my children."

"Of course they will," he said with a silky confidence that made her finally believe without a doubt that he was crazy. "That kind of thing happens all the time now. A woman becomes successful, sees what she can have if she isn't tied to anything—or anyone—and she leaves. People are shocked at first, disbelieving, but it's a sign of our times and they accept it."

She looked at him levelly. "We must know a different class of woman."

"We all want to be comfortable," he said. He took

the ledger and bank bag from her. "And you and I are going to be very comfortable, Georgia."

She looked at him, afraid to ask the question.

"In Mexico," he said. "I know it's unimaginative, but it's nearby and you can get completely lost in the little towns. The law can be bought."

She gulped back a sob and said lightly, "I don't speak the language."

"That's all right." He put a hand to her neck and rubbed a thumb along her bottom lip. When she flinched his hand tightened and his eyes became lustful as well as mad. "I'm not ever going to let you out of the house."

Her mind screamed for Ben. It was all she could do to keep from voicing the scream. Wally's hand at her throat tightened painfully, and *he* screamed, "Don't think about him! I've seen that look in your eyes. I know it's for him!" He quieted as suddenly as he'd exploded. He adjusted his tie and swallowed. "Don't think about him, Georgia," he said gently. "You've been mine since high school. I let Gary have you because he had been my friend. But Stratton can't have you. Not ever."

Terror subsided in a sense of unreality as Georgia followed Wally back down the stairs to the basement, Carl bringing up the rear. Wally loved her, if what he felt could be defined by that word. He'd loved her since high school. How could she have never known?

She was distracted from that question when they went back through the basement door into the tunnel. They followed the same route by which they'd come, presumably headed toward the car—except that Wally had told his driver to take the car home. Were they simply going to emerge from the tunnels on the corner of Eleventh and Duane covered in dust and carrying her ledger and a bank bag? Even as deserted as downtown was, that seemed like a big chance to take for a man who had planned ahead.

But they didn't climb out of the tunnel. Wally continued to lead them down the dark, dank passageway. Then they took a turn into an even darker tunnel. This part of the underground system of corridors carried the same smell of age but not of humanity, as though time and the river had invaded it but man had forgotten it.

Wally stopped abruptly, his flashlight picking out a pile of rock against what looked like the end of the tunnel. Wally pulled Georgia back, and Carl began to toss the rocks aside. A black hole opened where the rocks had been. Georgia peered at it, straining to see. Another tunnel? she wondered. She'd heard that sometime in the forties, one of the tunnels had collapsed on two police officers chasing a suspect. The suspect and one officer had been killed, the other officer seriously injured. That tunnel had been sealed off after the incident.

Wally confirmed the story as Carl began to wriggle almost comically through the hole. "This is the tunnel that's been closed off for more than forty years," he said. "It's been infinitely useful to me."

She suspected she would hate herself for asking, but she did anyway. "Why?"

He smiled at her blandly as Carl reached back through the hole to take her hands. "Because it leads to the basement of one of the two Jeremiah houses."

Carl pulled her through the opening without effort and kept a biting grip on her wrist as Wally crawled after them. She glowered at the thug, but the effort was wasted in the shadows. They proceeded in darkness for another hundred feet, then stopped again as Carl trained the light on what seemed to be another pile of rock against another wall. She was not surprised when he began to toss more rocks aside to reveal another hole. This time there was light beyond it. He went through, pulling Georgia along. He didn't have to hold her this time because she was immobilized by shock with what she saw. She was indeed in the basement of a house, with its ancient wood-burning furnace and laundry chute. But stacked all around the basement were cartons of small appliances, VCRs, personal computers and other electronic products. Hanging on a clothesline near one wall were men's and women's clothing carefully covered with plastic. There were small pieces of furniture, musical instruments, jewelry and several items she recognized as part of her own inventory.

Wally leaned an elbow on a stack of boxed video cameras and grinned at her, obviously pleased with himself and her stunned reaction. "Did you really think that I'd be satisfied with being a mere historian, devoting his life to keeping Astoria's past alive?"

"Yes," she replied, "and I liked you better when I thought that. The man I thought you were wouldn't steal from his friends and let down a whole community of people who believe in him."

He shook his head at her pityingly, his hand reaching out to stroke her chin. She drew back, and he let his hand fall. "You're such an infant, Georgia," he said with a sigh. "History's fascinating, but there's no money in it. Stolen goods can be very lucrative. For enough to keep them in beer and funny smokes, half a dozen kids have helped me fill this basement over the last year." He looked at Carl with mild contempt. "And they've had a good time doing it. I guess they have their own scores to settle. I don't know and I don't care. I just know that there's enough here to keep you and me in clover until I can make bigger plans." He straightened and patted the top carton in the stack. "This'll all be shipped out tomorrow in a garbage truck." He smiled modestly. "Everyone will think I'm cleaning the house out for the museum. You and I will be halfway to Mexico."

Shock and fear were beginning to give way to anger. Georgia looked around at the goods that belonged to her hardworking fellow merchants, thought about the kids whose weaknesses Wally had preyed upon, about her own abduction and the panic her family and friends must be feeling by now, and she nearly forgot she was in danger.

"Whatever makes you think," she demanded, "that I would want to go anywhere with you? You've robbed my friends, used children and frightened me and my family. God! You've even tried to kill me!"

Wally shook his head calmly. "Carl tried to run you down. I asked him to frighten you, and he got a little carried away, but you're still here, aren't you? I thought you might give up the notion of restoring these houses. I've had a good setup here. I've made more in a year of creative theft than in my last eight years as curator. Your damned competence has shot me down. I knew everyone would think Rob MacKay was responsible for everything that happened to you."

"You shot Phil at MacKay's house."

He smiled and nodded. "I'd been watching for him to come back. The friend who warned him to stay away became *my* friend for a few bucks and told him when it was 'safe' to come back." He frowned. "That didn't work as neatly as I'd hoped. The police were supposed to catch him.'' He sighed, as though dismissing past mistakes. ''Anyway, I'll have to take a lower price on all this stuff because I'll have to liquidate it in a hurry.'' He shook his head, looking less upset than he sounded. ''But having you instead of the full price of the goods has been a comforting prospect since I began to realize you weren't going to scare and my little scheme was going to fall down around my ears.''

Georgia looked heavenward and shook her head. ''I'd be more misery than comfort to you, Wally, believe me.''

''We'll see about that,'' he said, nudging her toward the stairs.

She resisted his push. It occurred to her that if she could provoke him, say something to hurt him, perhaps it would disorient him so that she could get to the stairs, through the house and out the door before he and Carl could catch her. Slowly and deliberately she said, ''You might be able to make me go with you to Mexico, Wally, but I'd always be thinking of Ben Stratton. Always.''

''Don't say that!'' he roared. He grabbed a fistful of her hair and yanked it back until her eyes teared, her scalp stung and her neck felt as though it would break. ''You're mine! Mine!''

It occurred to her that this wasn't working out quite right. She had hoped his reaction would have been a shove toward the stairs. She would have gone up them docilely until she reached the top, then she would have run for all she was worth. But now Wally was between her and the stairs, and Carl had moved closer, blood lust in his eyes. On the edge of panic, she wondered what to do, when a board creaked loudly overhead. Then she had to wonder how to continue breathing when Wally wrapped an arm around her throat and dragged her into the shadows under the stairs.

CHAPTER SEVENTEEN

"LOOKS LIKE REINFORCEMENTS are already here." As Ben screeched to a halt at the corner of Eleventh and Duane, Ragnar squinted through the windshield at the two patrol cars parked in front of Bishop's place. An officer was frisking a young man leaning on the car while Phil, supported by his cane, talked to him.

Ben was out of the car and beside Phil in an instant. "Where is she?" he demanded.

"That's what I'm trying to find out," Phil replied patiently. "This young man was sitting behind the wheel of Wally's Cadillac when we arrived. Okay, Lucius, you started to tell me about the tunnel."

Lucius hesitated a moment and Ben grabbed his shirt collar in one fist. "Look, punk—"

"Hey! Hey." Phil pulled Ben's hand away and smoothed the boy's shirt. "There are rules against that sort of thing. This is a crook. We have to treat him right." Phil smiled at the boy, then said quietly, "Now, Luke. You tell us about the tunnel, or I'll let this nice man have you."

Lucius looked at Ben, then back at Phil and cleared his throat. "It collapsed once, a long time ago. Bishop cleared it out and uses it to carry the stuff ripped off from downtown into the basement of that old house." He pointed to the closest of the two Jeremiah houses.

"And he's in there now," Phil said.

Luke nodded. "I just dropped him and Carl and the woman off at the entrance to the tunnels right behind her store. He was gonna get her to get some money, then he was gonna take her away."

Phil caught Ben's arm as he would have headed off toward the store. "I've already got two men there. Relax." He turned back to Lucius. "And you're sure they're still down there?"

Lucius pointed to the white Cadillac parked in front of the old house. "He told me to park the car there. He's taking it to Mexico."

"Okay." Phil put the boy in the back of the car and beckoned to one of the two officers waiting. "Kennet and Blake have found the tunnel? They're sure it's the one?"

"Right."

"Tell them to let us know when they're on the other side of the basement wall, then we'll go in." He turned to Ben. "You're going to have to wait here."

"No," Ben said evenly. "I'm not."

"I'm sorry. It's the law."

"You can bend it." When Phil looked at him impatiently, he insisted, "What if you were me and it was Karen in there with Bishop?"

Phil relented grimly. "You stay behind me or you're out of here."

When Ragnar fell into step beside Ben, Phil turned with a disgusted sigh. "Oh, now look! You can't come, Rags."

"You want to explain that to Bea?" Ragnar asked.

Phil appeared to weigh the pros and cons of that.

"They're at the basement wall, Phil," the officer reported, pocketing his radio. "They can hear Bishop talking, so we're sure he, at least, is in the basement."

"All right." Phil glared from Ben to Ragnar. "You stay behind us and not a sound!"

"Hard-nosed," Ragnar whispered to Ben as they fell in behind the officers.

Ben's heart was pounding. Fear ran through him like a fever, leaving him hot and chilled and feeling as though he had only a tenuous grip on reality. The possibility that Bishop could have disappeared with Georgia was too ugly to contemplate for very long. Up until now, he'd been prepared to live without her if that was what she wanted. He'd have hated it, but knowing she was in the loving circle of her family and friends would have made it tolerable. Imagining her hiding in some hole with Bishop—whom Phil was now convinced had completely flipped out—frightened, worried about her daughters, longing for this place she loved so much, would have driven him over the edge.

Climbing the back stairs behind Phil, who'd sent the other two officers ahead, Ben understood clearly how unimportant Portland and his personal freedom were to the man he'd become since meeting Georgia. He had to have her, whatever the conditions. If he had to spend his life helping her solve the mystery of how Gary died, he'd do it if it meant she would marry him.

Ben called himself back to the matter at hand when Phil jimmied the back door lock. One of the younger officers frowned at him. "I can bust it open for you. It's really rotted."

Phil shook his head, concentrating. "Bishop doesn't know we're here. And I don't want him to until we're at the inside door to the basement." He smiled, straightened and gently turned the knob. The door opened without a squeak. He glared at his companions, silently reminding everyone to be quiet.

The house smelled of mold, dust and wildlife. Thirty years of neglect had left it filled with cobwebs, curling linoleum, peeling wallpaper and light fixtures that hung drunkenly, rotting out of their connections. There were large, mud-colored stains on the walls and floor from leaky plumbing.

Phil moved stealthily through the kitchen and into a corridor where voices could be heard. Crowding Phil, Ben stiffened, hearing Georgia's voice clearly. ''You might be able to make me go with you to Mexico, Wally, but I'd always be thinking of Ben Stratton. Always.'' Her voice was high and gut-wrenchingly sincere. Feeling rose up in Ben to whip the fever. He made a move toward the basement stairs, but Phil yanked him back. Into the radio, Phil whispered urgently, ''Move in!''

BETWEEN THE OPEN BASEMENT stairs, Georgia watched an officer scramble through the hole from the tunnel. Wally covered her scream with his hand when Carl drew a pistol from inside his jacket and took aim at the officer. The big man was distracted from that purpose by a rush of officers and men down the stairs. Backed into a corner, he reluctantly relinquished his weapon.

Georgia watched the other officers move around the basement, searching, guns ready. Wally tightened his grip on her in a silent warning to be still. In the interest of hoping he would relax his painful hold on her, she would have complied, reasonably certain now that there was no way he could take her out of the basement. But then she saw Ben, and suddenly control and courage fled—along with every argument she'd ever held against spending the rest of her life with him. Because her mouth was covered, she could only moan, thinking how pitiful she sounded, realizing at last how pitifully in love she was.

Ben spun toward the sound instantly. An officer checking a stack of boxes nearby did the same, instinctively pointing his revolver. Georgia closed her eyes against the sight of the gun bore aimed menacingly in her direction.

"Come on now, Wally," Phil said reasonably as everyone converged near the shadowy underside of the stairs. "You don't even have a weapon."

"I'll break her neck!" Wally threatened, shifting his arm so that it was around Georgia's throat. "I can do it. I *will* do it if you don't let us out of here."

"She doesn't want to go with you."

Georgia opened her eyes at the sound of Ben's voice and found that he'd come closer. He was near enough to touch, but her hands were caught behind her in one of Wally's.

Ben looked away from the fear and exhaustion in her eyes in order to remain clearheaded. "I heard her tell you that she might have to go with you, but she'd always be thinking of me. She's mine, Wally."

"No!" Wally screamed. The sound reverberated in Georgia's ear like a pain that wouldn't stop. "Gary took her from me, but you won't!"

"Gary didn't *take* her. She loved him, and she went with him. Now she loves me, and she's staying with me. It's like history, Wally. You can't change it."

Wally's arm tightened convulsively, and Georgia's head filled with colored lights whirling in a circle. "But I love her," he said weakly.

Ben took another step and grasped the arm at Georgia's throat. "Then give her what she wants. Let her come to me."

Feeling the stiff muscle under his hand, Ben thought dispassionately that Wally had five seconds before he broke the arm. Then the muscle relaxed and Ben pushed the arm away, reaching for Georgia and pulling her aside. The officers were on Wally in an instant, cuffing him and reading him his rights as they took him away.

Georgia fell against Ben's chest and simply held him, unable to speak or think. Tears fell silently down her cheeks as he rocked her slowly from side to side.

Ben had to resist the need to crush her to him—she had to regain her breath after Bishop's manhandling. But he wanted to hold her forever, to smother her with kisses and assure her that he wasn't going anywhere. The frightened but steady sound of her voice would play back in his ears until the day he died. "I'd always be thinking of Ben Stratton. Always." He'd waited a lifetime to hear someone say that.

Ben looked up at Phil, who stood with Ragnar at the foot of the stairs. "Are you going to need her now?"

Phil shook his head. "Tomorrow's soon enough. Take her home. I'll meet you there in a while."

Ben gently pulled her face up from his chest and kissed her cheek. "Ready to go?"

She nuzzled him again. "No. Ask them to seal the door and the tunnel and leave us here." Her voice was stronger, with a hint of her customary humor.

"Will you still love me when I'm a skeleton?" he asked.

She looked up at him with an expression he would also remember until he died. Her eyes were dark and finally rid of shock and fear. They were filled with a love that seemed free of all restraint. "I will love you after every star in the universe is gone and everything is dark. There'll be a steady little glimmer somewhere that only God will be left to see, and He'll say, 'Aha! Georgia still loves Ben. What a match I made that time.'"

Speechless, his throat tight, Ben enveloped her in his arms again until Phil's and Ragnar's footsteps faded upstairs. "We're getting married," he said firmly, pulling her away to look into her eyes. "I'm going to stay here with you and the girls, and we're going to find out what Gary was doing."

"No." She shook her head calmly, and he knew one moment of cold panic. She smiled quickly, reading the look in his eyes and shaking him. "No. I guess that became so important to me because it helped me hold on to a part of my life that was over. I thought I was letting it go because I loved you, but I was just trying to pull you into the past with me. That won't work."

"Georgia…"

She wrapped her arms around his neck, silencing him with a small kiss. "I'll never really be 'over' Gary. We loved each other. That just about changes your molecular structure so that the person you were in the beginning of a relationship is different from who you are when it's over. He'll always be part of me. I just have to trust in that love and believe that he did." She smiled broadly, a positive glow invading her eyes. "And now I have this thing for you, Stratton, that really could cause fusion at room temperature, whether those guys at the University of Utah did it or not."

Laughing, Ben lifted her in his arms and started up the stairs. "Only problem is when you look at me like that *I* do not remain room temperature."

Ragnar drove home while Ben and Georgia sat together in a very small corner of the front seat. Bea,

Karen, Linda, Lacey and Shelly were waiting on the front lawn, Lacey and Karen jumping up and down, Bea wringing her hands, and Linda and Shelly holding each other. They swarmed the car, opening the door and pulling Georgia out.

"You okay, Mom?" Linda demanded, tears streaming down her cheeks.

Georgia hugged her, then reached for Lacey, assuring them that she was fine. She hadn't noticed Shelly and took her quick hug with a smile of surprise. "I'm glad you're okay, Mrs. Madison." She glanced around, apparently feeling out of place in the crush of family. She turned to Linda. "I'll call you tomorrow."

"Wait!" Shelly turned at Georgia's call. "Is your mom home?"

Shelly shook her head.

Georgia reached an arm around her and pushed her toward Linda. "Then why don't you stay with us until she comes home? You guys call for pizza and set the table." She hooked an arm around Bea and another around Karen, joy coming to full, bubbling life inside her. "You all have to stay for dinner. Phil's coming over."

Georgia leaned toward Bea to give her a hug as they walked to the house. "You okay, Bea?"

She sniffed. "Oh, quite. I've had the wits scared out of me, a pair of nearly hysterical girls to deal with, a nosy friend who refused to leave—" she indicated Karen with an imperious tilt of her eyebrow that didn't fool anyone "—and now I'm going to be subjected to pizza. Pepperoni, I suppose, with green pepper and onion. I'll have to sleep with the milk of magnesia tonight."

Karen giggled. "Will there be room for Ragnar?"

Bea stopped halfway across the patio, looking at Karen with a look of outraged morality…that changed subtly to a grin. "There's always room for Ragnar."

LINDA AND LACEY trapped Ben on the service porch. He'd gone for a bag of ice from the freezer and turned to find the doorway to the kitchen not only blocked by the girls, but closed, as well. They faced him, arms folded, a redhead and a brunette with determination in every fiber of their beings. He was reminded vaguely of high noon on some dusty little Texas street. He set the bag down on top of the freezer.

"You want me on the noon stage out of town because this town isn't big enough for both of us?"

The girls exchanged a look and took a few steps closer. "We want you to hang up your guns," Linda said, "and settle down. Raise a family."

Lacey nodded. "Us."

God, he thought. What had he done to deserve so much? "Just so happens that fits into my plans."

Their looks of stunned surprise at his easy capitulation forced him to smile.

"What about Portland and your business?" Lacey asked.

He opened his arms and the girls walked into them with comfortable ease. "I'll work from here until you two are out of high school, then we'll reconsider. My uncle's a great guy. I want you to get to know him."

"If you marry Mom, we can meet him at the wedding."

Ben nodded. "That's what we talked about on the way home. By *next* Saturday," he said, squeezing their shoulders, "I'll really belong here."

Linda hugged him tighter. "You belonged here from the beginning, Ben."

THEIR LITTLE IMPROMPTU PARTY lasted until midnight. Georgia prepared a salad to go with the pizzas, and Ragnar ran out for soft drinks and wine. Phil arrived later with two half gallons of ice cream and a cake from the bakery.

He and Karen left arm in arm, looking into each other's eyes with obvious plans for the next few hours.

"Don't forget to watch the road," Ben advised as he and Georgia accompanied them to their car. "It'd be a hell of a note if you were picked up for reckless driving."

Phil laughed. "Wouldn't it?" Then he looked back into Karen's eyes again as Ben closed the driver's door. Ben looked at Georgia over the top of the car. "You think it's safe to let them go?"

Georgia winced. "I wouldn't want to be responsible for making them stay. I have children in the house."

Phil rolled down his window and grinned at Ben. "We'll be fine. Guess I'll be seeing you around—in a social capacity, that is."

Ben stepped back from the car, smiling. "A lot. Take it easy."

Ben joined Georgia on the lawn as the car pulled away. He wrapped his arms around her, feeling a joy so complete it hurt. She leaned against him, rocking gently. The night smelled of honeysuckle.

Linda, Lacey and Shelly wandered out with Bea and Ragnar. "You're sure you don't want me to take the girls home with me tonight?" Bea asked. Then she added quickly, "Shelly can come, too."

Remembering how frightened the girls had looked

when she'd come home, Georgia's instinct was to refuse the offer in the interest of the girls' sense of security. Then it occurred to her that she now had someone else's feelings to consider, as well. She looked up at Ben.

The girls said nothing, merely waited, but he, too, remembered how they had looked when he'd brought Georgia home. He was desperate to be alone with her, but not at the expense of Linda's and Lacey's needs. The girls had invited him into their lives, and that was a responsibility he felt deeply, humbly.

"No, thanks," he said, grinning at them. "We'll just lock them in their rooms so they don't bother us."

The girls ran to him, giggling, and Georgia's grip around his waist was tight enough to turn him blue. *Good move, Stratton,* he congratulated himself. *Good move.*

"Well." Bea looked up at Ragnar as he unlocked the passenger door of his blue LeBaron. "I guess we can rent a truck tomorrow. Move our things to Portland. Put my house up for sale. After we get married, of course."

Ragnar leaned his forearm on the window as Bea sat on the edge of the seat and swung her legs in with all the grace of an uncorseted woman half her age. "What if I've changed my mind?"

She smiled at him sweetly. "I'll make you sorry."

Ragnar raised his eyebrows at his audience, a grin making them certain he considered that more of an interesting possibility than a threat.

Ben and Georgia held each other on the patio while the girls' laughter filtered out from the kitchen as they cleaned up. "Thank you for wanting them to stay," Georgia said softly into his throat.

Ben nuzzled her ear. "As long as you understand how noble it was of me to relegate myself to the workshop again."

"I do." She pulled back, feeling as though she had to explain. "We'll be married in a few days, and the last thing I want to do tonight is let you go, but I—"

He kissed her into silence. "It's okay. I understand."

Georgia nipped his earlobe, then whispered, "If you can stay awake a little while, I could make an early morning raid on the workshop."

"Something tells me I won't be sleeping at all until we're married." He held her to him one long, last moment, memorizing the imprint of her body against his. He sighed heavily and released her, kissing the hand he still held before reluctantly letting it go. "I'll be waiting."

Georgia winked at him and went inside.

NOTHING HAD CHANGED in the workshop, yet everything seemed different. Ben knew what it was immediately. He wasn't a visitor here anymore; he was the man who belonged in this shop. When he'd first stepped across this threshold last month, the room had defined Gary Madison: orderly, yet creatively cluttered, warm. Now it was only fairly orderly and a little more cluttered. But the warmth remained, and he understood why. What had given Gary Madison his unique perspective on life now belonged to him—the love of his wife and his daughters.

In the middle of the room, Ben closed his eyes and tried to make the connection with Gary he sometimes felt in the quiet of the night when he worked with his tools and the broken pieces of furniture. "I'll love them and take care of them," he promised. "And whatever the hell you were doing on that airplane, we believe in you—all of us.''

Knowing it was going to be a while before Georgia could get away, Ben repaired the last of the dining room chairs. The house had gone dark and the neighborhood was silent when he had finished, but he was still far from sleepy. He decided to tackle the small table in the corner. Georgia had insisted it wasn't immediately important, but it was something to do.

It sat overturned on a wooden crate, its sound legs pointing to the ceiling. Ben grabbed it by one and yanked it up, turning it toward the workbench. But the book caught his eye. It sat on top of the pile of knobs, handles and fittings in the box, a slender, leather-bound volume with the word ''JOURNAL'' tooled inside a simple border at the top. His heart gave a sudden, violent lurch. Putting the table down, he reached into the box and picked up the book. It smelled musty, and the leather was beginning to mold.

Almost afraid to consider what he might have, Ben took it to the workbench and flipped on the overhead fluorescent. Hesitating only a moment, he opened the cover and his heartbeat picked up speed. In black ink was written, ''Happy birthday, Gary. This is to help you harness some of those big ideas. Love, Mother.'' Ben opened the book in the middle and let the pages flip back, discovering that Gary had used it to make business notes as well as personal observations. He didn't use it daily but dated every entry at the top.

The possibility that this might hold the answer to Georgia's questions was very real. For a moment he wondered why no one had looked for this journal after Gary's death. Then it occurred to him that this was the kind of gift a man often received and put aside, particularly a man who did things rather than thought about doing them. But Gary must have had a pensive side he had preferred to keep to himself.

Ben had no right to open it. He should take it to Georgia. But what if there was something in it she'd be better off not knowing? He was making a God-like decision, but he'd rather be condemned to hell than see Georgia or either of the girls hurt any more. Taking a deep breath, he flipped to the back of the journal, passing empty pages to find the last entry. It was dated March 11, the day before Gary died.

Bill is flying Sara and me to an interview with Culver Freight in Portland. They're looking for a West Coast manager. If this works out, bringing my own secretary along isn't the only plus—I'd have bennies and perks a mile long. Haven't mentioned it to George on the chance it doesn't work out—don't want to get up her hopes that I have a job at last or worry her that she might have to move. She's such a champ—God, I've been a lucky man. There's nothing like having the ground fall out from under you to remind you what's important. Even if this doesn't work out, I still have George, my angels and Mom. But I hope it does.

Ben's eyes stung and there was a stone in his throat he couldn't swallow. He closed the book and put it down on the workbench. "I knew I was right not to doubt you, pal," he said.

"I knew I'd waited too long." Georgia closed the workshop door quietly behind her and ran toward him in a black negligee. It was low cut and transparent, but he hardly noticed. "You're talking to yourself. That's a bad sign, fella. You're going over the edge already, and you've only had us—''

She stopped midsentence, looking into his eyes. She had known it. She wasn't supposed to be this happy. It had all been a mistake. ''What's the matter?'' she asked, her mouth dry.

For an instant Ben considered not mentioning the book. She hadn't noticed it; he could guide her to the sofa and she'd never notice it until he could put it back in its hiding place at the first opportunity. She'd made the decision to love *him* now. But would she if she was made absolutely certain that Gary's last thought had been of her and how much he loved their family? After all, he shouldn't have opened it. It hadn't been his place. She hadn't looked in that box in two years; she might never look in it. He could marry her and they could love each other a lifetime and she need never know.

But he'd held her when she'd wept over the pain that not knowing had caused her, and he'd held Linda and seen what the pain had done to her. He couldn't withhold what would finally give them peace—even if it made *him* unnecessary. He reached beyond Georgia for the book and put it in her hands.

''What is it?'' she asked, obviously not recognizing it.

''Gary's journal,'' he replied. ''Read the last entry.''

She frowned at him. ''He didn't keep...'' she began, then she realized what she held—that there were answers in it that had plagued her for two long, lonely years. She looked at Ben, tears filling her eyes. She closed them, holding the book to her as one large tear slid down her face. ''What does it say?'' she asked.

"You have to read it," he insisted gently. "The last entry."

Oh, God. Georgia forced her eyes open, made herself flip through pages to find the last page of Gary's large, angled handwriting. She could take it. She could. Ben wanted her to read it so she could face the truth once and for all.

She tried to draw a breath, but she didn't seem to have any. There was fire in her lungs, her eyes, her stomach. She finally sobbed a breath and began to read. "Bill is flying.... Haven't mentioned it to George.... George, my angels and Mom."

She was sobbing and Ben didn't know what to do. Was she still his to hold and comfort? She solved the question for him by throwing herself into his arms. "Thank you, Ben," she wept against him. "Oh, God, thank you, Ben."

"It was in that box of fittings all the time," he said, rubbing her back, smoothing her hair. "Under that little overturned table."

"I had no idea he kept it. When he was alive, this workshop was his sanctum. When he died, I couldn't bear to come in here. I can't believe an answer was in front of my face all this time."

Ben held her and let the silence fall. He waited until she pulled away from him of her own accord and offered her his handkerchief. She glanced up at him, her eyelashes spiked with tears. "Your expression terrified me when I walked in here," she said. "You looked as though you'd lost everything. I thought you'd changed your mind or something."

He rubbed her arms gently. "I was afraid you might."

She looked at him in complete bafflement. "Why?"

"Because your memory of Gary is intact," he replied quietly. "I didn't know if you'd need me anymore."

For a moment he thought she might get angry, but her eyes filled with regret, instead. "Is that how I've made you feel? That you were just a bandage over my insecurities? I can't tell you how sorry I am." Tears brimmed and spilled over again. "You're life and light to me, Ben. Truly—if you weren't in my life, I wouldn't want to go on. Because of the girls, I'd have to, but I wouldn't care if I did or not. Knowing Gary loved me as much as I loved him right to the last day gives me peace, so that what we had can rest in peace. But I want to live with you, Ben, day after day of all the wonderful routine and mundane things that fill our lives, and the occasional bursts of absolute wonder and perfection. I love you." She emphasized each word, her eyes underlining, capitalizing, italicizing. "Please know that."

He took her in his arms again, absorbing the truth of her love, letting himself believe that at long, long last, he was loved and could love back.

"Do you want to wake the girls?" he asked.

"No." She put her arm around his waist and drew him to the sofa. "It's only a few hours until morning. We could invite Bea and Ragnar to breakfast and tell them all at the same time." She pushed him down and sat on his lap. "You're a completely selfless human being, Ben Stratton. If you were afraid my reading Gary's journal would make you superfluous, you could have put the book back and I'd have probably never known."

He shrugged and kissed her forehead. "I'd have known."

She turned to smile into his eyes. "That's what the hero always says."

Silhouette®

Romantic
SUSPENSE

**Sparked by Danger,
Fueled by Passion.**

Mission: Impassioned

A brand-new miniseries begins with

My Spy

By *USA TODAY* bestselling author

Marie Ferrarella

She had to trust him with her life....
It was the most daring mission of Joshua Lazlo's
career: rescuing the prime minister of England's
daughter from a gang of cold-blooded kidnappers.
But nothing prepared the shadowy secret agent
for a fiery woman whose touch ignited something
far more dangerous.

My Spy
#1472

Available July 2007 wherever you buy books!

Visit Silhouette Books at www.eHarlequin.com   SRS27542

SPECIAL EDITION™

Look for six new
MONTANA MAVERICKS
stories, beginning in July with

THE MAN WHO HAD EVERYTHING

by CHRISTINE RIMMER

When Grant Clifton decided to sell the
family ranch, he knew it would devastate
Stephanie Julen, the caretaker who'd always been
like a little sister to him. He wanted a new start,
but how could he tell her that she and her mother
would have to leave...especially now that he was
head over heels in love with her?

MONTANA MAVERICKS

Dreaming big—and winning hearts—in Big Sky Country

Visit Silhouette Books at www.eHarlequin.com   SSE24837

ATHENA FORCE

Heart-pounding romance and thrilling adventure.

A ruthless enemy rises against the women of Athena Academy. In a global chess game of vengeance, kidnapping and murder, every move exposes potential enemies—and lovers. This time the women must stand together... before their world is ripped apart.

THIS NEW 12-BOOK SERIES BEGINS WITH A BANG IN AUGUST 2007 WITH

TRUST
by Rachel Caine

Look for a new Athena Force adventure each month wherever books are sold.

www.eHarlequin.com   AFLAUNCH

THE GARRISONS

A brand-new family saga begins with

THE CEO'S SCANDALOUS AFFAIR

BY ROXANNE ST. CLAIRE

Eldest son Parker Garrison is preoccupied running his Miami hotel empire and dealing with his recently deceased father's secret second family. Since he has little time to date, taking his superefficient assistant to a charity event should have been a simple plan. Until passion takes them beyond business.

Don't miss any of the six exciting titles in THE GARRISONS continuity, beginning in July. Only from Silhouette Desire.

THE CEO'S SCANDALOUS AFFAIR

#1807

Available July 2007.

HARLEQUIN®

INTRIGUE®

ARE YOU AFRAID OF THE DARK?

The eerie text message was only part of a night to remember for security ace Shane Peters—one minute he was dancing with Princess Ariana LeBron, holding her in his arms at a soiree of world leaders, the next he was fighting for their lives when a blackout struck and gunmen held them hostage. Their demands were simple: give them the princess.

Part of a new miniseries:

LIGHTS OUT

ROYAL LOCKDOWN

BY RUTH GLICK

WRITING AS

REBECCA YORK

On sale June 2007.

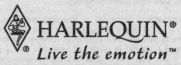

HARLEQUIN®
Live the emotion™

www.eHarlequin.com

HIMAY07

REQUEST YOUR FREE BOOKS!
2 FREE NOVELS PLUS 2 FREE GIFTS!

SPECIAL EDITION®
Life, Love and Family!

YES! Please send me 2 FREE Silhouette Special Edition® novels and my 2 FREE gifts. After receiving them, if I don't wish to receive any more books, I can return the shipping statement marked "cancel." If I don't cancel, I will receive 6 brand-new novels every month and be billed just $4.24 per book in the U.S., or $4.99 per book in Canada, plus 25¢ shipping and handling per book and applicable taxes, if any*. That's a savings of at least 15% off the cover price! I understand that accepting the 2 free books and gifts places me under no obligation to buy anything. I can always return a shipment and cancel at any time. Even if I never buy another book from Silhouette, the two free books and gifts are mine to keep forever.   235 SDN EEYU 335 SDN EEY6

Name	(PLEASE PRINT)

Address	Apt.

City	State/Prov.	Zip/Postal Code

Signature (if under 18, a parent or guardian must sign)

Mail to the Silhouette Reader Service™:
IN U.S.A.: P.O. Box 1867, Buffalo, NY 14240-1867
IN CANADA: P.O. Box 609, Fort Erie, Ontario L2A 5X3

Not valid to current Silhouette Special Edition subscribers.

Want to try two free books from another line?
Call 1-800-873-8635 or visit www.morefreebooks.com.

* Terms and prices subject to change without notice. NY residents add applicable sales tax. Canadian residents will be charged applicable provincial taxes and GST. This offer is limited to one order per household. All orders subject to approval. Credit or debit balances in a customer's account(s) may be offset by any other outstanding balance owed by or to the customer. Please allow 4 to 6 weeks for delivery.

Your Privacy: Silhouette is committed to protecting your privacy. Our Privacy Policy is available online at www.eHarlequin.com or upon request from the Reader Service. From time to time we make our lists of customers available to reputable firms who may have a product or service of interest to you. If you would prefer we not share your name and address, please check here. ☐

SSE07

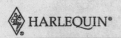

HARLEQUIN®

American ROMANCE®

**is proud to present a special treat this
Fourth of July with three stories
to kick off your summer!**

SUMMER LOVIN'
by
Marin Thomas,
Laura Marie Altom
Ann Roth

This year, celebrating the Fourth of July in Silver Cliff,
Colorado, is going to be special. There's an all-year
high school reunion taking place before the old
school building gets torn down. As old flames find
each other and new romances begin, this small
town is looking like the perfect place
for some summer lovin'!

*Available June 2007
wherever Harlequin books are sold.*

www.eHarlequin.com   HAR75169

HARLEQUIN®

Mediterranean NIGHTS™

Tycoon Elias Stamos is launching his newest luxury cruise ship from his home port in Greece. But someone from his past is eager to expose old secrets and to see the Stamos empire crumble.

Mediterranean Nights
launches in June 2007 with...

FROM RUSSIA, WITH LOVE
by *Ingrid Weaver*

Join the guests and crew of *Alexandra's Dream* as they are drawn into a world of glamour, romance and intrigue in this new 12-book series.

www.eHarlequin.com

MN1